ALSO BY GORDON JACK

The Boomerang Effect

YOUR OWN WORST ENEMY

GORDON JACK

YOUR OWN WORST ENEMY

HARPER TEEN

An Imprint of HarperCollinsPublishers

HarperTeen is an imprint of HarperCollins Publishers.

Your Own Worst Enemy
Copyright © 2018 by Gordon Jack
All rights reserved. Printed in the United States of America.
No part of this book may be used or reproduced in any manner whatsoever
without written permission except in the case of brief quotations embodied
in critical articles and reviews. For information address HarperCollins
Children's Books, a division of HarperCollins Publishers, 195 Broadway,
New York, NY 10007.
www.epicreads.com

Library of Congress Control Number: 2018941363
ISBN 978-0-06-239942-7 (trade bdg.)

Typography by Laura Eckes
18 19 20 21 22 PC/LSCH 10 9 8 7 6 5 4 3 2 1

First Edition

For Kathleen
My tightrope and my net

PROLOGUE

STACEY SHOULD HAVE run as soon as she saw the security guard's golf cart barreling toward her. That's what fugitives do, right? They run. But Stacey didn't feel like a criminal just yet. Her instincts were still those of a law-abiding citizen. Weird how your life can change in the matter of minutes, she mused. This morning she was the girl most likely to succeed. Now her name was trending with the hashtag #LockHerUp.

Sammy brought his golf cart to a screeching halt in front of her. What a ridiculous vehicle to give a man who was over six feet tall, and three hundred pounds. His hulking frame filled the two front seats, and he had to drive with his left leg dangling outside the cart's floorboard.

"I found her," he said roughly into his walkie-talkie. The thing looked like a flip phone in his giant hands.

Stacey had taken refuge on a bench outside the history

building—a fitting place for someone with no future. These open spaces used to be ugly concrete pathways, the freeways of Lincoln High School, where students moved en masse from one class to another. It was Stacey who advocated that the school beautify these barren thoroughfares with trees, bushes, and flowers. Now the campus was filled with tiny parklets that provided quiet, contemplative spaces for students to reflect on the ruin they had brought to their lives.

Stacey stood up and attempted to repair her damaged appearance. After the wrestling match in the quad, her pale skin had the texture of a sneaker sole. There was a wad of chewing gum stuck to the back pocket of her shorts. Her blond hair could be cast in a Mad Max movie. She tried to fix these defects by giving herself a preemptive pat down. All that did was kick up the dust and debris that had settled on her skin and clothes.

She wondered briefly if Sammy would take her in cuffs.

"I'll just get in the back," Stacey said, walking around Sammy and hopping onto the back seat. She wasn't going to fight this. She was tired of fighting. It wasn't just the brawl at brunch either. The whole election had exhausted her. She didn't realize how much until she had escaped to her bench after everyone had gone back to class. The quiet was intoxicating. She couldn't remember the last time she had sat still like that and cleared her mind of every item on her to-do list.

The back seat of the golf cart faced away from the driver. Stacey watched her sanctuary recede into the distance as Sammy drove down the covered hallway toward the main office. The walls on either side of her were still decorated with campaign posters urging students to vote in today's election. Stacey noticed that someone had torn down parts of the banner she'd hung next to the bathrooms in the English wing. Now instead of reading *Don't Waste Your Vote! Elect Stacey Wynn*, it read *Waste Stacey Wynn*. That wasn't very comforting. She pulled out her phone and checked the chatter on her social media feeds to see if anyone else was advocating assassination. Nope. Most were divided between calling her a bully and calling her a badass, but no one wanted to kill her.

The hallway dumped them onto the main quad, the heart of the campus, where the cafeteria, library, auditorium, and main office were located. The patchwork of lawns was still littered with debris, which the seagulls and crows huddled around like hungry Costco shoppers at a sampling tray. Along with the usual garbage that kids left after eating their morning snacks, Stacey saw a dropped poster with the words *Amor sin Fronteras* on the front. Someone from Julia's crew must have abandoned it when the fight broke out, which would make sense. It wouldn't look right to bash someone over the head with a sign saying love knows no boundaries.

A few feet away, Stacey spied that stupid astronaut

helmet Tony wore over his cow costume. The cheap plastic orb had cracked down the middle; probably the result of Julia yanking it off his head and hurling it into the crowd. Stacey turned around to ask Sammy if he wanted to collect it as evidence, but then stopped herself. It's not like the helmet was a smoking gun. If anything was responsible for the mayhem, it was these guns, Stacey thought, staring at her muscular calves. Ten years of Tae Kwon Do training had left her with beautifully toned legs. Even scraped and bruised, they were by far her best feature. And most leathal weapon.

Sammy parked in front of the administrative building and escorted Stacey to the principal's office. Stacey had been in Buckley's office plenty of times in her three years at Lincoln, but she was always invited in as a consultant, rather than perp walked in as a violent criminal. The administration had often asked Stacey to help organize or promote some school event, and she had always been happy to do it. She hoped Buckley would give her a pass in light of her good behavior. At the very least, she hoped Buckley wouldn't call her mother and tell her what had happened. If Mom suspected Stacey was venturing into a life of crime, she might force her to live with her and her new husband, so they could instill more discipline into her upbringing.

Any hope that Stacey's stellar reputation would win her a quick reprieve was promptly extinguished when she saw the principal's secretary. Rather than greet her with her usual cheerful smile and offer of candy, Ms. Hollenbeck nodded in the direction of the principal's door and scowled. "The principal's on her way," she said. Stacey had heard somewhere that jurors will not make eye contact with accused criminals if they are about to pass a guilty verdict. Hollenbeck didn't avert her eyes from her computer screen.

Julia and Tony were already seated in front of Buckley's cluttered desk. Sammy motioned for Stacey to take the empty middle seat between the princess and the cow. Stacey walked past Tony, exaggerating her limp so he'd feel bad for kicking her in the ankle. He was too busy playing with the udders on his costume to notice.

"Stop playing with those things," Julia said, clutching the silky folds of her dress in obvious frustration.

"I can't help it," Tony said. "It's like I have five penises."

"You're disgusting," Julia said. Her tiara still hung askew on her disheveled light-brown hair like an ancient ruin, evidence of a once-glorious civilization. Even after a fight, she managed to retain her nobility. Stacey, in her spring hiking attire, felt like a stable boy sitting next to her.

Tony kept swatting his pink, plastic udders, mesmerized by their rigidity. Stacey reached forward and pulled a pair of scissors off Buckley's desk and snipped one of the pink tubes from his costume.

"Hey!" Tony said. "That's kind of emasculating."

"Keep talking, and I'll remove the other four," she said, throwing the scissors back onto the desk.

Tony slumped in his seat, which made his udders protrude even more. Whoever designed his costume must have a sick sense of humor, Stacey figured. She grabbed a three-ring binder marked *Board Meetings 2017* and threw it in Tony's lap.

"I was just having some fun," he said.

"It wasn't time to have some fun," Julia said. "It was a serious occasion."

"You all looked so pretty," Tony said. "Like a princess parade."

"It was a protest, you idiot," Julia said, her brown eyes shooting daggers. "Didn't you read our signs?"

"I couldn't see anything with my space helmet on," Tony said. "Where is that anyway?"

"I saw it in the quad," Stacey said, rubbing her throbbing ankle. "It's busted."

"Aw, man," Tony said. "I got so high from smoking with that thing on my head."

"You're really not stereotypically Asian, are you?" Stacey asked, looking Tony squarely in the face. If he weren't so obnoxious, she'd almost find him cute. He had the dopey eyes of a toddler.

"My people hate me 'cause I keep it real," Tony said.

Principal Buckley burst through the doorway in her typical bulldozer style. The woman was a powerhouse. Prior to going into administration, she had been the athletic director for the school. She still approached every problem like it was a fat kid trying to climb a rope in gym class.

"Ladies and gentleman," she said, throwing her large body into an office chair that creaked under her weight. "Can somebody please explain what happened?"

"I was attacked," Tony said, holding up his torn costume as evidence. The hoof glove, torn from the sleeve, dangled limply from his wrist.

"Tony disrupted our peaceful protest," Julia said, leaning forward. Stacey caught a whiff of hair spray from her tousled locks. Her brown skin was scraped from where she fell against the pavement.

"I don't recall hearing about this protest," Buckley said, looking at Julia's overflowing pink gown. "Was it against evil stepmothers?"

Buckley was the only one who laughed at this joke. She hadn't seen the solemn display. Didn't realize how moving it had been.

"Be that as it may," Buckley said, getting her chortling under control. "Someone better come clean and take responsibility for the fight."

"Space Cow Massacre," Stacey said.

"Excuse me?" Buckley said.

"That's what they're calling it," Stacey said, holding up her phone so Buckley could see the Instagram story.

Buckley squinted at Stacey's screen and groaned. "This is why we need to ban those things from campus," she said. "We have a zero tolerance policy against this kind of behavior. So, whose fault is it?"

Stacey looked at her lap. She knew, just as the two people sitting on either side of her knew, that whoever took the hit for this would be suspended. And if they were suspended, they would be out of the presidential race. All the work they had done for the past three weeks would be for nothing. Their names would be removed from the ballot, erased from memory like some political rival in Soviet Russia. Or today's Russia. Either way, they would never be heard from again.

"It was my fault," Stacey said.

"It was my fault," Julia said.

"Me too," Tony said.

NOMINATIONS

1

DEBATE WAS RAGING inside room 401, meeting place of the Associated Student Body of Lincoln High School. Stacey sat in the back row of desks and tried to block out the discordant voices so that she could polish her acceptance speech, but it was proving to be difficult. Soaring, inspirational rhetoric wasn't created in rooms filled with people yelling about how awesome it would be to stick kids in inflatable balls and roll them across the quad.

"Have you ever been in one of those bubble balls, Dave?" Brandon asked. Brandon was the current ASB president and wanted to end his term on a high note with human curling. "It's like being stuck in a clothes dryer. Someone will hurl, I promise you."

"Let's hope so," Dave said. "We could increase those odds if we made the contestants eat one of the reheated breakfast burritos from the cafeteria."

Brandon looked to Mr. Nichols for support, but their adviser was busy laughing at something on his computer screen. "Shouldn't the goal of our activities be to bring people together in the spirit of healthy competition, not to publicly humiliate them?" Brandon asked. Stacey assumed it was a rhetorical question.

"Can't we do both?"

"Let's put it to a vote," Brandon said. "How many people think we should do bubble bowling for this Friday's brunch activity?"

Stacey paused in her editing to consider the word "brunch." Why did their school still use this term to describe the fifteen-minute break between second- and third-period classes? Why hadn't it disappeared like the many other elitist names Lincoln once used when it was largely white, affluent, and Christian? The school no longer called its February break "Ski Week" after all. Why hang on to "brunch" when it conjured up images of mimosas and scones and string quartets playing Vivaldi? Why weren't they debating alternative titles right now instead of arguing about whether they should stick someone's little brother in an inflatable hamster wheel?

Stacey looked up from her laptop to see how many hands were raised. Half the class had voted for bubble bowling. Damn it. That meant they'd have to spend more time on this pointless discussion. Why couldn't Brandon just make the executive decision and tell people they were doing human curling next Friday? He'd been wanting to do that activity ever since he saw a YouTube clip of some poor freshman smashing headfirst into the side of a building. He should just tell people, "We're putting kids on skateboards and rolling them across the quad this Friday" and be done with it. That's the way Stacey would do things when she was the ASB president. People might not always like her top-down decision-making, but they would thank her for saving them so much time in pointless debates.

She watched Brandon now as he tried to moderate a conversation that sounded like the kind of "would you rather" argument people had in the cafeteria at lunch. "Would you rather be shot out of a cannon or flushed down a toilet?" This was the problem with having student government sixth period; everyone was tired and slaphappy. No one took anything seriously after sitting for six hours taking everything seriously.

Stacey glanced over at Nichols and wondered, not for the first time, how he earned his salary for this class. It's not like he taught them anything about the finer points of government. That was done in the actual US Government class, the class everyone took their senior year. Until then, the students had to figure things out on their own, which resulted in a lot of time spent following complicated procedures to ensure no one's feelings got hurt. God forbid little Annie Tompkins didn't get to voice her opinion on any subject coming up for a vote.

Stacey watched as Nichols tipped his Starbucks cup back and sucked out the dregs of the coffee. Then he dropped the cup, traveler lid included, into the trash can next to his desk, and went back to scrolling through whatever social media feed he found so amusing. Stacey stared at the cup sitting atop the pile of trash and mentally sorted the detritus into three piles: waste, recycling, and compost. Then she envisioned dumping all three on Nichols's bald head and screaming, *Reduce, reuse, recycle, asshole!* She completed the fantasy with a roundhouse kick to Nichols's gut, just to make sure he never made the same mistake again.

"Stacey, what's your vote?" Brandon asked, staring at her intently.

Stacey snapped back to attention and took in the room. Brandon stood before her, smiling confidently. Jenny Ramirez, the current ASB secretary, was at the whiteboard waiting to record Stacey's answer. The vote was split between the two activities, so Stacey's choice would break the tie.

Stacey put her blond hair up with a pencil to buy her some time. As she twisted the strands around the back of her head, she calculated the advantages and disadvantages of supporting Brandon on this. *What* they were voting on might be pointless, but *how* they voted would be remembered. Brandon was president and had endorsed Stacey early in her candidacy, which was one of the reasons no one ran against her. But Brandon was graduating in two months, and his popularity had taken a recent nosedive after people learned that grad-night tickets were going to be three hundred dollars, a direct result of his fiscal mismanagement. Dave, on the other hand, was a junior and popular with the underclassmen. He could cause her trouble next year if he built a faction to oppose her.

"Bubble bowling," she said.

"Yes!" Dave said, and high-fived the students around him. Brandon just stared at her, his eyes bulging in surprise.

"Sorry, Brandon," Stacey said. "But bubble bowling is more of a spectacle, with or without the barf."

Brandon threw an eraser at the whiteboard. It bounced and landed at Jenny's feet, and she kicked it across the floor. It slid to the center of the room like a tiny demonstration of human curling.

"Nice job," James said, sitting down next to her after the other students started work on their various projects. "I saw that moment you paused, wondering if you should throw your mentor under the bus. Your foot hesitated over the brake and then hit the gas pedal hard."

"It's just a brunch activity, James," Stacey said. "Not a vote on health care."

Stacey stared at her laptop screen, hoping James would take the hint and go find someone else to choke with his cologne. Is this what things were going to be like next year when he was vice president? Was she going to have to pretend all year that James's nerdy glasses and bow tie didn't drive her crazy? His geek-chic attire seemed designed to broadcast how smart he was to everyone. It was almost as bad as when he slipped James Baldwin quotes into casual conversation.

"Can I help you?" Stacey asked after James showed no evidence of leaving.

James pulled out a MacBook Air from his leather messenger bag and opened Google docs. "I was thinking we should start talking about next year."

"A little premature, don't you think?" Stacey closed her computer so James wouldn't see the draft of her acceptance speech on the screen.

"Look at the board," he said, nodding in the direction of the whiteboard near the entrance. It was covered with a tally of names of kids running for the different student government positions at school. The class officers were written on the left, and the associated student body officers were on the right. Every position had two or three names listed under it.

The only people running unopposed were Stacey and James.

"There's still one day left in the nomination process," Stacey said. "I wouldn't get too cocky."

"C'mon, Stace," James said. That was another thing she disliked about James—his propensity to shorten people's names. "Stacey" became "Stace." "Jenny" became "Jen," "Brandon" became just "B." It was overly familiar. Like when people touched Stacey's arm to feel her biceps. "Who's going to run against us?"

James was right. After Stacey's and James's three years in student government, no one dared question their right to these top positions. Stacey had moved up the ranks in the ASB, first as secretary, then treasurer, and finally vice president. James had served consecutive terms as class president his sophomore and junior years. The only reason he didn't want to run for a third term was because senior class president was in charge of all high school reunions—for as long as people lived! "That is not a responsibility I care to have," he'd confided in Stacey when he announced his candidacy for vice president. "When I graduate, I never want to see any of these people again." As the openly gay African American student at Lincoln, James had a complicated relationship with his constituency.

"What do you want to talk about?" Stacey asked.

"I want our brunch activities to be more inclusive next

year," James said, running his long, slender fingers along the desk as if it were a grand piano.

Stacey wondered what was "exclusive" about stuffing someone in an inflatable ball and rolling them across the quad, but she kept her mouth shut. The last thing she wanted James to accuse her of was being heteronormative—a charge he made a little too frequently in her opinion. "What did you have in mind?" she asked.

"I don't know. Have you noticed that the only people who participate in these brunch activities are white?"

"That's because they're all friends and families of ASB officers," Stacey said. "Look around—we're pretty white."

"The activities are pretty white too," James said.

"What's so white about bubble bowling?"

"Black people will not let anyone roll them across campus in an inflatable ball."

"You're speaking for all black people?"

"I am."

"What do you propose, then?"

"I thought we could invite the cultural clubs to perform. Maybe have dancing competitions and Drop the Mic rap battles. Or karaoke."

"Sure, we could do that," Stacey said, trying to keep James from hearing the voice in her head screaming, *No way I'm spending my senior year listening to Ariana wannabes choke out her greatest hits.* "I was thinking we'd take the ASB in a more serious direction."

"How so?" James asked, sitting up straight. Stacey wondered if he was trying to make himself look as large as possible, the way you do when you stumble across a mountain lion on a nature hike.

"I want to make Lincoln a zero-waste school," Stacey said.

"Seriously, Stace?" James ran a hand over his buzz cut. "People don't care about composting."

"They will!" Stacey said. "Imagine if we found a way to work an environmental message into every school activity? We could have dramatic reenactments at rallies. Picture some football player getting reeducated by a squadron of cheerleaders after he carelessly drops his water bottle on the gymnasium floor. Doesn't that sound great?"

"It sounds like Communist China. You actually used the term 'reeducate' in your description of it."

"No, it would be funny. Although, I'm not opposed to there being stiffer penalties for students who ignore the clearly marked bins."

"Yes!" James said, suddenly becoming enthusiastic. "We could send all the dissidents to camps where they would rotate the soil in the compost bins for our community garden!"

"Exactly!" Stacey said. "Wait, were you being sarcastic? Because I actually think that's a good idea."

"Yes, I was being sarcastic, Chairman Mao."

Ugh. If only she could pick her running mate, she wouldn't have to put up with James's abuse. Who was it that thought it was a good idea to separate the vice president position from its conjoined twin anyway?

"I want to leave a lasting legacy when I graduate, James. Organizing dance parties and class competitions isn't going to help me do that."

"Your legacy will be that you ruined senior year for everyone. Is that what you want?"

"I don't think that's true. We can make composting fun. I know we can."

"You're hopeless," James said. The tremor of his eye roll seemed to dislodge his glasses. He made a big production of readjusting the frames before continuing. "I hope someone does run against you, and I hope that person overturns your ban on confetti and balloons."

"Those things clog our landfills, James," Stacey said. "While you're having the party, our planet is experiencing the hangover."

"Be careful, Stace," James said, shutting his laptop and putting it into his bag. "As the great James Baldwin once said, 'No one is more dangerous than he who imagines himself pure in heart; for his purity, by definition, is unassailable.'" He stood up, draped his messenger bag over his shoulder, and walked away.

Stacey watched his retreat and made a mental note to memorize her own set of lofty quotations, preferably from other civil rights leaders, to use against James next year. Why couldn't he be her gay best friend instead of her gay nemesis? Things would be so much easier if Brian was her vice president next year. Maybe she should convince him to run against James in the election. He was kind of gay. At least she thought he was. You'd think after being friends for three years she would know for sure. If he wasn't gay, he was definitely the *B* or *Q* in "LGBTQ."

She opened her laptop and texted him. After waiting five minutes and still getting no response, she started to worry. Normally, Brian answered her texts immediately with some emoji indicating his enthusiasm to help her in whatever she needed. What could be so important that he left her hanging like this?

2

BRIAN LITTLE HAD a boner he couldn't get rid of. He tried focusing on his biology teacher's explanation of the evolutionary relationship of carnivora depicted on his phylogenetic tree, but every path led him back to contemplating Julia's breasts. They were perfectly rounded and symmetrical, firm yet pliable (or so Brian imagined, or rather, was trying hard *not* to imagine). If you placed Julia's breasts on any phylogenetic tree, they would be a unique species, something that didn't exist in the family of teenage girls. How such a thing came to be was a mystery Brian could only half explain through evolutionary thinking. He knew breasts were needed to attract mates and suckle the young, but something as beautiful as Julia's breasts could only come from some intelligent design, and for this he thanked the gods.

Julia must have sensed Brian's struggle because she

glanced sideways and smiled, which only made things worse. Brian quickly averted his gaze away from Julia's chest and onto Mr. Cohen's pasty face and scrubby mustache. "In considering possible phylogenies for a species, we need to compare the molecular data for the species," he said in a voice that seemed designed to quell any curiosity or interest, sexual or otherwise, in the listener.

Brian nearly had his boner under control when the phone in his front pocket vibrated. "Damn it, Stacey," he muttered, squirming to separate the buzzing machine from his genitalia. He didn't need to look at the screen to see who was texting him. Only Stacey had the means, motive, and opportunity to contact him during sixth period. Student government was a class run by students, unlike AP bio. If Mr. Cohen caught Brian texting while he was lecturing, he'd confiscate Brian's phone for a week. If only he had a MacBook Pro like Julia, then he could text Stacey on his laptop and look like he was taking notes.

Brian glanced sideways and saw Julia's messaging screen open. She was an impressive multitasker, taking notes on Cohen's lecture while simultaneously carrying on a conversation in French. The girl was amazing. Brian couldn't believe his luck when she appeared in his AP bio class a few weeks ago as if emerging out of a clamshell to announce the birth of love and beauty. *Everyone, this is Julia Romero,* Mr. Cohen had

23

said in his typical monotone. *She's from Canada and will be joining us for the remainder of the term.* Even his dull recitation of facts couldn't refrigerate Brian's interest in the newcomer. Besides her breasts, Julia had magnificent hair—long and curly and the color of dark amber. Her light brown skin made Brian think she was Latina, but she could also be Filipina or maybe biracial. Her indeterminate cultural identity was part of what made her so fascinating. You couldn't place her in any census bureau racial identity box; she was Other—a beautiful, mysterious Other.

Stop race fetishizing, Stacey's voice reminded him. Her incoming texts felt like mini–electric shocks to condition his thinking and behavior toward a more enlightened view of women. Brian consciously shifted his thinking away from Julia's body and toward her mind. Julia had an amazing mind, from what he could tell. She got perfect scores on all her work and always knew the correct answer when called upon. Whereas some might describe her as haughty and aloof, Brian saw a shyness that spoke of humility and introversion. She didn't suck up to anyone, nor did she let others suck up to her. She was a strong, independent young woman whose thoughts and feelings were complex and interesting.

Why didn't this excite his body as much as the smell of her shampoo?

Brian's phone buzzed again, causing him to audibly groan.

"You're showing incredible restraint," Julia whispered.

"It's just Stacey," he said, feeling the need to focus the conversation away from his vibrating pants. "I'm sort of her campaign adviser."

"Campaign adviser?"

"Yeah, you know. For the student government elections? They're happening in two weeks."

"What do you do as her campaign adviser?" Julia whispered.

Brian looked up at Cohen to make sure their conversation wasn't interrupting his flow, and saw their teacher drawing a complicated diagram on the board, his sweaty back to the class. "Nothing really," Brian said. "No one's running against her."

"Why not?"

"I think she intimidates them," Brian said. "She's never lost an election. She's been in the ASB since our freshman year."

"ASB?"

"Associated Student Body. It's the student government class."

"You must be a good campaign adviser," Julia said.

"Gracias," Brian said. God, he was such a tool! Why was his mouth saying things without consulting him?

Brian had never had a good relationship with his body.

For years, it seemed to be under the impression that Brian was living in the Alaskan tundra and stored as much fat as possible to protect itself for the scarcity of winter. Brian ate well and exercised, but he couldn't shed the rolls of flesh that made his body look like a sugar cone overflowing with soft-serve ice cream. When he finally lost the weight, it wasn't because of any growth spurt or strong mental discipline; it was his body deciding to poison him by rupturing his appendix at the National Scout jamboree. This hospitalized him for a month. When he emerged from his adjustable bed–cocoon, he was thinner, weaker, and terrified of what his body would do next.

That's when the spontaneous boners started.

Brian had experienced boners before, but now he couldn't make them stop. At least he knew their cause: Julia. This both horrified and delighted him. Before her, there was no reliable trigger. He could be sitting on the couch, watching TV with his mom, and it would happen. He could be wrestling with the dog, and it would happen. One time it happened in the produce aisle of the supermarket. This left Brian very confused sexually. If this was the barometer by which you gauge your sexual attraction, he seemed to be attracted to everything. Now that his body was responding to Julia, he felt a little surer that he was on the hetero side of the spectrum but the jury might still be out on this. His body could fuck with him again at any time and send him spinning off in a whole other direction.

The bell rang, and everyone stood up to leave. Everyone except Brian. He didn't feel quite ready to stand, so he made a big production about copying down the weblike diagram Cohen had so painstakingly drawn on the board. Out of the corner of his eye, he saw Julia lingering. Brian made eye contact with her belly button, peeking out from under her T-shirt. It was going to be a while before he could stand again.

"Is it really hard?" Julia asked.

"Excuse me?" Brian looked up in horror.

"To get elected. Can anyone run?"

"Oh, sure." He took a breath. "You just have to submit your name to the ASB adviser."

"Who's that?"

"Mr. Nichols. He's in room 401."

"And you say no one is running against Stacey?"

Brian shook his head. This was the longest conversation he had had with Julia, and he didn't want it to stop. "Why? You interested?"

"Maybe," Julia said, smiling. "But I don't have a campaign adviser." She touched Brian's arm, and shot his whole body through with electricity. Brian clamped his mouth shut so he wouldn't say something stupid or start drooling.

"Miss Romero, can I see you a moment?" Mr. Cohen called

from his desk at the front of the room.

Julia rolled her eyes, a secret communication that Brian rejoiced in. She was unhappy to leave him! If it weren't for their stupid biology teacher, she might offer to continue their talk in the quad, or over coffee, or in some smoky nightclub they'd have to sneak into.

Brian's phone buzzed again.

Need your help on acceptance speech, Stacey wrote.

Brian's penis wilted like a dehydrated flower. Sure, he wrote. Where are you?

Right outside your door, she wrote.

Brian sighed and gathered his things, stole one last look at Julia, and then went outside to meet his best friend.

3

JULIA APPROACHED MR. Cohen's desk and tried to hide her annoyance at being pulled away from Brian. After weeks of sitting next to him in class, she had finally managed a conversation that wasn't textbook related and allowed her to smile and flirt and be a little physical. Julia was attracted to her seatmate, which was strange because Brian definitely wasn't her type. He was shy, awkward, and a little scrawny. So unlike the guys she dated at her old school, who usually started punching each other after a few beers. The fact that she liked him made her think this move to California had really changed her. She wouldn't describe herself as a butterfly emerging from a cocoon; more like a prickly cactus that was starting to flower.

"Miss Romero," Mr. Cohen said once she was standing in front of his desk. "I just wanted to tell you how happy I am that you're in my class."

"Thanks," Julia said. "I'm happy too."

"I've been trying to encourage more Latinas to take AP courses, but it's been difficult, as you can see."

Julia felt a familiar anger rising in her gut. People always made this assumption about her background, given her skin color and last name. Unfortunately, there wasn't an easy way of correcting them, so more often than not, Julia just stayed quiet.

"My family's from Argentina," Cohen clarified, "so I have a personal interest in diversifying our upper-division science courses."

Julia looked at Mr. Cohen as if he were something squishy under a microscope slide. His pinkish-white skin reminded her of the baby pigs they had dissected a few weeks ago. He didn't speak with an accent, either, but rather had the same nasal drone of everyone else at this school.

"Anyway," he went on. "I just wanted to let you know I think you're doing great, but if you need any help, don't hesitate to ask."

"Thanks," she said. "I appreciate that."

Outside the room, Julia tried to process her teacher's words of encouragement. She supposed she should be grateful, but part of her was pissed. Did he think she needed that pep talk? Was he going easy on her because he thought she was Latina? No, she had earned her high marks on his assignments. She was sure of that. So, why make this connection? To show that he "got" her? He knew nothing about her, except that she was brown and had a Spanish surname. Why not ask her what her ethnicity was before jumping to conclusions based on this scant evidence? Did he not hear her French accent or see all those Arcade Fire stickers on her binder?

She supposed she should be grateful he didn't ask about her complicated backstory. In Canada, whenever some naive or obnoxious kid wanted to know about her, the conversation was always awkward and ended with Julia feeling pretty shitty.

"So, like, what are you?" the person would ask.

"What do you mean?"

"Where are you from?"

"From Canada."

"No, I mean, like, originally?"

"My mom's family is from Italy."

"What about your dad?"

"I don't know. You want me to get you a fucking DNA sample?"

That usually shut people up. After a while, people stopped asking. Or they noticed that her dad wasn't around and made up their own stories, which were always much duller versions of what actually happened.

Julia's phone buzzed with a message from her aunt. Where are you?! You're supposed to be at the curb at 2:45.

Shit, Julia thought. She texted a quick reply: Meeting with bio teacher. Be there in a sec.

Are you in trouble? her aunt wrote back. Typical, Julia thought.

No, she wrote, picking up her pace and rushing past the other students who didn't have a seventh-period class. There was a group of cheerleaders gossiping by the bathrooms. She noted their mixed racial makeup and felt her dark mood suddenly brighten. Two white girls, an Asian, a Latina, and an African American. She felt an instinctive urge to rush over and perform a little cheer for them. *Two, four, six, eight. Who do I appreciate? You guys! You guys!* Back in Boucherville, that squad would be all white, as would the athletes, the refs, and the fans. Julia hadn't realized how blinded she had become to all that whiteness until she moved to California. When she first stepped onto the Lincoln campus, she felt like Dorothy, exiting her whiplashed house into the Technicolor land of Oz.

A group of brown boys hanging out in front of the library called something to her in Spanish as she hustled past them. She didn't understand what they'd said but felt sure it was derogatory in some way. You don't have to be fluent in Spanish to know that when a comment is shouted at you with a simultaneous crotch grab, it's probably not a polite inquiry about your day. She didn't care. She was happy to see them, happy to be seen by them, so she responded with her own crotch grab, which threw them into hysterics.

In the few weeks she'd been at Lincoln, Julia had observed how the social classes divided themselves at the end of the school day like boxers who retreated to their corners at the sound of the bell. The rich kids drove off in their own cars, the middle class were picked up in family cars, and the poor took the bus. The school might pride itself on throwing this diverse mix of kids into their melting pot, but at the end of the day, the students knew where they belonged.

If Aunt Gloria hadn't insisted on picking her up, she would have gladly joined those on the bus. Or better yet, ridden her bike. That's what she missed most about coming to America: her bike. In Boucherville, she rode everywhere when the weather was this nice. Her bike gave her her first sense of freedom. Now she was restricted to her aunt's car and schedule. But she supposed that was the point. Her mom didn't send Julia to live with her sister because she wanted Julia to be more independent; her mom had lost control and decided to ship her here.

Julia stood in front of the school's marquee and scanned the line of minivans parked along the white zone for her aunt's car. Her aunt hated getting stuck in this clogged drainpipe of a street, which is why she insisted Julia be at the curb immediately after class. She'd have to be extra helpful at dinner tonight to make up for this inconvenience.

"Hey," a boy said, sidling up to her on the sidewalk. "You're Julia, right?"

At first glance, Julia thought he was kind of cute. Tall, muscular, and a buzz cut of reddish hair. As he stepped closer, though, she felt an instinctive impulse to pull away. His face had been jackhammered by acne, and his yellow teeth were encased in iron. He smelled of dried sweat and some body spray made from sandalwood and spoiled fruit. Julia quickly reevaluated her first impression and decided that he would be handsome in a few years, but only if he survived the seven plagues of puberty.

"Yes," Julia said, continuing to look up and down the street for her aunt. If she caught her talking to this boy, she'd catch all kinds of shit.

"I'm Lance," he said, extending his hand.

Julia shook it and noticed he was a nail biter. Tiny specks of dried blood dotted his cuticles.

"I write for the school paper. Sorry, *used* to write for the school paper. I'm kind of on sabbatical right now."

"Sabbatical?"

"I had a disagreement with my editor over my doping-in-dodgeball investigation."

"What? Like, steroids?"

"Nothing that serious. The winning team got high before every game. My editor wanted me to bury the story because she's friends with the team captain." Lance paused. "I want to do a story about you."

A gob of spit flew from his mouth and landed on Julia's arm. Out of politeness, Julia waited a few seconds before rubbing her skin dry.

"I thought you said you were on sabbatical," Julia said.

"I have a blog. *Life at Lincoln.* Maybe you've heard of it?"

Julia shook her head.

"I like to profile new students and, well, you're new."

"Oh, I don't know."

"C'mon," Lance said, flashing a crooked smile. "People are curious about you."

"I'm sure they're not," Julia said. She heard the blare of an insistent horn and found her aunt leaning on her steering wheel four cars away. "I've got to go."

"I'll text you," Lance said.

"You don't know my number," Julia said.

"Here's mine," he said, grabbing her hand and writing a sequence of numbers on her palm.

Julia hurried away, hoping her aunt hadn't witnessed this little exchange. When she reached the van, she hopped in and greeted Gloria's ruddy face with a warm smile.

"I'm sorry I'm late," she said, strapping herself in.

Aunt Gloria grumbled something and pulled away from the curb. As they passed Lance on the sidewalk, he mimicked a phone call with his hand.

"Who is that boy?" Gloria said.

"I don't know," Julia said. "Some reporter, I think."

"Why does he look like the cat that just swallowed the canary?"

"What does that mean?" Julia asked. She didn't understand many of her aunt's euphemisms.

"Like he just had his way with you."

"Had his way with me?"

"Is this why you were late? Because you were with him?"

"No, I told you. My teacher wanted to talk after class. You can email him if you don't believe me."

"Hmpf," she said, and focused her attention on the road. No matter what the driving conditions, Gloria always looked like she was navigating an icy road with woodland creatures darting out from the underbrush. Her nervousness had caused her face to become lined with cracks like a piece of pottery left in the kiln too long.

"Say hello to the girls," Gloria reminded her.

"Bonjour," Julia said, turning to face her eight-year-old cousins strapped into their booster seats in the back, giggling over some secret communication. The girls freaked

Julia out, to be honest. The other day they got simultaneous nosebleeds on the way home.

"Madison, Olivia, respond," Aunt Gloria barked.

"Bonjour," the twins said in unison. One of Aunt Gloria's conditions for taking Julia was that she only speak to the twins in French. She hoped this immersive experience would develop their language skills and make them more cosmopolitan. Julia spoke to them mostly in swear words.

They drove a few blocks in silence before Gloria brought up Julia's infraction again. "I'm worried you're falling back into bad habits, Julia. What do you think your mom would say if I told her you were flirting with some playboy after school?"

"I wasn't. . . ."

"This is just a trial separation," her aunt cautioned. "If you can't show us that you're serious about changing your ways, it's back to Canada. Do you understand?"

"Yes," Julia said. "I promise you, I wasn't flirting with him. He's a reporter or blogger. Are they the same thing here?"

"They most certainly are not," Gloria said.

"He wanted to do a story on me because I'm running for student body president."

"You're what?" Gloria risked a quick turn, her pinched face momentarily softening the way a dried sponge does with a few drops of water.

"I've decided to get more involved," Julia said, improvising. "I want to give something back to my community."

"Well, that's great," her aunt conceded. "Your mom and I talked about channeling your energies into more positive directions. She'll be happy to hear about this."

Gloria reached out to pat Julia's knee but fell short a few inches and tapped the seat cushion instead. Julia stared at her aunt's pale skin already dotted with age spots, like an archipelago on a sepia-toned map, and thought of her mom. She and Gloria were twins too, although not identical like Madison and Olivia. Still, they shared enough qualities to make living with her aunt a challenge. Gloria was like an updated iPhone, something familiar but with questionable new features that took some getting used to.

Julia furtively glanced at Lance's number written on her hand. Tonight, she would friend him online, which meant creating brand-new social media accounts. Ugh. She hated the thought of getting caught up in all that cyberdrama again, but there was no other way of communicating with people her age. If she was serious about running for president, she would need an online presence. She only hoped the digital ghosts of her past didn't come back to haunt her.

4

14 DAYS TILL ELECTION DAY

TONY GUO DIDN'T like change. He especially didn't like it when he was high and craving his favorite snacks. He counted on a degree of normalcy in the school cafeteria, especially at brunch. The lunch menu might change from day to day, but for his morning meal, he could always count on there being a routine supply of blueberry muffins and chocolate milk. But not today. Today was different, and Tony didn't like different.

"What the fuck?" he said to no one in particular.

He looked at the rows of milk cartons neatly arranged inside the metal bin, hoping to see his beloved Space Cow. The cartoon icon was so cute the way it looked like it was dressed for space, its udders carefully concealed in a dotted jumpsuit, its face peering through a circular helmet. Tony loved it so much he adopted the DJ name Space Cow and infused all his mixes with loops of cowbells and gentle mooing. So far, his signature DJ stylings hadn't caught on with mainstream partygoers, but he knew genius sometimes took time to get recognized. That's what that nice lady said after those bar mitzvah kids booed him off the stage at his last gig anyway.

"Doris, where's the chocolate milk?" he asked the bosomy woman dishing out hash browns. Doris slid the potato square onto the tray in front of him and stared at Tony over the cat-eye glasses balancing on the bridge of her nose.

"Sorry, Tony. No more chocolate milk."

"You sold out?" This had never happened before in the three years he'd been at Lincoln. There was always chocolate milk, and Tony always drank it. He credited it for making him the tallest Asian at the school. It was his antidote to all the weed he smoked, which people said was supposed to stunt your growth.

"We're no longer serving it," Doris said.

"What?" Tony looked around the room for the hidden cameras. He was sure they were planted somewhere to catch his reaction to this horrible news. The skate rat next to him looked like he might have a GoPro stuck on him somewhere. Tony had to fight the urge to run his hand along the vertical bristles of the boy's blue Mohawk. "Is this some kind of joke?" He leaned down and asked the freshman.

"C'mon, man, you're holding up the line," the boy said.

The kid was right. There was a long line of munchkins

with trays full of reheated "food," waiting to check out. But Tony wasn't moving until he got some answers. None of these kids was going to hassle him anyway. As a six-foot-two junior, he ruled over them like that personal trainer on that TV show with all those fat kids stranded on a deserted island.

"Doris, please tell me this is some kind of joke," he said.

"No joke, Tony," Doris said. "School ruled that chocolate milk is not good for you. Too much sugar." Doris looked at him with sad eyes. She understood the pain he must be experiencing, having served him every day for the past three years. She didn't try to hurry him along. She knew he needed time to grieve.

"This isn't happening," Tony said, staring at the cartons of homogenized white milk. He couldn't imagine drinking such a bland and boring beverage. That left him with what? Orange juice? He picked up a carton and stared at the faceless orange stabbed in the head with a straw. "Can't do it," he said, placing the orange juice back in the tray.

"Fuckin' nanny state," the Mohawk kid next to him said.

"Totally."

Tony began moving down the line toward the cashier. It felt more like a funeral procession than a checkout lane. After paying for his items, he walked to his usual table in the back corner of the cafeteria and sat down. A group of nearby boys screamed about a devastating loss on *Alien Sniper*, their pungent BO from morning PE class adding to the already-ripe odor of the room. Mohawk sat down next to him with his egg-o-rito and orange juice, which was strange. The freshmen who filled this cafeteria usually preferred their own company and left him alone in the dark recesses of the cavernous space.

"They want to tell us what we can and can't drink," Mohawk said. "Next thing you know they'll be taking away your muffin. Lots of sugar and fat in that too."

Tony clutched the cellophane-wrapped blueberry muffin to his chest. "They'll have to pry it out of my cold, dead hands," he said.

"If you keep eating that junk, that won't be hard to do. That stuff will kill you."

"Wait? What?" He thought Mohawk was on his side.

"Listen, I'm on your side," Mohawk said, reading Tony's mind. Tony scooted his plastic chair away from this telepath lest he dig further into his consciousness and see his masturbatory fantasies involving Doris the lunch lady. "We have to stop this."

"Stop what?" Tony asked.

"Stop this government overreach. They can't just come in here and tell us what to do."

"Uhm, it's school," Tony said. "That's kind of the point."

"No, the point is to create informed citizens capable of making their own decisions."

Tony laughed at how worked up Mohawk was getting. The little kid's pale face was turning an angry rash-like pink. Tony broke the seal of his blueberry muffin and offered the boy a bite, which he refused. Tony had forgotten how nice it was to share a table with someone. Most of the time he dined alone and watched YouTube videos on his phone.

"We should stage a hunger strike," Mohawk said.

"Yeah, right." Tony peeled the bottom wrapper off his muffin and shoved the moist cake into his mouth. He closed his eyes in an ecstasy of chewing.

"We could talk to the principal."

Tony, mouth full of muffin, just shook his head. The last time he met with the principal, it was to assure her that Space Cow would not be performing at the annual talent show.

"We could take hostages," Mohawk whispered.

"Dude, you're trippin'. Do you mind?" Tony reached for Mohawk's orange juice and drank half of it. The acidic citrus taste a sharp reminder of what he'd lost.

"You're right," Mohawk said. "The only way to change things is from the inside."

"Inside the cafeteria?"

"No, the government. You know anyone on ASB?"

"What's that?"

"Student government," Mohawk said. "We need someone on the inside to fight for our cause."

"You want to run for student body president?" Tony said. This guy! First he sits at the big-kid table, then he talks about running for student body president.

"Not me. You."

"Me?"

"I think you'd be a natural. Like Kanye. You know he's planning a run for president."

"I would totally vote for Kanye."

"Just like people here would vote for you," Mohawk said, scooting closer. "Trust me on this. You're the only one who can bring back our chocolate milk."

Tony thought about this. Or tried to. It was a little hard with all the screaming going on. This place—with its open floor plan and high ceilings—amplified every conversation to cacophonous levels. Plus, he was still high from the wake-and-bake routine he had fallen into ever since his parents had left to attend that casino opening in Macao.

"Tony Guo for president," he said, trying out the words for size. They fit about as well as the tight shirts at Banana Republic.

"Sounds good, doesn't it?" Mohawk said.

Space Cow sounded better. Maybe this was a way to get noticed as a DJ. Tony imagined playing at campaign events, election rallies, and his inauguration. As president, he could probably pass a law that required the school to hire him for all dances. And graduation! No one liked listening to that same old stale tune every year. What was it called? "Pot and Circumstance"? What did that even mean anyway?

"Let me think about it," he said, and shoved the remaining half of his blueberry muffin into his mouth. By the time the bell rang, he had forgotten what they had been talking about.

5

STACEY WALKED INTO room 401 and found half the class crowded around the whiteboard. Her classmates looked like some nerdy football team gathered by the coach to learn some complicated play. James, dressed impeccably as usual in a crisp, white button-down and skinny jeans, was fielding questions at the front. When he saw Stacey enter, he immediately stopped talking, a cue everyone else took to turn around and stare.

"What's going on?" Stacey asked. Her feet instinctively positioned themselves into a fighter's stance. She didn't like surprises. Two years ago, she hook-kicked a cake platter out of Brian's hands when he surprised her for her birthday.

"Looks like you've got some company," James said, smiling, showing off his movie-star teeth. Their whiteness distracted Stacey for a second and made her think about James's orthodontic history.

The crowd parted to let Stacey through. The silence was complete. Stacey felt like she was moving underwater. The sounds of people outside the classroom became distant and muffled.

Stacey reached the nomination board and saw that there were two more names written on it. Under the office of ASB president, there was now Stacey Wynn, someone named Julia Romero, and Tony Guo.

The shock of seeing the names scribbled beneath hers was considerable. For a second, Stacey lost her ability to observe her behavior from outside her body and stood slack-jawed in front of the classroom like some freshman boy experiencing his first view of live breasts.

"Tony Guo?" Stacey said. "I thought he'd been transferred to New Horizons."

James shook his head. "His parents kept him out of that holding pen by building our new weight room."

Stacey wasn't as bothered by Tony's name as she was by Julia's. Tony was the class clown—not the kind that's stand-up-comedian funny but the kind that's village-idiot funny. He posed no threat in or out of Lincoln.

"Who's Julia Romero?" Stacey asked, trying hard not to sound like the evil queen talking to her mirror about Snow White.

"She's in my AP comp class," Leslie Knox, junior class secretary, said. "She's from Canada. Great hair. And smart.

Always quoting existential philosophers no one's heard of."

Stacey didn't care what Julia looked like or how smart she was. She could hold her own against an intellectual in a crop top. No, what concerned her was the last name. Romero was ethnic, and that could spell trouble for her at a school that was only 40 percent white.

"Great!" Stacey said through gritted teeth. "Nice to see more people getting involved in student government."

Once the class realized Stacey wasn't going to have a total breakdown, they dispersed and took their seats. Before James could walk away, Stacey grabbed him by the arm and yanked him close.

"Did you put them up to this?" she asked.

"What are you talking about?" The look of confusion on his face seemed genuine, but James was much better at faking sincerity than Stacey.

"Tony and Julia," Stacey said. "Did you encourage them to run against me?"

"Tony Guo?" James said, laughing. "You think if I wanted to put up a candidate to run against you, I'd pick that guy? I thought you knew me better than that, Stace."

"What about Julia Romero?"

"Never heard of her, which is weird 'cause I know most of the Latinas."

"Who is she?" Stacey said.

James must have registered the panic creeping into her

voice because the smile on his face disappeared, replaced by a look of genuine concern. "I don't know. Let's ask Jen."

James called Jenny Ramirez over with a snap of his hand. James, Jenny, and Odalis Rodriguez were the only black and brown people in student government and had developed a private communication style involving dramatic hand gestures and raised eyebrows.

"You know this girl?" he asked, pointing to Julia's name.

"Never heard of her," Jenny said, flipping her long, black hair behind her shoulders. "Whoever she is, the girl's got some ovaries." Jenny returned to her seat. Stacey watched her retreat and wondered how the girl made even a casual stroll seem like dancing.

"Stacey?" James said, drawing her attention back.

"Yes, sorry," Stacey said. "I was just surprised to see the names is all. Sorry to accuse you of trying to undermine me."

"Apology accepted," James said.

Stacey took a seat at her desk and tried to pretend everything was business as usual.

Fake it till you make it, her mother used to say whenever Stacey needed to present a positive front to her friends and followers. This psychobabble used to be Stacey's mantra, until her mom left her dad for Mr. Park, Stacey's Tae Kwon Do teacher. Now the phrase seemed like the slogan for pathological liars everywhere.

Her mom's abrupt departure was the last time Stacey had

been surprised, and she vowed it would never happen again. But how could she have foreseen this? She had anticipated every potential rival from the field of candidates in her student government class and spoke with each and every one of them to determine the likelihood of them competing against her. How could she have seen that a boy who recently drove into a math portable and a transfer student from Canada would decide to launch campaigns for the highest office at the school? It was impossible to predict, like the next earthquake or the mood of her English teacher.

Stacey tried to focus on the Stress-Free Students Club's proposal to bring puppies on campus during AP testing. She could use a puppy right now, although in her current state she might inadvertently break its neck a là Lenny in *Of Mice and Men*. All she could think about was how her votes were getting redistributed. Tony might get a sliver of support from the kids he partied with, but even those potheads might have enough brain cells left to realize he wasn't the best representative for their school. Stacey wouldn't be surprised if one of his friends put Tony's name on the board as some kind of joke. A prank to get even for the school's recent "Smart Choices!" campaign to curb teen drinking at sporting events.

Tony could be ignored. Julia, on the other hand, was a potential threat. Stacey flipped open her laptop and Googled Julia Romero but couldn't find anything that matched

Leslie's description of "Canada," "great hair," and "Sartre." Who was this girl, and why had Stacey not heard about her until today?

In the midst of her Googling, a message from her mom popped up on her screen. Don't forget we're going shopping for bridesmaid dresses next weekend. What do you think of this? Below the text was a picture of a floor-length dress the color of a Band-Aid. It was hideously bland, but better than the traditional Korean wedding attire Mom was considering when she first got engaged. Neither Stacey nor her mom could wear those dresses without looking like a culturally appropriating Barbie doll.

Yes, Stacey typed back as a quick reply.

"Stacey, what's your vote?" Brandon asked her.

"Yes," she said, hoping he was asking about the puppy proposal.

Why were all these people pressing her for answers when she needed to figure out her game plan? She opened a new document and started typing out a to-do list. First off, she needed to make posters. She had all the butcher paper and paints in her garage ready to go for that. She'd need a slogan. Something catchy that hinted at her vision for a zero-waste school. "Clean up your act!" she wrote, which sounded too much like a nagging parent. "Don't be trashy" she liked for the subtle dig at her rival. Should she go negative right off the bat? Stacey didn't think so. "Don't throw away your vote!" made her smile. She'd run that one by Brian after school. She'd need his help making these banners in order to have them ready to hang by tonight. She'd also need him to help her revise her acceptance speech into a stump speech that would persuade students to vote for her. Was her composting platform too narrow to win her votes? She wrote "Focus group message" down at the bottom of her to-do list.

As soon as the bell rang, Stacey ran over to Brian's AP bio class, slaloming between students like a waitress in a crowded restaurant. The halls were crammed with so many kids; Stacey registered their faces as blurs of black, brown, and white. How could she, or anyone, appeal to such a diverse collection of interests? She couldn't serve all these different people the same dish, but if she tailored her message to each of these constituencies, she ran the risk of sounding like a suck-up. How did she create a menu to please both the carnivores and the vegetarians? She needed to find the item that pleased both. French fries, she thought. She needed to run on a platform of French fries.

Stacey reached Brian's class a little sweaty and out of breath and waited for him to exit the room. The flood of students turned into a trickle and then stopped altogether. Did Brian stay home today? They had texted at lunch while Stacey was at the Environmental Club meeting. Almost all of

Stacey's free time at school was taken up with club or student government meetings, so she usually didn't see Brian until after school.

Stacey poked her head in and saw Brian talking to a girl sitting on the desk, facing him. The girl's legs, and who knew what else, were directly in Brian's line of sight, preventing him from seeing Stacey waving from the doorway. Stacey couldn't see who the floozy was from her position, but whoever it was had great hair. Looking at its honeyed shine in the fluorescent light, Stacey recalled a myth she'd read in elementary school about a golden fleece and the powers it brought to whoever possessed it.

And then she realized it. "Fuck," she breathed.

This was Julia.

6

BRIAN DIDN'T NOTICE Stacey standing in the classroom doorway with Julia's smooth and tanned legs on display right in front of him. They were like an athlete's, only with none of the scars or bruises that come from competitive sports. Brian kept trying to focus on whatever it was Julia was saying. Something about the project they had just been assigned? They had to explain the genetic variations in some organism? He hadn't paid attention to anything Mr. Cohen said after Julia leaned over and whispered, "Will you be my partner?" Brian must have nodded because here they were, staying after class talking about sexual reproduction and giraffe necks.

And suddenly there was Stacey, standing next to them, wearing an expression of anger and despair, like someone showing up to a costume party in a sexy nurse outfit only to learn they're at a bar mitzvah.

"Stacey," Brian said. "What's up?"

"I need to talk to you," Stacey said flatly.

The silence that followed probably only lasted for a few seconds, but it felt like hours to Brian. The three of them sat there in the awkward space between conversations. Brian looked down. He knew he should be the one to say something here. Introduce the girls to each other. Make a joke. But something in Stacey's hostile demeanor made him hesitate. Instinctively, he sought to protect Julia by keeping her as anonymous as possible.

Julia just looked back and forth between Brian and Stacey, until finally, Stacey thrust a hand out to her. "My name's Stacey," she said. Julia shook her hand gently.

"Julia."

"I understand you're my rival," she said.

"Julia and I are just lab partners," Brian said.

Stacey rolled her eyes. "I'm talking about the election, dumbass."

"Oh, right. Wait. What?"

"Julia's running for student body president."

"She is?" Brian looked at Julia. "You are?"

"Yes," Julia said.

"Really? That's weird. I mean, it's great. I guess." Brian felt trapped suddenly. Nothing he could say to one would go over well with the other. His best move would be to shut up, but he had as much control over the words coming out of his mouth as he had over his penis. "Why do you want to be student body president?" he asked.

Julia shrugged. "I think it would be fun."

"Oh God," Brian mumbled. That was not the way to describe student government to Stacey.

Stacey stumbled back, as if she'd been slapped. "Fun?"

"Yes."

"It's a lot of work," Stacey said.

"I like working," Julia said.

"Do you know anything about this school and its traditions?"

Julia shrugged again. "I know enough."

"What does that even mean?" Stacey said. Brian could tell she was getting heated. Stacey wasn't good when she let her emotions take over like this. She came across as intolerant and condescending. Underclassmen didn't like her for that reason. In the last opinion poll Brian conducted, they overwhelmingly said Stacey reminded them of their mean older sister.

"It means, in my opinion, that some of your traditions only serve to divide the school, rather than bring people together."

"Like what?"

"I don't know. Take homecoming for example."

Stacey made a choking sound.

"You want to get rid of homecoming?" Brian asked for Stacey, who had lost the ability to speak.

"I don't know about getting rid of it, but don't you find it a little, I don't know, démodé?"

"I think the word you're looking for is 'historic,'" Stacey said.

"Yes," Julia said. "It's historic. Like slavery."

Stacey laughed and sputtered. "You're equating homecoming with *slavery*?" She was on the verge of hyperventilating at this point.

"Not slavery per se. Maybe more like colonialism. I don't understand your desire to be ruled by kings and queens. And frankly, the whole thing is oppressive to anyone not conforming to binary gender norms."

"Oh please," Stacey said. "Seriously?"

"I'm sure you'd see it too if you weren't so indoctrinated by the school."

"Now who's sounding like the colonialist?" Stacey said.

"Do you mean colonizer?" Julia said.

"You know what I mean. You're trying to impose your foreign values on our school culture."

"Maybe." Julia said. "I'll present my point of view and let the voters decide which system they favor. That's what's so wonderful about democracy, right?"

Brian knew he should be on Stacey's side, but he was in awe of Julia's oratorical style. While Stacey visibly shook with righteous indignation, Julia never lost her cool. If this were a debate, he'd clearly have to hand the victory to her. In five minutes of conversation, she had made him question his allegiance to a system that continuously rewarded the rich and athletic.

"I think you two are going to give the students a lot to think about," he said pathetically. His comment was meant to end the conversation on an optimistic note, but judging from the dour expressions on both Stacey's and Julia's faces, he may as well have asked them what they planned to wear for the swimsuit competition.

"*Merde,*" Julia said, glancing at her buzzing phone. "I have to go." She threw all her things into her bag and stood up to leave. "It was a pleasure meeting you, Stacey. Brian, we'll talk tonight about the project?"

Brian nodded and stood up as well. He and Stacey watched Julia sashay out the door and into the bright sunlight of the day.

"You can't be working with her," Stacey said, whipping around.

"We're just lab partners," Brian said.

"She's evil."

"She's not evil," Brian said. "She's Canadian."

"She wants to get rid of homecoming!"

"She didn't say that," Brian said. "She just used it as an example of one of the things she'd like to change."

"But who is she to want to change anything?" Stacey said. "She's been a student here for what? A month?"

"I think it's great that she wants to get involved."

"Brian, I need you to swear your loyalty to me right now."

"Are you serious? Now you do sound like a colonizer."

"I don't care. We've been friends for three years. Who beat up Chester Jespersen when he tried to nickname you 'Slim'?"

"You did," Brian said, cringing at the memory.

"Who brought you that towel after your swimsuit split open at the waterslides?"

"You did."

"Who brought you cookies every day you were in the hospital when your appendix burst?"

"Okay, I get it," Brian said. Stacey had been his only friend since he started high school, a fact for which he was both grateful and resentful—two emotions he didn't think he could experience simultaneously. "I hereby swear my loyalty to you, my superior queen."

"That's better," Stacey said. "What's her background anyway?"

"She's from Canada. The Quebec Province, I think. She speaks fluent French."

"That's not what I mean," Stacey said.

"I don't know. She's definitely not white."

"Duh," Stacey muttered.

"Everybody loves you, Stacey," Brian said. "More important, they respect you. There's no way someone new to the school can beat you, not even someone as hot as Julia."

Stacey punched him in the shoulder. Hard. "Can you come over tonight and help me with my banners? I'll bake you those gluten-free cookies you like so much."

"Yum," Brian said. "I'm there."

"You don't even have a wheat allergy," she said. "Why do you like those things?"

"I don't know, I just do." There were lots of things he liked that he wasn't supposed to. Figuring out if this made him unique or freakish consumed most of Brian's mental energies.

"You guys about done here?" Mr. Cohen said from his desk at the front of the room. Brian and Stacey looked up in surprise. He had been so quiet up there grading lab reports that neither had noticed him in the room.

"Sorry, Mr. Cohen," Brian said, sweeping his notebook and binder into his backpack. He and Stacey hustled out of the classroom and into the bright afternoon. As Stacey walked him through her ambitious to-do list, he nodded in agreement, all the while mentally scheduling her demands around his phone date with Julia.

7

JULIA WAS LATE again. She texted her aunt saying there was a mandatory meeting for all the ASB candidates and she would be curbside in five minutes. Take your time, Gloria texted her back. Clearly, Julia's involvement in student government had relaxed her aunt somewhat. Julia hoped the campaign could win back even more of her freedom. She'd love to better acquaint herself with her new hometown. She hadn't even visited the new ice cream store everyone was talking about. Supposedly, they had a barbecue ranch flavor that was like licking a potato chip.

Julia walked through campus, luxuriating in the warm spring day. The school seemed designed to soak up this sunshine, from the expansive lawns and benches in the center quad to the canopy of solar panels that covered the student parking lot. Unlike her old school, which was almost

Tetris-like in its brick-and-stone construction, Lincoln looked like a vacation resort. Each single-story building was separated from the others by open cement pathways, and patios made out of paving stones, and landscaped with desert flowers and trees. Maybe the Club Med atmosphere was responsible for the students' sunny dispositions.

On her way to the front, she passed two brown girls happily chatting near the entrance to the library. The girls were clearly California natives with their tank tops and short shorts. Julia wished she could pull off such a springtime casual look, but her body was too curvy and round. Both these girls had such skinny athletic figures, their clothes draped on them and looked almost elegant. The casual glamour seemed at odds with the field hockey equipment scattered on the ground in front of them.

Julia again found herself smiling. To be in the presence of so many brown faces! It was a reward, not a punishment, for her crime. She supposed she should feel guilty about that, but she was too happy to let those complicated feelings bother her. Besides, hadn't she been the one who suffered for sixteen years being the only brown girl in a sea of white faces? Of course she was going to lash out eventually at the people who treated her as "the Other" for so long.

One of the girls—the one with the long, silky black hair—smiled back as she passed. "Are you Julia?" she asked.

"Yes," Julia said.

"I'm Jenny," the girl said, extending a hand to shake. "You're running for student body president?"

"I am," Julia said. "How did you know?"

"I'm the ASB secretary," she said. "This is Rosa."

Rosa held up her hand in a shy wave. Her face was a bit harder than Jenny's, outlined in heavy eyeliner and lipstick.

"Nice to meet you," Julia said.

"I was so psyched to see your name on the nomination board," Jenny said. "I'm, like, the only Latina in that class. It's hella awkward."

"Oh, I don't know—" Julia started.

"Odalis is in the ASB," Rosa said.

Jenny rolled her eyes. "Girl, she don't count. She only hangs with the cheer squad."

"You can't say she doesn't count. Her family's Nicaraguan."

Jenny held up a hand to quiet her friend. "I love your accent," she said to Julia. "Where you from?"

"Canada."

"There many Latinos in Canada?" Rosa asked.

"Some."

"So, you're, like, trilingual?" Jenny said.

"Actually, I never learned Spanish," Julia confessed.

"Me neither!" Rosa said. "My parents worried it would hold me back."

"What?" Julia said. "That makes no sense."

"I know, right? Meanwhile, my white neighbor is fluent because his parents put him in a Spanish immersion school. He can talk to my *abuela* better than I can."

Julia's phone buzzed again. Gloria must be getting impatient. "I'm sorry, I've got to go," she said. "My aunt's waiting for me."

"Nice to meet you," Jenny said. "Glad you're putting yourself out there. You got my vote."

"Mine too," Rosa said.

Julia thanked the girls and rushed to meet her ride. What had she gotten herself into? If her legs hadn't been moving, they might have buckled under the surge of anxiety flooding her system. What had seemed like an ingenious way to gain her freedom had just put her in a new cage.

Julia scanned the convoy of minivans lined up at the curb, looking for her aunt's car. When she spotted it, she was surprised to see Lance leaning into the passenger window. What the hell was he doing talking to her aunt? She never agreed to being profiled on his blog. Was he trying to dig into her background? What would Aunt Gloria reveal? Surely, she'd want to keep Julia's secrets safe from this tabloid reporter. Or maybe she'd tell him everything and then use his article as an excuse to ship her back to Canada. Neither Lance's nor Gloria's motivations were clear to her. She only knew she had to stop this conversation right now.

Julia picked up her pace, speed walking to the mini-van. As she approached, she was treated to a view of Lance's underwear poking above his hanging jeans. She fought the urge to grab the waistband with both hands and lift the guy into a giant wedgie.

"Lance, hi," Julia said, a little breathless.

"Hi, Julia," he said, turning around and opening her door for her like a valet. "I was just talking with your aunt here about your move."

"Really?" Julia said, strapping herself into the passenger seat. "Bonjour!" she said to the twins in the back. She needed to slow her heart rate down, and she hoped following the regular pick-up routine would help. The twins just stared back at her with unblinking eyes and smiled.

"J'accuse!" one of them said, although Julia was so freaked out she might have imagined it.

"Yes, dear," Gloria said, placing a calming hand on Julia's thigh. "I just told Lance here why you moved to California."

"You did?" Julia said. She kept her eyes locked on her aunt, not trusting her ability to hide her panic from Lance.

"Yes," Gloria said. "It makes so much sense to establish residency if you want to go to an American university."

Julia closed her eyes and exhaled, feeling her panic abate somewhat. Her aunt had covered for her. This was the first time Gloria had done something to indicate that Julia was a welcome guest instead of a fugitive from justice. Had her change of heart come about just because Julia decided to run for student body president? It seemed like such a small thing to swap for her aunt's trust and support.

"I knew you were smart," Lance said. "Out-of-state tuition at UC is killer."

"Yes, well, I'm just lucky I have such a generous and loving family," Julia said to Gloria. "They really . . . How do you say? Have my back."

"Now that you're running for ASB president, I'd love to do that profile we talked about," Lance said, leaning on the passenger door, giving everyone in the car a sample of his BO. It was like being spritzed by *Eau de Gym Locker*. "It could really help voters get to know you."

"That's a great idea," Julia said. "I'll call you tonight."

"Looking forward to it," Lance said, stepping back from the car. He waved goodbye to the twins in the back, who growled in response.

"That boy seems shifty," Gloria said, pulling away from the curb.

"I agree," Julia said.

"But he could be useful in your campaign."

Julia looked into the rearview mirror and saw Lance standing by the school marquee, typing into his phone.

"So you think I should let him interview me?" Julia asked.

"I would, but I wouldn't let him get too close, if you know what I mean."

"Thanks, Aunt Gloria," Julia said. "For not telling him about . . . you know." Julia glanced back at the twins, who were laughing at something on their iPads.

"I know I've been hard on you," Gloria said. "But that's only because I felt you lacked structure." Gloria leaned over and dropped her voice. "What happened back in Canada only happened because your mother wasn't looking after you."

Julia wanted to object, but she kept her mouth shut. What happened had nothing to do with how much her mom monitored Julia's behavior. It happened because Julia believed a boy who had every reason to lie.

"I really want to be a better person," Julia said.

"I believe you," Gloria said. "That's why I'm so proud about this step you're taking. You know, I see a bit of myself in you."

"Really? How so?"

"When I was your age, I wanted to be class president too, but then your mom went and got herself arrested, and I became guilty by association. I dropped out of the race, and I've always regretted it."

"What did Mom do?"

"Oh, I don't know. She was always protesting something.

Back then it was nuclear power, I think. The point is, I gave up on my dreams. I don't want you making the same mistake."

"Part of me thinks it would be better to maintain a low profile," Julia said.

"Now, that's what got you into trouble back home, isn't it? Living on the internet? Sunlight is the best disinfectant, Julia. Trust me on this. You put yourself out there, and you'll be surprised at what can happen."

"You think so?"

"I know so. And listen, running a campaign is a lot of work, which will require more time at school. It might be a good time to start using that bike of yours so you're not stuck to my schedule."

"Seriously? I would love that." Julia wrapped her arms around her aunt's shoulders, making sure she didn't block her view of the road.

"Careful," Gloria said, gripping the steering wheel more forcefully.

Julia bounced up and down in excitement. It was such a small thing—biking to school—but it would change everything. She would celebrate her newfound freedom by taking Brian to ice cream after class tomorrow. He could pedal while she rode on the handlebars.

"I need a campaign poster," Julia said. "Can you help me make one?"

"I'd love to," Gloria said. "Right after dinner."

Julia opened the passenger-side window and let the warm breeze blow through her hair. She caught a glimpse of herself in the side mirror and smiled at the girl staring back at her. She could do this. It didn't matter if she lost; the victory would come in Gloria seeing her act responsibly. Afterward, she'd have more freedom, and who knows, maybe a few friends? Like Jenny and Rosa. She would find some way to tell them she wasn't Latina, at least not in the way they defined the term. They might freak out at first, but eventually, they would come to accept her. She was sure of it.

8

TONY STARED AT Mrs. Zhang as she *tsk*ed her way through his Mandarin Chinese exam. He had skipped class yesterday because he hadn't studied, but he didn't use the extra time to prepare for his makeup. This taught him an important lesson: cutting class on the day of a test doesn't result in better grades; it just means more time with your teacher after school. He hoped he would remember this the next time a major assignment was due.

"You failed," Mrs. Zhang said, reaching across her cluttered desk and handing him his chapter exam. On the top of the page she had scribbled the score 28/50. That didn't seem like failing to Tony. He was actually impressed he got more than half the questions right.

"Dang," Tony said, trying to sound as disappointed in himself as Mrs. Zhang. She stared at him through large, round glasses, blinking a Morse code of admonishments.

"You should not be failing my class, Tony," she said. "Both your parents are Chinese."

"That's kinda racist, Mrs. Zhang."

"You can't be racist against your own race," she said dismissively.

"Sure you can. No one expects English speakers to cruise through English. Why should I be expected to pass Mandarin just 'cause my parents are Chinese?"

Tony felt like he had been fighting the model-minority stereotype his whole life. Everyone assumed he was smart and hardworking just because he was Asian and lived in a mansion in the hills. But his parents weren't smart or hardworking either. As far as Tony knew, his dad had inherited all his wealth from his father, who owned a real-estate empire in Fuzhou. Mr. Guo made occasional trips back for board meetings, but other than that, his dad and mom spent most of their time traveling the globe, winning and losing their fortune in casinos on every continent.

"What language do you speak at home?" Mrs. Zhang asked.

"Romanian."

"What?"

"The people who take care of our house—they're from Moldova, I think."

"Where are your parents?"

Tony had to be careful here. His dad left him strict instructions on what to tell the school if they ever asked about their whereabouts. "My dad's in China on business," he said.

"What about your mom?"

"I'd prefer not to talk about that," Tony said, casting his eyes downward.

Just as his father had predicted, that shut Mrs. Zhang up quickly. She shuffled some papers on her desk, trying to think of a way to depersonalize this conversation. "Well," she said. "I can help find you a tutor if you want."

"That's cool," Tony said, stuffing his failed test into his backpack and heading toward the door. "I promise to try harder next time."

The campus was empty as Tony made his way to the parking lot. He didn't like how quiet everything was. It reminded him of a recurring nightmare, where he was the only one to survive a nuclear holocaust. In his dream, the sky is an ashy gray, and there's a breeze that blows crumpled-up pieces of paper across the quad like tumbleweeds. Tony lumbers through the hallways, checking doors and finding them all locked. There's no one on campus. Just him. The worst part of the dream is that on that day, Tony has finally done all his homework.

Today wasn't like that exactly. First off, he hadn't done any of his homework. Second, it was a beautiful spring day, pleasant even at four p.m. Tony stepped out from under the awning that shaded the exterior hallway and let the afternoon sun warm his face.

The student parking lot was mostly empty. Off in the distance he saw some kid skateboarding dangerously close to Tony's shimmering Mercedes. As he got closer, he recognized the munchkin with the blue Mohawk he talked to yesterday in the cafeteria. The kid saw him approach and rolled over to greet him.

"What's up?" Mohawk said.

"Nothin'," Tony said. "What are you doing near my car?"

"Waiting for you. Sweet ride." Mohawk motioned toward the Mercedes.

"It's my dad's," Tony said. "I drive it when he's away."

"Have you thought any more about my idea?" Mohawk asked, doing an ollie. Tony was impressed he could execute the move and maintain eye contact.

"What idea?"

"About you running for student body president."

"Dude, I thought you were kidding."

"I wasn't. If you really want to see chocolate milk back in the cafeteria, it's the only way to go."

"But I don't want to be president."

"You wouldn't get elected," Mohawk said. "You'd just run for office."

"I don't get it. Why run if I don't want to get elected?"

Mohawk took a deep breath, which is just what Tony's dad did when he explained things he thought should be obvious. Like why it's important to walk the dog or brush your teeth at night. Tony didn't like being treated this way by a skate rat. He was about to tell him off but then realized it would take too much effort.

"You run to bring chocolate milk back to the cafeteria," Mohawk said. "Your campaign is, like, your megaphone. It allows your voice to be heard. It lets you speak truth to power."

"So, I say I'm running for president, but really, I'm just telling everyone about the chocolate milk crisis."

"Exactly. Think about it. While the other candidates are boring everyone with their speeches about their experience and lame ideas, you'll focus solely on the injustice of depriving students of this delicious, nutritious beverage. People will love you."

"What makes you so sure?"

"Because you're different. You're not like all the other politicians talking about spirit rallies and food drives. You're Tony Guo, a hilarious dude people can relate to."

"What if I win?"

"Then you win. What's wrong with that?"

"I don't want to, you know, do any work or anything."

"So you delegate. There's a whole class of overachievers you can make work for you."

Tony liked that idea. He was starting to worry that everyone at Lincoln was passing him by. He didn't know how he had become a piece of deadweight that needed to be tossed overboard. He suspected his failure at school had something to do with the amount of pot he smoked, but he didn't want to reflect too deeply on his favorite pastime lest he be forced to give it up. The promise Mohawk seemed to be making was that Tony's pot smoking could actually help him get elected. Somehow, Mohawk saw it as an asset the other candidates lacked. Maybe Tony could be, like, a role model for other Asians who failed their Mandarin Chinese exams. Tony Guo: Winning by Subverting the Stereotype! The campaign slogan appeared in his head like a soap bubble, then popped and quickly evaporated.

"Okay, I'll do it," Tony said. "Where do I sign up?"

"I already took the liberty of nominating you," Mohawk said, skating out of Tony's reach.

Tony shook his head. "You what?"

"I knew how much chocolate milk meant to you, and I was near the ASB classroom so . . ."

"Dude. Not cool."

"It's no big deal. If you said no, I would have taken your name off the list." Mohawk jumped off his skateboard and kicked it vertical. He walked cautiously back to where Tony was standing.

"Who else is running?" Tony asked.

"Two girls. Stacey Wynn and Julia Romero."

"Don't know either one of them."

"Don't worry. You'll crush them."

"And you'll do all the work?"

"I got this covered, bruh," Mohawk said, extending a hand for Tony to shake. "Don't you worry about a thing."

CAMPAIGN ADS

9

ANY DOUBT THAT Stacey had about Brian's loyalty was erased after he came over to her house and helped her paint her campaign banners. Stacey wanted to make twenty, but he wisely counseled her against oversaturating the market. "Too many posters, and you look desperate," he said. "You want to show you're in it to win it, but you don't want people to get sick of you." They decided ten banners would be enough to communicate this message, and they worked until Brian's mom called him home to dinner.

"I'll meet you at school tonight and help you hang them," he said before driving away.

Stacey thought the banners should be up when the first students arrived at school in the morning. Technically, campaign posters weren't allowed on campus until tomorrow, but Stacey wanted to grab the high-traffic areas before anyone else. The school grounds at Lincoln were open, giving her access to the quad and hallways. The only security the campus had was the custodial staff, but Stacey had already spoken with them to make sure they wouldn't remove her banners as part of their evening cleaning.

Stacey went back into the garage, which they had converted into a printmaking studio, and put away the brushes, paint, and markers. The lettering on the posters was still a little damp, so Stacey left the eight-foot-long strips of butcher paper drying on the floor. She didn't want to roll them up too early because then the ends would curl, and she'd prefer that they looked ironed flat when they hung from the walls of her school. She painted a quick *No Parking* sign to hang on the garage door to warn her dad that the space was being occupied. He was used to her commandeering the garage for her various projects. Just a few months ago, the area was filled with boxes of canned peaches from her holiday food drive.

On her way to the stairs leading to the kitchen, Stacey passed the collection of cardboard boxes her mom was supposed to move to her new place. They still occupied a large corner of the garage, and Stacey was tempted to throw them out. What had it been? Four months? Surely Mom had time to collect these things that were so important they had to be removed from the house and stored here. Stacey glanced at the labels her mom had affixed to each of the moving boxes. *Kitchen, Office, Shoes.* Stacey was tempted to dribble an open can of paint into each one. *Sorry, Mom,* she'd say all innocent-like. *I don't know how that happened.*

There was a large box in the back with Stacey's name written on top in Sharpie. Stacey had avoided it for months, worried about its contents. What mementos from Stacey's childhood would her mom deem important enough to take to her new home? She pictured baby blankets, finger paintings, lanyards, and other childhood detritus crammed inside. What Stacey didn't want to see were folded baby clothes. Her mom was in her late thirties, old but still young enough to have another child. What if the box was filled with Stacey's hand-me-downs? The cute outfits she'd give her new baby? The one she'd raise in a happy home, with a stable family, and twenty-four-hour access to a martial arts studio?

Fuck it, Stacey decided, pulling the container free from its location. This box might as well have "Pandora" written on top. Whatever lay inside was going to upset her. Might as well rip off the packing tape like a Band-Aid and stop worrying about getting hurt.

As she folded back the cardboard lid, the first thing Stacey thought was that this was her mom's treasure chest. She had only written her daughter's name on top to hide the fact that it was filled with pieces of gold. Then she realized the objects inside were only gold-plated figures of girls posed as athletes and scholars. The statues looked like toy dolls that had been turned to stone by some tiny Medusa.

Looking at the collection of trophies, Stacey wasn't sure what was more depressing: the fact that these were the only mementos her mom cared about or the fact that she left the box in a neglected corner of the garage. She picked up the largest trophy—the one she won at her last Tae Kwon Do tournament—and held it over her head, as if in tribute to her crowds of adoring fans. Then, in one sweeping motion, she brought the statue down onto the cement floor and broke the gold figure off with a crack. The plastic girl, forever frozen in a fighting stance, bounced a few times before finally landing on her side next to a twenty-pound-bag of cat food.

Stacey took a deep breath and inhaled the garage's odor of wet paint and motor oil. That felt good. She should do that more often. Imagine her mom's face when she opened this cardboard trophy case and found all her daughter's statues decapitated. What a fitting metaphor, Stacey decided. Her mom would get to keep all the awards; Stacey would keep all the girls.

Just as she was lifting another gold-plated figure above her head, her dad drove up. She quickly threw the trophy back into the box, sealed the lid, and placed the container back in its original place.

"What's all this?" her dad said, getting out of his ancient

Volvo. The car, like him, was in need of a wash. Stacey had to start laying out his clothes the night before classes to make sure he didn't dress like a slob. His look was less absent-minded professor and more midlife-crisis hobo.

"Brian came over and helped me with some banners," Stacey said.

"I thought you were running unopposed."

"Not anymore."

Seeing the clutter, her dad detoured and entered the house through the front door. Stacey walked up the stairs to the kitchen entrance and hit the button that brought the garage door sliding down from the ceiling.

"I thought I'd heat up that lasagna for dinner," Stacey said. "That is, if you're not sick of it." Stacey had too much going on at school to give herself daily assignments in the kitchen, so she made meals that could be portioned out for weeks.

"That sounds great, honey," her dad said, dropping onto the couch.

Stacey tried not to let his sagging energy level frustrate her. The divorce had been hard on him. The marriage had been hard on him too. If Stacey felt pressured by her ambitious mother to succeed, she couldn't imagine the stress her eggheaded father felt. All he wanted to do was tinker in his lab and teach a few physics classes at the university, not create the next billion-dollar mobile app.

At least he was leaving the house every day. That positive step had come about only after Stacey persuaded her dad to teach one class this term. After the divorce, her dad had taken a sabbatical (i.e. vacation) from the university so he could research (i.e. drink beer and binge-watch *Cosmos*) his book (i.e. proposal) on relativistic energy. The Intro to Physics class he was teaching this quarter was probably a no-brainer for him; it was the act of getting out of bed that required the most effort.

"Dad, I need your help with a project," Stacey announced, bringing him his dinner. She placed their plates of reheated lasagna and side salad onto the coffee table. Before he could get up and get a glass of wine, she marched back to the kitchen, filled two glasses with ice water, and placed them on coasters in front of him. Her dad looked like a child who'd just been given fruit for dessert.

"What's up?" he said.

"I want to build a drone," Stacey said. She didn't really want to build a drone. She wanted her dad to build a drone. Now that she had gotten him busy during the day, she needed to find a way to occupy his nights. This was the perfect project for him. And it would make a nice gift to the ASB on her first day in office. She wasn't sure what the ASB would do with a drone, exactly, but she was sure she could find a way to use it. Aerial views of football games, perhaps. Or a spy cam to catch careless polluters.

Stacey threw a copy of *Make* magazine in front of him and watched him slowly become absorbed by the step-by-step instructions. Pretty soon he was talking less to her and more to the pages of the magazine. When he was done with his meal, she cleared his empty plate and went back to the garage to put the banners into her car.

"You think it's doable?" she asked, coming back in to say goodbye.

"Yes," he said. "I have to order some of these parts, but I've got most of the tools."

"Great!" Stacey went over and gave her dad a kiss on the cheek. "I gotta go hang some banners."

Stacey drove to school, swinging by the Tea House on her way to pick up Brian's usual order. She wanted to do something nice to thank him for all his help, and she didn't have time to make another batch of gluten-free cookies. There were only so many men she could take care of, she thought. Besides, if she didn't stop baking for Brian, he'd be as chubby as he was freshman year.

When she entered the darkened student lot, Brian's car was already parked near the entrance to the school. She pulled up next to him and handed over the milky Earl Grey he loved so much.

"Decaf?" he asked.

"Of course," she said, wishing she felt as confident in her order as she sounded. "Sorry for flipping out on you today."

"That's okay," Brian said, taking a sip. "I know how you feel about surprises."

"I really appreciate your help." Stacey popped the rear door of her Honda Fit and pulled out the rolled banners.

"Happy to do it. The less time I spend at home with Kyle, the better."

"How's his therapy going?"

Brian shrugged. "It hasn't made him any nicer."

"Maybe you should have bullied him more growing up. That's what most older brothers do. You're too nice."

"Thanks, Janet."

Janet was Stacey's mother. Brian was always quick to remind Stacey of her lineage whenever she adopted her mom's tough-love talk. He knew how terrified she was of turning into Janet and did his best to lightly nudge her away from the dark side. Stacey thanked him by dumping the pile of rolled-up banners in his arms. "C'mon. Let's hang these."

They hit the high-traffic areas first, hanging banners in the quad, by the gym, and near every bathroom. When they moved in the direction of the science wing, Brian started lagging behind.

"Why are we heading back this way?" he asked.

"I've mapped out all the events taking place on campus this week," Stacey said, grabbing him by the arm and hustling down the empty hallways weakly illuminated by sporadic lighting. "Hackfest is Thursday, which means the science building will be packed with students who want free pizza."

"Genius," Brian said.

"There's also a big calculus test on Friday, so people are going to be using the tutorial center more. I thought we'd head there next."

They finished twenty minutes later. After taping up the last banner, they paused and took in the quiet of the campus at night. Off in the distance, a bent man pushed a cleaning cart down an illuminated hallway. "We're all done, Oscar!" Stacey shouted from the walkway that connected the student parking lot to the main quad. Oscar turned and waved and then continued on his way.

The two walked back to their cars on the empty lot. On their way, they passed a bike chained to the racks that hadn't been there before. Stacey looked at her watch. It was nearly ten o'clock. "Whose bike is this?" she asked.

"Yeah, who would be crazy enough to come to school at this hour?" Brian said, nudging Stacey.

"Shut up," she said. "Don't you think that's weird?"

Brian shrugged. "Not really. It's probably some freshman who needed something in his locker."

Brian pulled Stacey back to their cars. Before getting in, Stacey gave Brian a big hug and thanked him again for all his help.

Brian drove off, leaving Stacey alone in the empty lot. She knew she should race home and start working on the homework she had put off, but she had to know who the owner of the bike was. It was a surprise seeing it appear like this, and Stacey didn't like surprises. After waiting thirty minutes and still seeing no one appear, it was even more unsettling. She was just about to go investigate when her father texted her, demanding she return home at once. After telling him she was on her way, she started her car and pulled out of the parking lot, making sure to watch the campus through her rearview mirror for any signs of movement.

10

THE MORNING SUN lit up Brian's room like a migraine. He tried to smother out the burning rays with his pillow, but it was no use. The light had frightened sleep away, and it would not be returning until fifth-period trigonometry.

Brian yanked himself free of the covers, stood up, and rubbed his eyes. There was a reason he slept with his curtains open, wasn't there? He liked to rise with the sun, rather than be awoken by Skinny and the Mooch on the radio. Why was this morning so difficult?

It was because he couldn't get to sleep last night. After helping Stacey hang her banners, he raced home to call Julia. They talked a bit about their biology project and then segued to other topics, like music (their love of Mitski, specifically), movies (Brian liked comedies; Julia, foreign films), and travel (Machu Picchu was on both their bucket lists).

Julia told Brian about all the things she found strange about Lincoln—the open campus, the devotion to group work, the ubiquitous technology. Before he knew it, it was one a.m. and Julia had to go. Brian was so keyed up by the conversation, or by the tea Stacey had given him, that he didn't fall asleep for another hour.

Now he was stumbling across his carpet like a zombie looking for caffeinated brains. He plugged in the electric kettle on his desk and waited for the steam to emerge from the spout. When the water had boiled, Brian dug through his tin of tea until he found an Earl Grey bag. He plucked it from the metal container and dropped it in his Garfield-shaped mug that had *I Hate Mondays* on it. Stacey had given it to him as a joke a few years ago, but it turned out to be the perfect size for his morning brew.

He blew the rising steam emanating from Garfield's head and stared at the photo tacked up on his bulletin board of him and Stacey dressed as Harry and Hermione last Halloween. He shouldn't feel guilty for talking to Julia last night, right? It's not like he told her any of Stacey's campaign secrets. As long as they focused on biology and other nonelection topics, there wasn't a conflict of interest. So, why did he feel the need to keep his conversation secret from his best friend? Did Stacey feel threatened by Julia because she was running for president or because Brian liked her? Brian wished he had someone he could talk to about this.

James, maybe? He was another thorn in Stacey's side, but at least he wasn't a threat politically or romantically. Now that the nomination process was over and no one was running against him for ASB vice president, James might have some time to help him work through his feelings. That is, if James would agree to a meeting, which Brian doubted he would.

Brian leaned over and took down the photo of him and James at the National Scouts jamboree from a few years ago, pinned just below the Halloween photo. The two of them stood in the center, their uniforms crisply ironed and covered in badges. James was already wearing his signature oversize glasses, advancing the geek look before it was trendy. If he could have fit a bow tie on the uniform without breaking regulations, he probably would have. The other boys surrounding them were sloppily attired, their neckerchiefs as crooked as their smiles. No one in the troop took scouting as seriously as Brian and James, both of whom sought to maintain high standards of conduct at all meetings and jamborees. When James finally dropped out, it left Brian with no other rule follower. On the last camping trip, the other boys tied him to a tree and put a banana slug down his pants. Brian quit Scouts soon after that.

Given the unpleasant end of his Scouts experience, it was strange that Brian kept this photo tacked to his bulletin board. He should probably take the picture down, but it was the only evidence he had of guy friends, and for some reason this comforted him. Why didn't he like the things most guys liked? Even his tea drinking was suspect. "You tea bagging it today, bruh?" his little brother, Kyle, was fond of saying when he saw him with his cup, which was part of the reason he drank his beverage in the privacy of his room. Maybe if he switched to coffee, he would blend in more. Or beer. That's a manly drink, especially when it's poured into your mouth from the tap of a keg while a bunch of football players hold you upside down.

After showering and getting dressed, he headed down the hallway for breakfast. The nice part about having a mom who wrote fantasy novels was that she was always home in the mornings. When Brian entered the kitchen, she would stop working and join him, sometimes making his favorite French toast if she knew he had a stressful day ahead.

"Morning, honey," she said as he stumbled in.

"Morning," he said. He grabbed a bowl of cereal and sat down at the kitchen counter. "Kyle up yet?"

"What do you think?"

Most days, Kyle didn't emerge from his bedroom until Brian was walking out the door, which was fine by him. Brian liked to get to school early—to get a head start on his day—whereas Kyle skateboarded in, usually arriving late to first period. Mom called them yin and yang, never identifying who was dominated by darkness and who by light. But it wasn't hard to guess. Only one of them was in therapy, and it wasn't Brian.

"Why don't you wake him up?" Brian asked.

"You want to wade through that minefield?" his mom asked. It was true. Besides the piles of dirty clothes, shoes, and skateboards, Kyle had booby-trapped his room to keep out unwanted visitors. The other day, Brian had activated a trip wire that launched a partially eaten meatball at his head.

His mom got up and poured herself a cup of coffee. "What do you think is the better superpower: Shape-shifting or mind control?"

"Hmmm." Brian thought about it. "Are we talking world domination here?"

"Yes," his mom said.

"Then mind control, for sure. But I'd rather be a shape-shifter."

"Why?"

"Well, shape-shifting lets you transform yourself into anything, whereas as mind control gives you control over others' thoughts and perceptions. One gives you power over the body, and the other power over the mind."

"Yes?"

"I'd rather have control over my body."

"What do you mean?"

"I don't know." Brian felt trapped. His mom often did this—cloak personal topics under the veil of fantasy. A discussion on dragons could somehow magically segue into a talk about masturbation. "It would be cool to be able to change into an eagle and fly, I guess."

His mom sighed. "You're right. Mind control is more powerful, but it's kind of boring, unless there's some way to stop it. Like Magneto with his helmet."

"Yeah, why don't all the X-Men villains wear those?" Brian asked. It was a question that bothered him.

"Maybe the materials are hard to come by," his mom said. "Like kryptonite. If everyone carried a chunk of kryptonite in their pocket, then Superman would be powerless."

"Every superhero needs a weakness to be interesting."

Brian heard his phone buzz from the hallway table. His parents held his phone hostage there at night so he wouldn't stay up late texting. They had no idea his computer came with fifteen different messaging apps, including FaceTime, which he used to talk with Julia.

"That thing has been vibrating since you went into the shower," his mom said.

"Why didn't you tell me?" Brian said, running to retrieve the device. He picked it up and scrolled through the texts. They were all from Stacey in full freak-out mode.

This is everywhere!!!!!!!! her first text said, only with a lot more exclamation points. When Brian clicked on the link, he was taken to a blog called *Life at Lincoln* by Lance Haber. "Campaign Poster Vandalized with Racial Slur," the headline read. Brian's first thought was that someone had graffitied over one of Stacey's banners, but when he scrolled down, he saw it was Julia's sign that had been defaced. She had hung a tiny 2' x 2' poster on the library window with the words "Julia for Student Body President" written in big, bold, rainbow-colored letters. Underneath this generic message, someone had Sharpied "Build That Wall!" Brian scrolled down and read the "web exclusive."

"CAMPAIGN POSTER VANDALIZED WITH RACIAL SLUR"
by Lance Haber

Last night, someone vandalized the campaign poster of Julia Romero with an anti-immigrant rallying cry.

Romero, a recent transfer student from Canada, is running for student body president against Stacey Wynn. Wynn's campaign banners, hung throughout the school, were untouched, which leads many to believe this was a hate crime.

"I know this kind of racist speech doesn't represent the majority of students at Lincoln," Romero said in response to the incident.

The administration has removed the poster but has not commented on their investigation.

"Everyone needs to take a stand against this kind bigoted, intolerant attitude," Lauren Andrews said. "I've already started an Instagram hashtag #WeWelcomeYouJulia, which I hope everyone uses to express our support for Julia and her campaign."

Brian clicked over to Instagram and scrolled through the hundreds of messages that students had posted in support of Julia. "I know we don't really know each other," Tanisha Baker wrote, in a typical reply. "But if you want to talk, I'm here for you. This is NOT who we are."

Brian wanted to join the chorus of supporters with his own "I love you, Julia," but he didn't know if this would be misinterpreted by Julia. He knew it would be misinterpreted by Stacey, so instead, he clicked back to Stacey and expressed his shock and disbelief. Holy shit, he wrote. His phone rang a few seconds later.

"Are you seeing this?" Stacey said.

"I can't believe it. It's like . . . Wow."

"I'm so dead."

"You didn't . . ."

"What? No! How can you even . . . ? Brian, you know I would never. . . ."

"I know," Brian said. "When you said 'I'm so dead,' I thought . . ."

"I meant politically. People are either going to assume I did it or one of my supporters did it. Either way, I'm labeled as a racist unless I petition the pope to make Julia a saint. Did you see how many friends she has? In one hour, she increased her followers by seven hundred and sixty-three people on Instagram alone!"

"People feel sorry for her. That doesn't mean they'll vote for her."

"Of course they will! No one wants to be seen as a racist. If she locks in the Latino vote, we're through. That's forty percent of our student body right there."

"Who would do something like this?" Brian asked.

"Exactly! We don't have racists at Lincoln. Not overt ones anyway."

"There was that article in the paper last month about the racial disparity in suspensions."

"I'm not saying there's no institutional racism. But students don't fuck with each other like this." Stacey paused and then said in a whisper, "You know what I can't figure out?"

Brian waited for Stacey to continue, but she seemed to be weighing her words carefully. Either that or practicing her newly discovered telepathy skills. "What?" he finally said.

"The timing."

"What do you mean?"

"Think about it. We left campus around ten o'clock, right?

Julia's poster wasn't up then. So, that means she must have hung it between ten last night and six this morning."

Brian wanted to correct her to account for the time he was talking to Julia on the phone last night, but he kept his mouth shut.

"You still there?" Stacey asked.

"Still here."

"'Cause here's where things get confusing: Julia hangs her poster in the middle of the night. Then our racist tagger comes on campus. This person assumes Julia's from Mexico and writes that horrible thing on her poster. Then he or she or someone else takes a photo of the poster and sends it to Lance, so he can write his web exclusive before seven o'clock this morning."

"Maybe it was all Lance," Brian offered. "That guy's pretty shady. Didn't he send you a dick pic last year?"

"It was a promposal," Stacey said. "With the words 'Let's have bun at prom' written on his butt."

"Right," Brian said. "It got him suspended for a week."

"I don't think it was him," Stacey said. "He's an idiot. He's not smart enough to know that defacing Julia's poster would be the best way to get the sympathy vote. You know who is smart enough to know that?"

Brian didn't like where Stacey was going with this.

"Julia," she said.

Boom. There it was. "No," he said. "She wouldn't do something so . . ."

"Evil? Sure she would. Think about it, with one crappy poster, a student who's been at school less than a month is now the front-runner for the highest position in student government. I'll bet you anything that bike we saw last night was Julia's. She probably came to school with her poster, saw my banners hanging everywhere, and defaced her own campaign ad. Then she came to school early to take a photo and send it to Lance so he could write his web exclusive and send it to everyone."

Brian didn't want to believe it, but Stacey's explanation made sense. Had they been outplayed by a political genius? Was last night's phone call just an alibi Julia needed to cover up her crime? Why did this not extinguish his desire for Stacey's political rival? He felt his traitorous boner rise in salute to this Machiavellian fiend.

"What's going on?" a voice from behind him said. It was Kyle, just waking up and still in his boxers. The guy didn't have an ounce of body fat on him, which was number seven on Brian's list of annoying things about his little brother. All that skateboarding must burn every calorie he consumed in the school cafeteria every day.

"Nothing," Brian said, stepping away.

"Is that Kyle?" Stacey asked.

"Yes, unfortunately," Brian said. "Listen, you may have lost the Latino vote, but there are still lots of other groups on campus to win over. Now that this thing's all over the web, you need to build up your presence on social media."

"You talking to your girlfriend?" Kyle asked, sneaking up behind Brian and pinching him on a love handle.

"Fuck off," Brian said.

"Brian!" his mom said.

"Tell him to leave me alone, Mom. I'm on an important call."

"Kyle, come over here and eat something."

"Not hungry," Kyle said, stepping over to the hallway table and picking up his phone. He scrolled through his feed for a few seconds before saying, "Holy shit. Stacey's so fucked."

"That's it," his mom said, standing up and going over to the cabinet above the sink. She pulled down an empty spaghetti sauce jar and slammed it on the counter. "The swear jar's coming out again. Both of you owe me a dollar."

"Your house sounds insane," Stacey said.

Brian pulled out his wallet from his back pocket and withdrew a dollar. "I gotta get out of here," he said, dropping the bill into the jar.

"What does Stacey have against immigrants, Brian?" Kyle asked. "The students at Lincoln want to know."

"Bye, Mom," Brian said, grabbing his keys and heading toward the door.

"Bye, honey," his mom said. She looked pained to be refereeing a fight so early in the morning.

"Hate's not welcome here, Brian," Kyle yelled from behind. "Tell your girlfriend that Lincoln needs a uniter, not a divider."

"Fuck off, Kyle," Brian said, slamming the front door. He'd put a dollar in the jar when he got home later.

11

AFTER PURCHASING HIS blueberry muffin and flavorless milk, Tony entered the cafeteria and scanned the crowds for Mohawk. It was the usual brunch-time crowd—freshmen boys yelling at one another while staring at their screens. What attracted these munchkins to this place? Tony wondered. It couldn't be the food. Even stoned, Tony knew it was prison bad. It couldn't be the atmosphere. The place was as comfortable as one of those cavernous hotel ballrooms Tony had visited with his parents, only without the carpet, cushioned chairs, or air-conditioning. The general odor of the place was a mixture of dried sweat, stale farts, and cooking oil. So why did he come here every day? Why hadn't he moved on like most of the guys he used to hang out with his freshman year?

Tony didn't have an answer to that question, except to

say he was a creature of habit. The more he followed a regular routine, the less he had to think. And he didn't like to think, so this worked for him. He began every day by smoking a bowl or two, then he ate a big bowl of Lucky Charms, then he masturbated in the shower, then he drove to school, slept through periods one and two, and then came to the cafeteria for brunch.

Now that he thought about it, he was a bit like a robot, following a schedule that had been programmed into him by some invisible software engineer. If his parents were around more, he'd probably follow their directions to eat healthy, do his homework, and exercise, but they weren't, so some other force had written his code. Now Mohawk had hacked into his mainframe and was making him do different things like run for president. He tried to fight the munchkin, but it was easier to let Mohawk move him in the direction he wanted.

Tony didn't see the freshman's spikey blue hair anywhere, so he shuffled over to his table, the one the other munchkins left empty for him. It might as well have a sign on it saying *Reserved for Hulking Asian*. He sat down and kicked his feet up on a chair and dug into his muffin.

Where was Mohawk? They had only hung out a couple times, but he already missed his company. The little guy was so sure of everything, including Tony. He'd never met anyone who was so confident in who Tony could become. Tony's guidance counselor certainly didn't have that kind of positive outlook. At their last meeting, his counselor actually asked Tony if he'd be interested in a career as an Uber driver.

Tony saw Mohawk enter the cafeteria and felt a rush of relief flood his body. He needed this little guy, almost as much as he needed Space Cow's chocolate milk. Mohawk saw something in Tony that others didn't. He made Tony think that his problems weren't his own—they weren't even problems. Tony didn't have to conform to his parents' or school's expectations to be successful; he could be successful as he was. To hear Mohawk tell it, the fact that he was a lazy, stupid stoner was the best thing he had going for him.

"Wassup, my man," Mohawk said, holding up his palm for Tony to high-five. He was in an unusually chipper mood this morning, judging from the smile on his face. Even his Mohawk seemed to stand straighter than usual.

Tony slapped the munchkin's hand and kicked out a plastic chair for him to sit on.

"You hear what happened to Julia's poster?" Mohawk said, sitting down and ripping open the wrapping to his strawberry Pop-Tart.

Tony nodded. "My English teacher stopped her lesson on *The Scarlet Letter* this morning to discuss the president's role in creating such a hostile environment for immigrants. People are ready to wreak Puritan vengeance on whoever did this."

Mohawk was smiling, which was not the expression most people wore when discussing a hate crime.

"Why are you in such a good mood?" Tony asked.

"No reason," Mohawk said, and then burst into a fit of stifled laughter.

"Seriously, bruh. Explain yourself."

Mohawk leaned in and whispered something Tony didn't catch. It sounded like he said he wrote that shit on Julia's poster. "I can't hear you," Tony said.

"I wrote that shit on Julia's poster," Mohawk said again.

It took a moment for the words to register, despite the repetition. "What the fuck, man," Tony finally said. His first instinct was to punch Mohawk in the face, but it was still early, and slamming his fist into another person would take more energy than he had right now.

"I did it for you, Tony," Mohawk whispered. "For the campaign."

"I should turn you in right now," Tony said.

Mohawk's smile vanished, replaced by something closer to a snarl. "I don't think that would be a good idea," he said. "What do you think people are going to think when they hear your campaign adviser wrote a racist slur on the competition's poster?"

"You're not my campaign adviser," Tony said.

"Sure I am. This is the second time we've met in front of

all these witnesses." Mohawk pointed to all the other munchkins crammed into circular tables around them. "You tell anyone, and who do you think they're going to blame? The six-foot-two junior or the five-foot-three freshman? Who looks more in control here?"

"Dude, you're, like, evil. Racist and fucking evil."

"I'm not evil. I'm strategic. Listen, you think I give a fuck where Julia Romero's from? I don't. But, just so you know, she's from Canada, not Mexico. I'm not even sure she's Latina. I only wrote that thing because I knew it would make everyone at school rush to her defense. I did it to *help* her."

"I don't understand," Tony said.

"The only way to break Stacey Wynn's lock on the presidency is to draw votes away from her. Last night, I followed my brother out and watched him and Stacey blanket the campus with her stupid banners. I was just about to tear them all down when I saw Julia show up and hang her pathetic campaign ad. That's when I realized the best way to bring Stacey down wasn't to silence her but to amplify her opponent, which I did by defacing Julia's poster. Now everyone loves Julia, which will force Stacey to focus all her attention on bringing her down. While the two girls fight each other, you'll sneak up with your healing message of chocolate milk and win the election."

"I don't know. It still sounds evil."

"You have to trust me on this. Everyone was ready to hand Stacey the presidency on a silver platter for all the 'work' she's done for the school. Do you know what that would mean for us? Every leadership position at the school would be held by a girl. Every one! Every class president is a girl. Most club presidents are girls. The newspaper and yearbook editors are both girls. The class valedictorian for the past five years? All girls. Our principal is a girl. Guys are becoming obsolete. We're retreating into the cafeteria with our devices and letting women take over the world. It has to stop! We're the only ones who can make that happen!"

Tony backed his chair away from Mohawk, who looked like he was about to grab a plastic fork and take hostages. "Dude, you need to chill," he said.

Mohawk closed his eyes and took some deep breaths. Tony watched him slip into a coma. When he emerged, he was calmer, but his left leg bounced with energy.

"Sorry," he said. "I can get a little worked up about this stuff."

"'S cool," Tony said, passing the little dude his unopened carton of milk. "You need something to drink?"

"I do, but not that," he said. Mohawk reached into his backpack and took out a pint-size carton of chocolate milk. Space Cow's smiling face immediately brightened the mood at the table. That's the effect the mascot had on people.

"Aw, man, thanks!" Tony said, reaching for the carton and hugging it to his chest.

Mohawk then pulled out a bottle of chocolate syrup from his bag. With an acrobatic leap onto his chair, he raised the syrup high above his head and addressed the crowd. "Anyone here want their chocolate milk back?"

A few tentative cheers erupted from the tables nearby.

"The administration has taken away the one delicious thing this cafeteria has on its menu," Mohawk continued. "Tony Guo says enough! He wants you to have your chocolate milk and drink it too. If you agree, come over here, get some chocolate, and raise your cartons to the end of tyranny!"

The applause that erupted in the cavernous hall was deafening. Groups of boys rushed to Tony's table, holding their white milk cartons open for a squirt of Hershey's syrup like they were starving orphans. Tony heard the opening words of the US Constitution ring in his ears—"Give us your poor and your needy"—and forgot all about the horrible thing Mohawk had done. All he saw was a long line of munchkins, waiting for him to squirt chocolate syrup into their cartons.

12

SO, THE STORIES she'd heard about America were true. Julia couldn't believe it. For weeks, she'd let these daily displays of multiculturalism brainwash her into thinking that everyone got along like characters on a TV sitcom. But it turned out one of the characters on *We're All in This Together* was a white supremacist. Was it Veronica, the cute barista with the trendy bob? Or Jake, the lovably nerdy astrophysicist? Tune in next week to find out!

She thought she'd avoided all the ignorant, racist fucks by coming to mellow, tolerant California, but it turned out these assholes were everywhere, even hidden behind palm trees and iPhone billboards. This "melting pot" was just a boiling cauldron of hate that condensed anyone trapped inside into a gooey paste, without texture or flavor. Why was she so desperate to stay in this country again? Oh, that's right. Because back home, *she* was the bully everyone hated.

When Lance texted her the picture of her defaced poster this morning and asked for a comment, she was speechless. First off, how did "Build That Wall!" even apply to her? Wasn't that a slur directed at people south of the border? Then she realized the tagger assumed that's where she was from. She managed to choke out a forgiving response, but inside, she was seething. It wasn't the macro-aggression that infuriated her, although that was pretty bad. She was angrier at herself for letting her guard down and thinking she was safe from this kind of attack now that she wasn't the only brown person at school. She had even convinced herself that Lincoln students might elect her student body president!

Immediately after Lance posted his blog entry, she was inundated with Facebook friend requests and Instagram followers. The response was overwhelming. At school, people she had never met before stopped her in the halls and hugged her like she was a grieving widow. Even the guys who normally greeted her by grabbing their crotches were deferential in their greeting, pounding their fists against their chests and raising them high in salute.

Lance ambushed Julia outside her fourth-period classroom at the start of lunch. As soon as Julia emerged from the door, he grabbed her by the arm and yanked her into a selfie.

"I can't believe how many hits I'm getting with this story," he said.

"Did you take the photo of my poster?" Julia asked. The question had been bothering her all morning. After the shock of the vandalism subsided, she couldn't figure out what Lance had been doing on campus so early.

Lance shook his head. "It appeared in my in-box this morning. Someone obviously wanted people to know the administration was covering up a hate crime. This guy or girl is my Deep Throat."

Julia had no idea what "Deep Throat" was and saved the term in her mental "to be translated later" file, along with "Relaysh" and "That's so dank!"

"We've got to do a follow-up article," he said, pulling Julia out of the flow of lunch traffic. "Something focusing on your cultural heritage. You didn't really talk about much of that in our phone interview last night."

For a good reason, Julia thought. "I don't know," she said. "I kind of want all this to go away."

"What are you talking about?" Lance said, placing both hands on her shoulders. "This is the best thing that's happened to us."

"To us?"

"Yes, us. Your campaign has taken off, and my blog has a wider circulation than the school newspaper. Take that, Abby!"

"Who's Abby?"

"The editor I told you about," Lance said. "The one who got me kicked off the paper."

"I thought you said you were on sabbatical?"

"I was joking," Lance said. "So, when do you want to meet? I'm free after school today."

Julia squirmed, trying to shake free from his grasp. Lance's pockmarked face was uncomfortably close, and she felt the instinctive urge to head butt him. She'd always wanted to do that, and now seemed like the perfect opportunity.

Then, before she knew what was happening, she was engulfed in a sea of black hair. Lance's odor of sweat and Cheetos was instantly replaced by the sweet fragrance of jasmine and vanilla.

Jenny had wrapped her arm around Julia's shoulder and pulled her close. "This guy bothering you?" she asked.

One of Jenny's friends, a girl with dark burgundy lips and the painted eyes of an Egyptian queen, pushed Lance backward with two hands. "Step off, asshole," she said.

"I wrote the article," Lance said, holding up his hands in mock surrender.

"It's okay," Julia said, putting her arm around Jenny. Even though the girls had just come to her rescue, she didn't feel like a victim in their presence. Standing in formation like this, she was a warrior. This posse wasn't going to let anyone hassle her.

"I'm on your side," Lance said to the group of girls standing in front of him. "I want to find the asshole who did this."

"How do we know you're not the asshole who did this?" one of the girls asked.

"Yeah, you look like one of them preppy racists to me," another one said.

"What? No! I want Julia to be president. I fuckin' hate Stacey Wynn."

"Not very objective, are you?" Jenny said.

"I can separate my personal feelings from my work," Lance said, fumbling for his phone. "Hey, any of you care to comment on Stacey's role in creating this hostile environment for Latinos?"

The girls turned their attention away from Lance and his phone to focus on Julia.

"LSU is holding a special meeting tomorrow to talk about our response to what happened," Jenny said. "Can you come?"

"LSU?"

"The Latino Student Union," Rosa said. "Didn't they have one at your old school?"

"They didn't have Latinos at my old school," Julia said.

"You should have started your own club," Jenny said.

"Girl, you can't have a club with only one member," Rosa said.

"Do you have to be Latino to join the club?" Lance asked.

The girls looked at Lance like he'd just burped up orange Fanta.

"No, but it helps," the girl who pushed him said, getting up in his face again.

"Of course anyone can join," Jenny said, stepping between the two. She turned to the other girls and said, "We need allies for this fight."

The aggressive girl backed off, rolling her eyes.

"Great! I'll see you ladies tomorrow, then."

Lance spun around and strutted down the hallway, stopping people along the way and thrusting his iPhone in their face for comments.

"God, that guy is a tool," Rosa said.

"I bet he's the one who wrote that on Julia's poster," Egyptian Eyes said. "He looks hella racist to me."

"If it wasn't for him, no one would know what happened to Julia's poster," Jenny said. "The administration took it down this morning before anyone saw it."

Julia counted this as a mixed blessing. If no one had seen the vandalism, Julia would have just assumed one of her opponents or their supporters had torn it down. Lance's story had created an outpouring of encouragement, but it also put Julia in the uncomfortable position of being the most aggrieved Latina at Lincoln High School.

"Where's the LSU meeting tomorrow?" Julia asked.

"Room 309," Jenny said. "Don't worry, I'll take you."

The girls escorted Julia to their designated spot on the quad—on the concrete stairs leading from the theater to the expansive lawn. This elevated position gave them a great vantage point to comment on those gathered below and yell out compliments to any passing boy they thought was cute.

"See that guy over there?" Jenny said, directing Julia's attention to a tall, muscular dark-skinned boy with a Giants baseball cap turned backward on his head. "That's Pedro Ruiz, captain of the baseball team. He's hella fine. I think you should date him."

Pedro registered the girls' stares and nodded in their direction, which sent Jenny and the others into a fit of laughter. Julia turned away, not wanting to send any signals that Pedro might misinterpret. All day long, she'd been looking forward to seeing Brian, her shy, awkward lab partner. They'd had such a great conversation last night. Bits and pieces of it popped up pleasantly this morning, pushing the horrible incident of her poster to the far corners of her consciousness. What kind words would he say in response to what happened? Should she play up her sadness a bit, just to make him work a little harder to comfort her?

By the time she reached sixth-period biology, she could barely contain her excitement, which made her performance as a tragic hero somewhat difficult. She watched Brian enter the class looking distracted and nervous. When he sat down next to her, he barely glanced in her direction. Instead, he busied himself flipping through his textbook and extracting sheets of paper from his binder. His silence lasted the entire class period, despite Julia's best efforts to draw his attention away from Cohen's boring lecture. When the bell finally rang, she had had enough.

"Did Stacey do it?" she asked, just outside the classroom door.

"What?" Brian pulled hard on the straps of his backpack. "The poster thing?"

"Yeah, the poster thing."

"Of course not. Stacey would never do something like that."

"Then why the silent treatment?" Julia asked.

"What? I didn't . . ."

"You've been ignoring me all class. What's wrong?"

Brian broke eye contact and stared at his shoes. "Did you do it?"

"What?"

"Did you write that on your poster?"

Julia felt her face catch fire. "Are you fucking kidding me? Why would I do that?"

"To make people feel sorry for you. To win the election."

Julia stared at him for a moment. This was by far the

worst thing she had heard all day. Worse than the "Build That Wall" comment because it had come from someone she liked, not some anonymous asshole. How could he even suspect such a thing? She thought they had really connected last night. But he didn't see her as a person; she was only a threat to his candidate. Before she started to cry, she stormed off. Unfortunately, it wasn't in the direction of the bike racks. But that didn't matter. All that mattered was that she get away from Brian and his stupid face with its cute freckles and button nose.

Halfway down the hallway, she heard the slap of his sneakers behind her and turned around to confront him. He was standing below one of Stacey's enormous banners with that slogan that told everyone that a vote for Julia was a wasted one.

"You know, I thought you were different," she said. "I thought you were a nice guy, but you're just an asshole. Worse, you're an asshole who pretends to be a nice guy. At least the other guys I liked didn't hide the fact that they were miserable cretins."

"Wait," Brian said, smiling. "You like me?"

"Liked!" Julia shouted, and turned and walked away.

"Julia, I'm sorry," Brian said, running to catch up with her. "It was a horrible thing to say. Nothing like this has ever happened at Lincoln."

"Maybe because no one has ever challenged the status quo."

"Maybe. Stacey's freaking out, and I guess I let her panic get to me. I'm really sorry."

Julia stood there and debated how forgiving she should be. Brian really seemed remorseful. He waited a safe distance away for Julia to make up her mind about him. She liked how vulnerable he appeared in that moment, the way he seemed to stand in front of her like he was in his underwear. She really wanted this shitty day to end on a more positive note. And it could if she trusted her instincts about this guy standing in front of her with the kind eyes and shy smile.

"I'll accept your apology on one condition," she said.

"Anything."

"You buy me ice cream."

13

JULIA INSISTED THEY ride their bikes to iCream. "You see more of a place if you move slower through it," she said. Brian hadn't used his bike since he got his driver's license, but he was pretty sure his old Trek was still functional. Since his house was near the ice cream store, he made plans to meet Julia there, and they would bike the rest of the way together.

This plan worked out for two reasons. First it gave Brian time to make sure Stacey was preoccupied and not anywhere near the route he'd take with Julia. If she saw him with her rival now, she would flip out, especially in light of Julia's ascendance in popularity. You wanna get tea? he texted her before leaving the student parking lot.

Can't, she responded. Meeting with the Christian Club to discuss possible fund-raiser. I need their thoughts, prayers, and votes more than ever now.

Go with God, Brian wrote back, and then sped out of the parking lot.

Meeting Julia at his home also gave Brian a few minutes to calm the fuck down before his first date with her. Had she really asked him out? After he said that horrible thing to her? How could he have been so stupid? He would have punched himself in the face, except he wanted his face to look good right now.

Brian pulled to a stop in front of his garage, happy to see the family car wasn't parked anywhere nearby. That meant that his mom must have taken Kyle to his therapist appointment and he had the house to himself. Brian didn't want Kyle to know anything about his relationship with Julia. If Kyle even thought Brian liked her, his little brother would find some way to use it against him. Unlike the other times Kyle tortured him, this was something he could use to inflict real damage.

Brian entered his house and went straight to the bathroom. He had about five minutes before Julia arrived. Not enough time to shower, so instead he dampened a towel and wiped himself clean. Then he brushed his hair and teeth and reapplied his deodorant. Would it look weird if he changed outfits? Probably. He needed to appear casual, like biking to get ice cream with the most beautiful girl in the world was something he did every day.

Brian entered the garage from the kitchen and found his bike lying on the cement floor like a murder victim. "Oh shit, oh shit, oh shit," he said, kneeling down in front of it, preparing to do chest compressions. He prayed to God to save his bike for one last ride. "If you fix this thing now, I promise to attend the next two Christian Club meetings with Stacey." Brian lifted his bike up, and it appeared to be in perfect working order minus the deflated tires, which he easily fixed. This meant Brian was contractually obligated to God, the Christian Club, and Stacey, in that order.

He opened the garage door and found Julia waiting patiently by the sidewalk on her cruiser. "Were you talking to someone in there?" she asked.

"Me? No! Must have been someone else praying to God." He didn't say this last bit out loud. At least he hoped he didn't.

"Let's go," she said, pushing away from the curb and setting her bike in motion.

It felt like a dream. Or a perfume ad. Julia pedaled in front of him, occasionally glancing back and smiling, her long, brown hair blowing in the gentle breeze. The streets were mostly quiet in Brian's neighborhood. He listened to the light grinding his bike chain made in its easy rotation. He passed a single-story home and heard someone inside practicing piano. It would be nice if they had this accompanying soundtrack on their way downtown. The light and buoyant tune perfectly matched the warm afternoon. Maybe this was a preview of what his summer was going to be like, Brian thought hopefully, although he'd have to find alternative destinations to the ice cream shop if he wanted to avoid returning to his freshman size. He didn't have another appendix to help him lose weight by leaking poison into his body.

The two arrived at iCream, a self-serve, soft-serve ice cream shop at the end of downtown. The place was designed to look like an Apple store, with gleaming, metallic dispensers that oozed their contents into paper cups or waffle cones. An island in the middle of the store contained every topping imaginable, from your fruits and nuts to your Skittles and chocolate-covered espresso beans. Brian actually preferred the old-fashioned parlor that had been here since he was a child, with its limited choices and judgmental scoopers. Now it was up to him to limit his intake, which was a responsibility he didn't feel ready for.

The place was empty so Brian and Julia spent the first twenty minutes going from machine to machine sampling the different flavors, trying to decide which would taste best mixed together. In the end, they were pretty full, so they only filled their cups halfway with their favorite flavors. Julia had mango and strawberry with white chocolate chips, and Brian went with the vanilla bean and pomegranate, no topping.

"My treat," Brian said when they went to pay.

"Okay, but I get the next one," Julia said, smoothly implying that this was not going to be their only date.

The two grabbed a table outside and watched the day draw to a close. The leaves of the tree-lined street almost glowed in the late-afternoon sun. It was very European, Brian thought, sitting curbside and talking with a French Canadian. He remembered seeing whole neighborhoods take breaks like this when his family took him to Paris last summer. It was amazing to witness so many people doing nothing at once.

Julia swirled the flavors in her cup together and brought the spoon to her mouth. Brian found himself staring at her lips. They were the most beautiful objects in the world, he decided. They were more expressive than the eyes because they were both singular and a pair, like two dancers performing their separate moves in sync.

"Can I ask you something?" Brian said.

"Sure."

"Why do you want to be the ASB president? I mean, I know you said you thought it would be 'fun,' but there has to be another reason, right? It's such a big responsibility."

Julia paused. "My aunt wants to send me back to Canada."

"What? Why?"

Julia shrugged. "She's afraid I may do something shameful."

"That's ridiculous."

"Not really. But she is a bit more paranoid than I expected. I thought that if I had some big responsibility at the school, it would show her I had changed. Make it harder to get rid of me."

"So, you never thought it would be fun?"

"I just wanted to get under Stacey's skin. I felt bad as soon as I said it. That's the kind of person I hoped to leave behind in Canada. The girl who said mean things to get reactions out of people."

"You don't seem like that kind of person."

"I'm trying to reinvent myself. You ever want to do that?"

"Yes," Brian said.

"I feel like this is my opportunity to become someone new." Julia stabbed her ice cream with her spoon. "It's weird. I've only been here a month, but I already feel like I belong in California more than Quebec."

"Really? That's great," Brian said. He tried to keep the surprise out of his voice.

"You're surprised," Julia said.

"No, it's just . . . after the horrible things that happened today, I would think you hated this place."

Julia grew silent. "What happened today was awful. But in a weird way, it made me feel safer than I ever felt at my old school. People said casually racist things all the time there, but I didn't have anyone I could talk to about it."

"I'm sure you had lots of friends," Brian said. Julia was always texting people during AP biology. He assumed she was popular.

"All my friends were white. None of them really understood what it's like to be different."

"I get that, I think."

"Really?" Julia said. "Did you grow up in an African village?"

"I grew up fat," Brian said.

Julia leaned back in her chair and examined Brian as if he were an abstract painting. "I can't see it."

"Three years ago, there was a lot more of me to see," he said. "It didn't help that my last name is Little. Kids loved calling me 'Big Little.' One time in middle school, my English teacher was teaching us about oxymorons and asked students to think of one. Shelly Taylor used me as her example. After that, 'Oxymoron' became my nickname for a while."

"That's terrible."

"It sort of became the way I saw myself. Like I was this walking contradiction: a fat kid in a skinny family."

Julia looked away and followed a young mother as she chased after her tottering daughter, still dressed in her one-piece bathing suit. "Yes," she said. "I get that."

"When my appendix burst, it was like a metamorphosis. I

became a new person physically, and I wanted a new personality as well. I looked around for the person who seemed the happiest and most confident, and that was Stacey. I followed her lead in just about everything."

"Interesting that you chose her as your role model."

"You mean, instead of a guy?"

"Yeah."

"I've thought about that too. I think if I played sports, I might have followed someone else. But I was fat, so I never got good at sports. I was always picked last on teams and then got blamed for losing the game because of some stupid error. So instead, I worked harder at school stuff and got smarter, which made it even harder to be friends with the jocks."

"That's not fair. Lots of athletes are smart."

"That's true. But the ones I know prefer to talk about what's in the sports section rather than what's on the front page."

"Now that you're a hottie, I bet the girls regret not being nicer to you."

"I don't know about that. I think girls still think of me as that fat kid."

"No, they just assume you're dating Stacey. You two are always together."

"We're just friends," Brian said.

"Really?"

"Really."

"You know, some people think that it's impossible for men and women to be friends."

"That's stupid. Why can't men and women be friends?"

"Biology."

"My parents have a great marriage *because* they're friends."

"Friends who have sex with each other."

"Ew. Gross."

"Sorry, but sex will always affect male-to-female relationships."

"Not every guy thinks of girls as a means to an end."

"That's sweet," Julia said. She placed a hand on Brian's thigh and started caressing it. "It's wrong, but it's sweet."

Brian jerked his leg away from Julia's touch. If he was to get a boner here and now, it would not only be embarrassing, but it would disprove all his enlightened ideas about platonic relationships. Before his dick knew what he was doing, Brian scooped up the empty containers from the table and went inside the store to throw them away. When he came back, he had everything back in control.

"It's getting dark," he said. "We should probably go."

The two of them biked home in the dusk of evening, talking about easy things like their favorite YouTube videos and Mr. Cohen's irritating habit of answering his own questions. When they reached Brian's street, they paused and started circling each other in the intersection.

"Where do you live?" Brian asked.

"About a mile south," Julia said, pointing.

"I'll bike home with you."

"No need. Besides, my aunt is very strict, and I don't want her hassling me with questions about the handsome boy who kept me out so late."

Brian blushed. He hoped Julia couldn't see it in the darkening sky. Why was his body so determined to embarrass him in front of the girl he liked? It was like he was allergic to Julia, only instead of watery eyes and sneezing, he suffered from heart palpitations and sudden speech impediments.

Julia brought her bike close to his and stopped. "I've embarrassed you," she said.

"What? No. The bike ride. It must have winded me."

Julia leaned in and kissed him on the lips. Brian felt every organ in his body pause in astonishment and wonder.

And before he could really think about what was happening, Julia pulled back, said "Good night," and pedaled away.

14

KYLE COULD TELL his mom was only pretend reading. He sat next to her in the therapist's waiting room and watched her eyeballs. They weren't moving left to right, indicating someone absorbed in a newspaper story; her gaze was locked onto an image on the page and had been for the last five minutes. It was a photo of a suspected terrorist captured by police, just as he was boarding a crowded subway car in New York City with an assault rifle and high-capacity magazines.

After staring at the page for five minutes, his mom finally threw the newspaper onto the empty seat next to her and got up to find something more lighthearted to read. She came back with a *Highlights* magazine.

"The pickings here are pretty slim," she said to the other parent in the room, a stout woman with gray hair wound tightly into a bun. The woman smiled in response and went back to reading on her Kindle. Kyle was sure his mom wanted to talk, but the silence in the small space discouraged conversation. Instead, she opened up the magazine to the puzzle page and used her finger to find the right path on a maze to reunite the lost camper with his family.

Kyle shifted in his seat. He didn't feel comfortable either, being in a room with only one entrance and exit. He supposed if some crazed former patient came in, he could leap across the counter and hide behind the receptionist, who was probably playing a game right now on her computer. Using her body as a shield, he could make his way back to Shirley's office, where there was a window from which he could escape. The office was on the first floor of the building, so the drop wouldn't hurt as long as he didn't land on any glass shards. But that would mean leaving Mom behind, and that just wasn't acceptable. No, Kyle would have to fight the assailant with whatever makeshift weapon he could get his hands on, like a pen or chair. Kyle got up and stood by the door to the lobby. This would give him the advantage of surprise if someone came in shooting.

Kyle's secret-service-agent pose made the receptionist nervous, he could tell. She was new and probably still trying to figure out how Kyle, a scabby kid with a blue Mohawk, was related to the woman who looked like everyone's favorite librarian. Maybe the woman thought he was adopted. She probably saw his mom as some kind lady who rescued this creepy kid from a refugee camp for child soldiers. Did they have those in the Northern Hemisphere? Kyle asked himself. If so, he should look into training there.

"The doctor will see you in just a minute," the woman said, trying to shoo Kyle away. Kyle wondered if she had some concealed weapon under her desk. He'd arm himself with something given the number of whack jobs Shirley saw on a daily basis.

"She's not a doctor," Kyle said. "She's a licensed therapist."

"Kyle," his mother cautioned from her seat. Mom didn't like Kyle starting unnecessary arguments, but he couldn't help himself. When Kyle was bored, arguing was the only thing that kept his mind engaged.

A few minutes later, Shirley opened her door and escorted a young girl into the arms of her waiting mother. The mother put her e-reader away and stood up, assessing her daughter the way one might examine a piece of clothing from the dry cleaner for any evidence of a stain. When the inspection was complete, the two walked out the door without saying anything to each other. Kyle took this opportunity to peek out the open door and felt calmed when he saw the empty hallway.

"Hi, Kyle," Shirley said. "You ready?"

Kyle nodded. He felt a little shy around his therapist because of her new appearance. She had recently stopped dyeing her hair, and now it was a patchwork of copper and silvery gray. In the span of a month, she seemed to have aged ten years.

"I'll wait for you outside," Mom said, making her way to the door. She clearly didn't want to spend any more time in this barren landscape.

Kyle followed Shirley into her office and took his seat on the couch facing her chair. He watched her lock the door behind them, a request Kyle had made early in their sessions, which she honored in order to help him relax. *Our goal is for you to feel comfortable with open doors,* she had told him. So far, that goal remained a distant one.

"How are you doing?" Shirley began, settling down into her squeaky vinyl chair and taking out her notepad.

"Great," Kyle said, staring at his therapist's scarf. The folds made it hard to tell if the print was made up of cacti or pineapples.

"Your mom told me there was an altercation at a convenience store?"

"It was no big deal."

"Not according to your mom. She says you've been banned from shopping there."

"I thought these guys were going to jump me, so I jumped them first."

"What made you think the guys were going to jump you?"

"The way they walked. The way they looked at me. I could tell they wanted to fight."

"Did you practice any of the breathing exercises we've been working on?"

"There wasn't time."

"Kyle, the skills we practice here need to be applied to situations outside this office."

"I know," Kyle said. "But in here, it's easy. Out there, it's hard."

"I understand that," Shirley said. "But you have to try. Remember what I told you about your brain."

"Yes," Kyle said.

"Tell me," Shirley said.

"The amygdala controls the fight-or-flight instinct," Kyle said robotically.

"What else?"

"It makes me see everything as a threat, unless it's controlled by my prefrontal cortex."

"And what do we know about the prefrontal cortex?"

"It's not fully developed until my twenties."

"Which is why you need to practice the strategies that will help you calm yourself into a less emotional state. What's our slogan?"

"Feelings are not facts," Kyle replied.

"Exactly."

"What you're asking me to do is to not trust my instincts."

"I'm asking you to check those instincts against logic and rational thought."

"You want me to wait until someone puts a gun to my head before I decide to do something. By then it's too late."

"You have to stop thinking that every human interaction ends with someone putting a gun to your head."

"I don't think *every* human interaction ends that way."

"Just the ones that take place in convenience stores," Shirley said.

"You should have seen these guys," Kyle said. "They were devious."

Shirley took a deep breath, clearly using her own techniques to calm her emotional response. "Let's practice some more, shall we? I'm going to unlock the door, and I want you to regulate your emotional response through the deep breathing we've been practicing."

She stood up and walked over to the door. Kyle heard the click of the doorknob being turned and felt his breathing quicken.

"Deep belly breaths, Kyle," Shirley reminded him.

Kyle breathed in through his nose until his lungs were fully inflated, then he held the breath for a few seconds before exhaling through his mouth.

"Tell yourself there is no assassin outside the door."

"There is no assassin outside the door," he repeated.

"Just because I *feel* bad, doesn't mean it *is* bad."

"Just because I feel bad, doesn't mean it is bad," he said flatly.

"Good," Shirley said in her most relaxed, comforting voice.

They sat there in silence with Kyle focusing on his breathing rather than the fact that the room was not secured or the fact that even in California it was easy for the mentally ill to purchase a handgun.

"Talk to me about school," Shirley said.

"We had a code-red drill on Monday," Kyle said. Deep breathing, he reminded himself. He sucked in another lungful of air, held it, and then let it out. "The school had us hide in place, which is a surefire way to get us all killed, unless, of course, they allow us to carry firearms, which is what—"

"Have you tried getting more involved?" Shirley said, trying to move Kyle on to another subject than his school's woefully inept methods for handling a crisis. "Looked for clubs to join?"

"I'm sorta involved with student government," Kyle said.

"That's great. Tell me about it."

"I'm the campaign adviser for one of the candidates running for student body president."

"Campaign adviser? That sounds like a lot of responsibility."

"It is. I was hoping you could help me, actually."

"Help you? How?"

"I'd like to run psychological profiles on our opponents. It might help my guy do better if he could mess with their heads. How do I do that?"

"Let's talk about why you want to mess with their heads, shall we?"

Shit. Kyle had been too honest with his therapist, which was always a mistake. He slumped a little in his chair, trying to think of a way to backtrack. He was really hoping Shirley could help him wage psychological warfare on Stacey and Julia. And his brother. But she wouldn't help him unless he gave her something first.

"I don't want to mess with their heads, exactly," Kyle said. "More like I want to understand my enemy."

"They're not your enemies, Kyle. They're teens interested in public service."

"We still have to beat them, which means helping people see why my candidate is better."

"Why is your candidate better?"

"Because he's *my* candidate."

"Okay. But what makes him your candidate? Why support him over these other people?"

Kyle thought about that. There wasn't anything especially interesting or charismatic about Tony. He was Kyle's candidate because he did what Kyle wanted him to do, unlike Brian, who fought him on everything. Things had been so much better when his older brother was fat and depressed. With one dig about his weight, Kyle could send his brother crying into his room for hours. He liked having that kind of control over someone.

Then Stacey came around and ruined everything.

She may not have caused Brian's appendix to burst—although Kyle had his own theories about that—but she helped him learn to stand up for himself. Now Kyle had no power over his older brother. The slave he had so carefully and painstakingly manipulated over the years had found his freedom and become his parents' golden child. If Kyle was being honest (and this was therapy so he supposed he should be honest, at least to himself), Tony was his candidate because it was through him that he could bring down Stacey and, by extension, Brian.

"I guess I like his stand on childhood obesity," Kyle finally told his therapist. "That's a real concern for me."

"POSTERGATE COVER-UP"

by Lance Haber

To be successful at politics means you've got to be a good liar. "I did not collude with the Russians." "If you like your health care, you can keep your health care." "Saddam Hussein has weapons of mass destruction." "I did not sleep with that woman." The list goes on and on, and I haven't even backed up to Iran-Contra or Watergate yet. (Don't worry if these terms don't look familiar to you. My US history class stopped at the Vietnam War too.)

So when presidential candidate Stacey Wynn says she did not write a hateful slur on her opponent's poster, should we believe her?

When criminal prosecutors are trying to prove their case to a jury, they focus on the accused's means, motive, and opportunity. Let's apply this standard to our prime suspect.

MEANS

"Means" refers to a suspect's ability to commit the crime. In this case, the weapon used to deface Julia's poster was a Sharpie. Let me think . . . Does Stacey have access to a Sharpie? I refer you to exhibit A: the ten campaign banners hanging throughout the school decorated with planet earth cartoons, all drawn in . . . you guessed it: Sharpie.

MOTIVE

It's pretty obvious that Stacey has the best motive for attacking Julia in such a despicable way; by inciting people's fears and prejudices against immigrants, she can appear as the safest choice for president. Hey, it worked for President Trump; why wouldn't it work for her?

OPPORTUNITY

This is the area most critical to proving guilt of a suspect. Did the person have the opportunity to commit the crime, or does she have an ironclad alibi? Stacey claims she was at home when the vandalism took place, but this reporter has confirmed from multiple evening custodians that Stacey was on campus between the hours of nine p.m. and ten p.m.

Stacey has always advocated for a cleaner school. This reporter now wonders if this platform is a result of some kind of "you clean up my trash and I'll clean up yours" quid pro quo agreement with the powerful custodial union. Is this why they looked the other way when she hung her banners *ten hours before* it was permissible to do so?

Stacey Wynn declined to comment on this story, but Tony Guo, the other contender in the presidential race, appeared worried when confronted with the facts. "What?" he said, in a way I can only describe as perplexed.

I'm not saying Stacey is guilty, but the case is certainly damaging. If she did vandalize Julia's poster in some quick attempt to discredit her, it has had the opposite effect. Students at Lincoln have rallied behind Julia's candidacy, seeing in her a new type of leader—one who holds herself to the highest principles of behavior and restraint.

ENDORSEMENTS

15

STACEY BEGAN THE next day by trying to fill every vacant hour on her calendar. There was nothing she could do about the time taken up by classes, but she could structure all the open slots in her day by meeting with various influential members of her school community. Before school, she planned a sit-down with Abby Spencer, editor of the school paper, to provide her side of the Postergate story. No way she was talking to that hack Lance Haber, despite his repeated requests for an interview. Then at brunch, she was meeting with Megan Oh, president of the Asian Student Union, to try to gauge the group's feelings about Tony's candidacy. She was pretty sure they loathed him, but she wanted to confirm that she could still count on the group's support. Lunch was reserved for her Amnesty International meeting. They were working on their official statement against the persecution of China's Muslim Uighurs, a statement Stacey hoped to use to quiet some of the criticism that she didn't care enough about minority rights.

Somehow during all these appointments, she needed to find time to sit down with Priya Chaudhary and convince her to sign on as Stacey's media consultant.

As soon as Brian mentioned having a stronger online presence, Stacey immediately thought of Lincoln's reigning social media queen. Following all her accounts, Stacey kept close tabs on the girl throughout the day. Somehow, Priya managed to post during every period, despite the school's ban on cell phone use during class time. At 9:00 a.m. there was a tweet about the new Cosmic Junkies single. At 9:30 there was an Instagram post of the braid she had made of some girl's hair. At 9:45 she reevaluated her opinion of the Cosmic Junkies single from four stars to three. At 10:00, she posted an image of the bruised fruit in the cafeteria with the hashtag #cafeteriacrime. At 10:45, Priya posted three Snapchat photos of her history teacher using the exploding-volcano-head filter. At 11:00 she tweeted an endorsement of some girl's sandals and then followed that up two minutes later by sharing a link to a Black Lives Matter protest happening that afternoon in the city. How had this girl not had her cell phone confiscated? Stacey wondered. It took all her concentration and energy just to read Priya's posts throughout the day without getting caught. If Stacey hadn't mastered the art of the semipertinent question/comment, her teachers would have taken her phone away hours ago.

When Priya posted a photo of a book-poem with the spines reading:

The Happiness Project
This Is Where It Ends
I, Robot

Stacey knew it was time to act. Priya was in the library, and with only twenty minutes to go before the lunch bell scattered kids to the four corners of the quad, Stacey had to move now. She raised her hand and asked Mr. Delacourt if she could go to the bathroom.

She raced to the library instead and signed in saying her teacher sent her to find a book on *Marbury v. Madison*. When the librarian tried to escort her to the right stack, Stacey waved her off and speed walked to the social sciences section. She pulled the first book she found and then moved quickly through the stacks like a lab rat looking for its slice of cheese. *I, Robot* was a science-fiction book, so Stacey went to the fiction section first. Nothing. *The Happiness Project* sounded like one of those lame titles in pop psychology, so she backtracked to the 100 stacks. Nothing again. Damn, she was quickly approaching the allotted amount of time her teacher gave for bathroom breaks. If she didn't find Priya soon, she'd have to manufacture some lie involving her period, which she was loath to do, especially to a young, male teacher who would hold this against her gender when it came time to vote in the general election.

Now running through the library at top speed, she finally stumbled across Priya in the most remote and lonely of sections: California history. The girl was sitting on the floor next to her backpack and typing furiously on her phone, completely oblivious of Stacey's presence.

Stacey waited for her to stop typing before clearing her throat and then saying, "Priya?"

The girl looked up at Stacey with her large, round, brown eyes. Stacey had the distinct impression that Priya was a blind person. She looked at her, but Stacey wasn't sure Priya actually *saw* her. She showed no emotion, other than mild irritation at being distracted from her screen.

"I'm Stacey Wynn," she began. "I wanted to talk with you about something."

"I'm supporting Julia Romero," Priya said, turning back to her phone. "Sorry."

"Oh, that's cool," Stacey said. *Fuck!* She should have known when she saw the Black Lives Matter post that Priya would throw her support to someone suffering from systemic racism. She had to think fast. The more time she fumbled for words in front of Priya, the greater likelihood she would post something disparaging about her. What mattered to Priya more than the civil rights of an oppressed people?

"Nice phone," Stacey said.

"Thanks," Priya said.

"How'd you get to keep it?" Stacey asked. She assumed Priya was in the library because she'd been kicked out of class for using it.

"I have two. When I get caught, I just give them the burner."

"Smart," Stacey said. She sat down next to her and looked at Priya more closely. She was cute in a Powerpuff Girl kind of way, with black hair in a pixie cut, and a short, compact body. Priya barely had to bend her legs to fit into the narrow passage between book stacks, whereas Stacey had to pull her knees to her chest to squeeze into the space. "You know, I could use someone like you on my team."

"I told you. I'm supporting Julia." Priya smiled at something on her phone and then paused before typing a reply.

"Because of the poster?" Stacey asked.

"Not just because of that."

"Why else?"

"I don't know. She's different. No offense." Priya shrugged. "I like her hair."

"I get it," Stacey said. She couldn't decide if this girl was a genius or a moron. Maybe a little of both. "Can I ask you a question?"

"Sure," Priya said while typing. Stacey prayed it wasn't about her.

"What changes do you want to see happen at this school?"

"Changes? Like what?"

"I've been following you online, and you seem to have strong opinions about the cafeteria food, police brutality, sandals." Stacey tried to make these things sound equally important, but the list sounded like something off a crazy person's dating profile.

"Yeah, so?" Priya said.

"Well, student government can help make your opinions heard. Take our cell phone policy for example," Stacey said, pointing to Priya's phone. "Would you like to see that changed?"

"Yeah, right. Like that will ever happen," Priya said.

"Those devices are learning tools," Stacey said, improvising. "Most schools around here have already relaxed their policies about when and where they can be used. Did you know that?"

"No."

"It's true." Stacey glanced at the clock on the wall behind Priya. Her bathroom break time was officially over. Looks like her period would have to come two weeks early after all. "Everett High is actually encouraging teachers to have students use their phones in classes."

"For what?"

"For all sorts of things. Doing research. Taking polls. Having discussions. Reading books. Education is online, and if you deny students access to that environment, you're depriving them of the resources that foster success and achievement."

"I thought you only cared about composting," Priya said.

"It's not all I care about," Stacey said slowly, an idea forming in her head. "Actually, changing our device policy fits in perfectly with my platform. The more we go digital, the less paper we'll waste on worksheets, quizzes, and stuff."

"You think you could change the school's policy?"

"I do. I have good relationships with all our administrators. Plus, I have connections to Everett and other schools who have become more digitally friendly. I want to move our school into the twenty-first century and make these devices as common as the textbook."

"That would be awesome," Priya said.

For the first time in their conversation, Stacey saw Priya become more interested in her than the phone she clutched in her tiny, nimble fingers. At the same moment, Stacey felt a twinge of apprehension. Could she deliver on this promise?

Would it be good for Priya if she did? These questions would have to be figured out later. What she needed to do now was close the deal.

"I love Julia too," Stacey said. "But as a new student at the school, she just doesn't have the contacts I have to make a thing like this happen. Believe me, it won't be easy. But we can do it. You and I. What do you say? Will you be on my team?"

Priya looked down at her phone, then looked at Stacey. It was like Stacey was asking her to conscript her only child into the army. "Let me think about it," Priya said.

"That's all I ask," Stacey said, standing up and speed walking toward the door. She ran back to class. Just before she reentered the room, her phone buzzed. It was a post from Priya. She had taken a photo of one of Stacey's banners and written, "After much thought and deliberation, I've decided to support Stacey Wynn for ASB president, and you should too. #notwasted."

Stacey jumped and high-fived the air above her. She quickly liked and reposted Priya's message with the comment: "You're the best, Priya!!!" Maybe she hadn't lost this election after all. With Priya in charge of social media, and Brian attending all the club meetings she couldn't, she had effectively cloned herself. She texted Brian to remind him about the Gay-Straight Alliance meeting at lunch. He was a much better ambassador to James's group than she could ever be. Who knows? Maybe the meeting would reunite these former friends and help Brian work through the struggles with his sexual identity. It sure would help Stacey if her gay best friend and gay nemesis hooked up and threw her a fabulous inauguration party.

Stacey opened her classroom door just as the bell rang, excusing the students for lunch. Mr. Delacourt called her over and demanded an explanation for her twenty-minute absence.

"Sorry, Mr. Delacourt," Stacey said. "It's that time of the month."

16

BRIAN SAT IN a room with four other students and wondered again why this meeting was so important to Stacey.

"The Gay-Straight Alliance might be small in number, but they have a lot of influence," she said. "Everyone wants to support the gays, so I need them to support me."

"If it's so important, why aren't you going to the meeting?" Brian asked.

"Because it conflicts with Amnesty International," Stacey said. "Besides, James is in charge of the Gay-Straight Alliance, and he'll say I'm pandering for votes."

"Won't he accuse me of the same thing?"

"No. You're, like, the perfect ambassador. You and James were friends once, right?"

Any hope that James's attitude toward him had softened since they last squared off at Speech and Debate quickly evaporated when Brian walked into the room. "This is the GSA meeting," James said coldly, unwrapping his sandwich from its tightly sealed aluminum-foil container.

"I know," Brian said, nodding at the other members. The other students were much friendlier and smiled when they introduced themselves. Sierra was model thin, with pink hair and a nose ring. Justin was an Asian boy with a thin mustache sprouting on his upper lip. And Michael was a trans boy in a trench coat and combat boots. Brian said hello and squeezed himself into a seat.

Brian and James had been friendly rivals before becoming hostile rivals. Back when they were Scouts, their competition for merit badges pushed them to excel in backpacking, bugling, and basketry. As the most dedicated Scouts in their troop, they were often used as models for the other boys to follow, which only served to isolate them from the kids who didn't take insect study as seriously as they should have.

Things got weird after they kissed during a sleepover.

It wasn't a big deal. At least not to Brian. They were young and just fooling around. Brian didn't remember how they had started kissing. He remembered laughing mostly, as if it was a funny thing they were doing, like blowing mouth farts into the crook of their arms. It wasn't until much later, when the boys in the Scout troop started making fun of James's fastidious way of eating, dressing, and speaking that Brian felt uneasy about the memory. He never let these feelings inter-fere with his friendship with James though. It was James who rejected him, eventually leaving the troop and turning down future playdate requests because of "violin practice."

James was very comfortable with his sexuality now, which Brian envied in the same way he envied the devoutly religious. How lucky, he thought, to know yourself so well you can come out to everyone in a speech for sophomore class president at a school assembly. Sure, James most cer-tainly suffered from people's fears and prejudices, but Brian would accept the scorn of the assholes for the confidence in knowing who you are.

"So, why are you joining us today?" James asked, staring at Brian through his thick frames. He chewed his sandwich aggressively, as if it were a tough piece of steak instead of tuna fish.

"Stacey would be here too if the meeting didn't conflict with Amnesty International," Brian said. "She's president of that club and works tirelessly for human rights across the globe." He thought this was a nice plug for Stacey. It not only demonstrated that she was aligned with the group's inter-ests, but that she was taking them to a more global level.

"You're trolling for votes, then."

"I wouldn't say *trolling*," Brian said. "Stacey and I were talking the other day about how the GSA should take a more active role on campus."

The group stared at him, waiting for Brian to continue. As he and Stacey had had no such meeting, he had to imagine the conversation in his head before he could describe it for his audience. "We thought, you know, how important gay rights are, and that, uhm, we should do more to, you know, advance them."

"And how do you think we should advance gay rights?" James asked, cradling his chin in his hands. Brian didn't have time to deconstruct the pose to tell if it was serious or mocking. He hadn't anticipated this kind of involvement. All Stacey said he'd have to do was listen to the concerns of the members and say Stacey agreed with everything they said.

"I don't know. Like bathrooms and stuff?" Brian was hoping this group was as obsessed with this issue as the rest of the nation was.

"We have unisex bathrooms," Michael said between sips of his bottled water.

"What about, I don't know, homecoming?" Brian said.

"What about it?" James asked.

"Don't you think it kind of, I don't know, reinforces traditional binary gender norms?"

"Now you sound like Julia," James said.

"I'm sorry. Who?"

James smiled. "Julia Romero? She's running for ASB

president? Maybe you heard of her? Some asshole vandalized her poster."

"Oh, *that* Julia," Brian said.

James sighed. "Let's move on to the first item on our agenda. Michael, where are we on our website?"

Michael flipped open his laptop decorated with a Banksy gun-toting panda and started typing. "I'm nearly finished. But I need everyone's content. It's not much of a site unless we have content, people."

"I submitted my coming out story," James said. "Sierra? Justin?"

Sierra and Justin suddenly became very interested in the contents of their Tupperware.

"What's holding you guys up?"

"I don't have much of a story," Sierra said, nibbling on a pretzel. "I told my girlfriend. We kissed. End of story."

"Wait, you told your girlfriend?" James asked. "That implies that she already knew you were gay."

"Like I said. It's not much of a story."

"Justin?"

Justin shook his head.

"Does that mean you haven't turned one in or you're not turning one in?"

"The last one," Justin said.

"Okay, when we brainstormed this last week, we said

we'd tell our stories on the site to encourage other people to tell theirs. As the great James Baldwin said, 'Love takes off the masks that we fear we cannot live without and know we cannot live within.' That's the purpose of the website: to take off our masks and show the world who we are. It can be anonymous, Justin, if you're worried about someone seeing it."

"Do they have to be coming out stories?" Brian asked. He was just supposed to be listening, but he couldn't help himself. He was a serial participator, unable to stop himself from contributing to a discussion, even if he knew nothing about the topic.

"Yes, Brian. That's kind of the point," James said flatly, and kind of annoyed. He adjusted his bow tie. How he wore that and swallowed his food was something Brian never understood. "Why? You ready to come out?"

"In a way," Brian said. "It's complicated."

The others in the room all laughed. Apparently, his was not the only complicated love story out there.

"Tell us," Sierra said, leaning forward. "This is a safe place."

Brian looked around. Despite James's cold condescension, it did feel like a safe place. On the surface, this was probably the most diverse group of people Brian had ever seen at a meeting. The thing that connected them lay hidden under the surface. They could have kept this secret from one another, but instead they shared this part of themselves and became stronger. Brian had this kind of trust with Stacey, but his secret crush on Julia had made him lock a room in the house they shared. Every day he heard her rattle the doorknob to this inaccessible place and inquire, "What's in there?"

"I've never been physically attracted to anyone," Brian began. "I mean, I knew if a person was good-looking or not, but I never lusted after them the way I've heard guys are supposed to lust after someone. I never wanted to jump anyone's bones or get in anyone's pants or anything."

The group laughed at this, nodding to one another in a way that made Brian think he wasn't alone in this feeling.

"Recently though, I met someone who I do feel this way about," Brian said. "It wasn't a conscious thing. One day, I'm sitting next to them in class and . . ." Brian made a gesture to his lap and hoped the group would understand his nonverbal cue. Judging from their laughter, they all did.

"It felt like my body suddenly woke up. Now it's doing things it's never done before, in ways I can't control. The problem is, this person I like, I can't like them. If I follow what my body wants me to do, it would ruin everything. So now I'm in this perpetual conflict between what my mind wants and what my body wants. You guys ever feel this way?"

"Every day," Justin said quietly. The others, including

James, all nodded their heads solemnly.

"Thank you for sharing," James said. For the first time since their ill-fated kiss, Brian heard the voice of his old friend. The one who used to disentangle the knots Brian so carefully constructed.

"That story clearly has universal appeal," James went on, "but if the object of your affection isn't another boy, it doesn't belong on our site."

"I understand," Brian said. "It helped to share it. Justin, maybe it will help you too."

Justin smiled shyly and went back to his sandwich.

Maybe after the election, Brian could tell his story. But only if Stacey won. It wouldn't seem like much of a betrayal if she were president. If she lost, it would only serve to kick her when she was down.

17

TWO WINGS DOWN, Julia sat in a crowded room with a group of Latino students who had taken her on as their cause célèbre. Julia checked herself. She couldn't speak French at this meeting, and unfortunately, she didn't know any Spanish. The best she could do was put a Spanish accent on her Quebec French and claim it was Basque.

But so far, the members of the Latino Student Union weren't interested in hearing her speak. They were too upset over what happened to her poster to pay much attention to her. All she had to do was sit quietly, martyr-like, and let the group treat her as a symbol for the dormant racism that pervaded Lincoln High.

"We need to either sit in or walk out," Maria Cervantes said. She was the president of the LSU; a girl who was heading off to Stanford next year on a full scholarship. Julia heard that she single-handedly saved the language of an indigenous people in a remote region of Ecuador.

The room erupted in conversation, which was the pattern of the meeting so far. Maria would say something, people would react, and then Maria would tell them to shut up and then call on individuals for comment. The freewheeling meeting style seemed less influenced by culture than it was by space. There were fifty-plus people crammed into a room that had seats for only thirty-five.

Julia watched the proceedings with a mixture of awe and disbelief. She couldn't believe that in her sixteen years, she had never been in a room with this many brown people. Sure, there were variations of color. Julia fell somewhere in the middle of the spectrum, between the girl with the dark Afro-Caribbean features and the boy who was white enough to be cast on *Friends*. What tied these people together? Julia wondered. It certainly wasn't their melanin production. They all came from different places with different customs. They all spoke varying degrees of Spanish, based on, Julia assumed, how long their family had lived in the country. The fact that this diverse group of people could be categorized as a single entity seemed vaguely insulting to Julia, but she wasn't going to voice this opinion aloud. She was probably the least qualified person to be sitting in this room, having been raised by a white mother in a white community. So why did she feel such a strong need to belong to this club? Was it some instinct buried deep within her DNA? Or some narcissistic need to see her face reflected back at her?

Maria slapped the desk and brought people to order. A girl in the back raised her hand, and Maria called on her.

"My mom will kill me if I miss any more school," the girl said. There was some murmur of agreement, although Julia couldn't tell if the reaction was to the girl's point or the green highlights in her hair.

"Your mom won't kill you when you tell her what happened to Julia," Maria said, placing a hand on Julia's shoulder. "They told her to go back to Mexico."

"Actually, they wrote 'Build That Wall,'" someone in the back corrected.

"Same thing," Jenny chimed in. She was sitting next to Julia, providing moral support.

"We have to take a stand against these white supremacists," Maria said.

The audience grumbled loudly. Julia heard quite a few people say things in Spanish she assumed translated to "those small dick motherfuckers."

"You don't know it's a 'they,'" a tall, gangly boy in a well-worn David Bowie T-shirt said. "It could be a he or a she."

"It's definitely a 'they,'" Lance said. Julia heard Jenny groan softly at her side. Lance had been waiting outside the class and walked them in, as if he were their escort. "The administration wants to pretend we live in a postracial society, but we don't. Bigots are everywhere, and they're getting bolder."

There was some grumbling in response to this. Julia wondered if Lance's readership fluctuated depending on the population's outrage. If so, he had a vested interest in keeping people angry.

"It's not a 'they,'" a cute girl with delicate, doll-like features and long black hair said. She was so short, she had to stand on her chair to be heard. "Before this happened, when did any of you feel attacked for your race at school? I get more hassles from the Salvis on my street."

Julia wanted to ask who or what a Salvi was, but she worried this might make her seem like an outsider. She was desperate to be a part of this group, and not just as a political candidate or the girl who needed defending.

"Those guys are the worst," another girl said. "But they're sexist, not racist." A couple of boys, who Julia assumed were Salvis, high-fived in agreement with the girl's assessment.

"People!" Maria said, trying to get control of the crowd. "We need to stay focused here. What happened to Julia was wrong. I don't want it intimidating other Latinos from running for office. How many of us are in student government?"

This was the first time the crowd went quiet. Jenny raised

her hand, suddenly uncomfortable with all the attention.

"Jenny is the ASB secretary," Maria pointed out. "That's it. We're the biggest group on campus, yet we don't have any representation. It's all the white and Asian kids. We need someone like Julia to speak for us."

Julia smiled, but inside she had started to panic. Speak for them? How could she do that when she didn't even know their language? This might have been a horrible mistake, she realized. What if someone asked her about her heritage? How would she answer that question? Lying by omission is one thing; she didn't think she could lie to people's faces. This characteristic should probably disqualify her from holding public office now that she thought about it.

"What does the ASB do anyway?" someone in the back asked.

Everyone looked at Jenny for the answer. Julia turned and saw Jenny staring at the crowd like a cat that's just fallen from a tree into a dog park.

"We plan rallies and stuff," she fumbled. "Every month we recognize a student for whatever."

"That's it?"

"We do more," Jenny whined. "I'm just blanking out right now."

"Ask Julia," someone said. "She's the one who wants to be president."

Julia felt the room's attention suddenly shift toward her. This was it, she thought, clearing her throat and standing up. You should come clean, a voice in her head said. Tell everyone the truth. If you're truly one of them, they will forgive you.

"Uh, to be honest," she began. "I don't know what the ASB does. I'm new to this school and country and still trying to figure out some of your customs and traditions." Julia paused. This was as far as she could go with her confession. She would tell the whole truth eventually, but she'd rather it come out as a trickle instead of a flood.

"As a recent immigrant," she went on, "I see things a little differently. What I see from the outside looking in is that the school is divided between the Haves and the Have-Nots."

"That's right," someone in the back said.

"The Haves are able to devote their whole lives to school. They take the hardest classes, participate in after-school sports, and hold practically every leadership position on campus. The Have-Nots don't have this luxury. They live farther away and have to take two or three buses to get here. They have family or work responsibilities in addition to all their schoolwork. They're surviving day to day, and because of this, they can't plan for the future like the Haves can. It's an uneven playing field that just results in the Haves getting more and the Have-Nots getting less."

Jenny clapped her hands and encouraged others in the audience to follow suit.

"Here's a question I have for the ASB: What are you doing to get more kids involved in school activities? How many of you guys would participate in student government or sports or whatever if you had more time?"

Every hand in the room went up. Well, almost every hand. The boy in the David Bowie T-shirt was either not interested or too busy pouring a bag of Skittles into his mouth.

"That's what I thought," Julia said. "It's not lack of interest that keeps us from getting involved. It's lack of time. Our lives are too busy."

"Amen," someone shouted. Or Julia imagined someone shouted. She was kind of lost in her own biopic at this point. This was the scene when she makes the inspirational speech to her squad, just before sending them back on the court to wipe out their opponents' fifty-point lead.

"We can't do anything about our family commitments," Julia went on. "So we need to change things at school." Julia paused for effect here. She hoped no one would fart or burp and ruin the moment. The only sound in the crowded room was the Bowie kid chewing his candy.

"Here's what I'd like to change. I'd like to stop doing one hundred problem sets in trig just to demonstrate I understand the material."

The people who had survived Mr. Hopper's trigonometry

class all nodded their heads in agreement.

"I'd like to stop covering a decade a week in US History and maybe learn something about how minorities contributed to this country."

Julia saw more heads nodding across the room.

"I'd like my classwork to inspire me, not just keep me busy. I'd like for the ASB to demand more from our teachers and administrators. If student government isn't the place to talk about these issues, where can we go to demand change?"

The whole room started clapping. Some even broke into chanting Julia's name. Jenny stood up, grabbed Julia's hand, and squeezed it tight.

"Here's what I'm thinking," Maria said. "Instead of a sit-in or walkout, we hold a campaign rally for Julia."

More cheers and applause.

"We can't do that," Jenny said, waving her hands high in the air to get people's attention. "The school doesn't allow campaign events for people running for public office. They don't want this turning into a popularity contest."

"We don't have to call it a campaign event," a pudgy boy said. "It could just be a party."

"But the election is almost two weeks away," someone said. "How can we organize a party in time?"

"Besides, everyone's going to Isabel's quince on Saturday," someone said.

"What's a quince?" Julia asked.

The second she said it, she knew it was a mistake. She cursed herself for voicing her question out loud, but she had been swept away with the enthusiasm of the room. That enthusiasm evaporated the moment the words left her mouth. Everyone looked at Julia as if she had mixed up the punch line of one joke with another.

"Sorry, what?" Maria asked.

"I . . . I . . ." Julia struggled to come up with some way to save face. "I never had a quince," she choked. A quince was something you had, right? Like a party? That's what Jenny had been talking about, right? Please let that be the thing Jenny had been talking about!

The room stayed silent, but somehow the mood shifted from "Wha?!" to "Aww!" As if Julia were a pit bull puppy who lunged at a small child, only to lick its face.

"You never had your quinceañera?" Maria said.

"Nope," Julia said.

The consensus of the room, both verbalized and communicated through wide eyes and slack jaws was that this was a terrible thing.

"We have to throw you a quince," Jenny said, hugging Julia tight.

"That's not necessary," Julia protested.

"It's perfect!" Maria said. "We'll throw a quinceañera protest party, like they did in Texas."

"What are you talking about?" someone yelled.

"Texas passed some hella strict immigration law that gave the police permission to ask for papers if you were brown or spoke with an accent," Maria said. "So, a bunch of girls protested by showing up at the state capitol in their quinceañera dresses."

"Did they get the law changed?"

"Hell no," Maria said. "But they got attention and called out the governor for his racist attack against our community."

"Can we choreograph a dance?" Jenny said. "Please!" Julia tried to match the enthusiasm on Jenny's face, but it was hard to do when she was about to vomit. Things had suddenly spiraled out of control. It was like getting caught in a summer storm. One moment you're biking along in shorts and a tank top, the next you're looking for shelter and wondering why you didn't wear a bra.

"How many of you still have your quince dresses?" Maria asked the crowd.

All the upperclassman girls raised their hands. There were nearly twenty of them.

"You can borrow my sister's dress if you don't have one," Jenny offered.

"Thanks," Julia said.

"It's settled, then," Maria said, addressing the crowd.

"Next week, we learn Jenny's quince dance. Then on voting day, we come to school in our quince dresses, with a few signs expressing how we feel about what happened to Julia. We won't let this asshole attack our community and get away with it."

Maria and Jenny each grabbed one of Julia's hands and lifted them in a show of solidarity. Julia felt a little vulnerable in this position, almost like she was a criminal caught in the act. *Hands where I can see them,* the police say in situations like this, just before they cuff the offender and haul her off to prison.

The bell rang, and the club participants dispersed to their fifth-period classes. Some came up and high-fived Julia before they left. When the room emptied out, Julia grabbed Jenny by the wrist and pulled her in close.

"I need to talk to you," Julia said.

"Sure, let's walk to class. What do you have fifth period?"

"English," Julia said.

"Me too!" Jenny said. "You in AP?"

Julia nodded.

"Thought so. I thought about taking AP."

"What stopped you?"

"Time. Just like you said. The homework in that class is insane, isn't it?"

Julia nodded.

"Yeah, that's what I heard. Between ASB, field hockey, and babysitting, I don't have time to do all the reading. And I love reading."

"See, that's just wrong," Julia said.

The two girls joined the crowds filling the hallways. Julia couldn't think of the right way to make her confession, especially with these people bumping into them on all sides. Jenny was friends with everyone and didn't miss an opportunity to wave or say hello to anyone close by. Why isn't she running for ASB president? Julia wondered. She'd surely win the popular vote if this meet and greet was any indication.

When they finally reached Jenny's classroom, Julia pulled her aside and sat her on the bench on the other side of the open hallway. Julia stared up at the blue sky, hoping for some inspirational skywriter to provide the words she needed to say next.

"Girl, you're going to make me late for class," Jenny said.

"I'm not Latina," Julia blurted out. She figured it would be easier to rip off the Band-Aid.

"Excuse me?"

"Ms. Ramirez?" a young, bookish man with a neatly trimmed beard said from the doorway.

"Just a sec, Mr. Baxter," Jenny said.

Julia couldn't look Jenny in the eye. She waited for her to either spit in her face or walk away, but instead, she grabbed her hand and waited for Julia to continue.

"My mom's family is from Italy," Julia began. "That's where Romero comes from. I never knew my dad."

"Didn't your mom tell you anything about him?" Jenny asked.

"Ms. Ramirez?" Mr. Baxter said again from the doorway.

"Girl, I need you to start crying right now," Jenny whispered. "Otherwise, I'm going to have to go to class."

Julia had no trouble producing tears. She had been keeping so many secrets from people, the two biggest being the one about her ethnicity and the one about the crime that brought her to California. Telling Jenny the truth about the first had pricked a hole in a balloon that was filled to bursting with water. Her eyes flooded with relief and sorrow, and before she knew it, she was bawling.

"Okay, tone it down a notch, girl," Jenny whispered, "or Baxter will call the front office." Jenny stood up and walked over to her teacher and spoke privately with him. She returned a few minutes later and said, "I think I bought us five minutes."

"My mom doesn't know who my dad is either," Julia said, getting her sobbing under control. "It's complicated." She couldn't go into her whole backstory in five minutes. She would tell Jenny everything eventually, but she needed to know the most important information first. "I feel like such a fraud. I want so much to be a part of the LSU and to fight for your cause, but I don't think I'm the best spokesperson."

"But you're the spokesperson we got," Jenny said. "And a damn good one."

Jenny folded her hands in her lap and tapped her foot against gravel. After a few minutes of silence, she turned toward Julia and grabbed her hands. "You've got to be Latina," she said. "Not to get all mystical and shit, but with you . . . I don't feel this kind of connection with people outside my race."

"I feel a connection too," Julia said.

"That's good enough for me," Jenny said. "The fact that you're choosing to be Latina is better, actually. You know how many people in my family choose to be white? My aunt got her skin bleached last year. How fucked up is that?"

"I need to know for sure though," Julia said.

"Then do a DNA test," Jenny said.

"My mom won't let me. She wants me to choose my own destiny, not let my chromosomes do it for me."

"But you're not living with your mom," Jenny said. "Right?"

"Yeah."

"So, let's do it. These online services don't care about parental permission; they just want your saliva and your money."

"What do I do while we're waiting for the results?"

"We follow our instincts. We both know that the test will only confirm what we know in our hearts. You're Latina, and in two weeks, you'll be our first Latina ASB president."

"You sure? It feels a little like cultural appropriation to me."

"I don't know what that shit is."

"It's when you adopt a cultural practice that's not your own. Like me putting on a quinceañera dress as part of a pro-test against racial profiling."

"Then don't think about it in that way," Jenny said. "Just tell yourself you're supporting your friends in their struggle against oppression. White folk do it all the time, and people thank them."

"I'm not white," Julia said. She'd never made such an open declaration before. Living in Canada, it would have been sacrilegious to declare such independence from her mom's tribe. But here, it felt liberating. She wasn't white. No matter how much her mom wanted her to forge her own path, inde-pendent of her biology, she still lived in a world that created barriers and detours because her skin was brown.

"We've got to get to class before Baxter calls security," Jenny said, standing up.

"Please don't tell anyone about . . . you know," Julia said.

"Your secret's safe with me," Jenny said. "Order the DNA

test online today. I don't need to know the results, but I'm thinking you do."

The girls hugged and then went to their separate doors. Julia walked in and saw all the white and Asian faces turn to stare at her. Besides the handful of Indian students, she was the only brown face in the room, a fact she took pride in, even while it isolated her.

18

WHEN LUNCH BEGAN, Tony headed out to the student parking lot, hoping inspiration would strike before he reached his car. He usually drove to one of the many fast-food restaurants within the five-mile radius of school, but today, he didn't know what he was in the mood for. A burrito sounded good, but if he went to Chipotle, he'd have to get out of his car, and he didn't feel like making the extra effort. The drive-throughs were all burger joints though, and Tony had been eating at them for weeks and had grown tired of their identical menus. Why can't all restaurants serve you in your car? Tony wondered. Is there something so special about sushi that prevents people from passing it through a drive-through window?

As he reached the outskirts of the parking lot, Tony saw his old friend Doug waiting at the curb and texting.

"Wassup, dog?" Doug said, looking up from his phone and holding his pale palm out for Tony to slap.

Doug and Tony were good friends their freshman year. At least, Tony thought they were. As soon as Doug started playing football and taking honors classes, they sort of drifted apart. For a while, it was like he and Doug were the only guys on a deserted beach. But then the beach filled with tourists until eventually, Tony looked around and couldn't find his buddy in the crowd anymore.

"Where you goin' for lunch?" Tony asked, hoping for inspiration. Or a ride. Sitting shotgun in someone else's car would really solve all his problems. He could just go wherever the driver took him.

"We're hitting Italian Deli," Doug said, scanning the area for his ride. Tony noticed Doug had sideburns now. They extended down from the edge of his baseball cap like narrow earflaps.

A Honda Civic peeled around a corner of the lot, nearly running over a girl walking while texting, and pulled up in front of where Tony and Doug were standing.

"I'd invite you to come along, but the car's kinda full," Doug said.

Tony looked into the car and saw it crammed with other dudes with baseball caps and sideburns.

"'S cool," he said.

"Hey, your parents going on another vacation soon?" Doug said, opening the back door.

"They're gone now," Tony said. "For a couple more weeks."

"Dude, have another party," Doug said. "That last one was epic."

"Sure," Tony said. "Next weekend, maybe?"

"Awesome," Doug said. He took his seat in the car and yelled, "Dudes, party at Tony's next weekend."

The guys cheered from inside the vehicle and then drove off, leaving Tony standing at the curb alone.

Tony stood there wishing he hadn't told Doug about his parents being gone. Last time Doug and his friends came over, they kinda trashed the place. It took the Moldovan cleaning crew all day to repair the burn holes in the carpet. They said someone also vomited in the birdbath.

"Tony!" someone yelled from behind him. Tony turned around and saw Mohawk carrying four boxes of pizza. "Why are you standing out here?"

Tony tried to think, but it was hard to do with the delicious pizza smells distracting him. He was really pretty hungry.

"C'mon, we're late," Mohawk said. "Here, you bring these in. It'll look better for your audience."

"Audience?" Tony said.

"You don't remember, do you?" Mohawk said. "We're

having a pizza party in the cafeteria today. I promised the guys you'd deliver."

Tony did not remember having this conversation with Mohawk, although to be fair, he didn't remember most of his conversations with the little guy. Things were so chaotic at brunch in the cafeteria now that he was running for president. Still, he trusted his campaign adviser to know what was up, so he followed him back to school.

"Dude, where'd you get the pizzas?" Tony asked.

"I had them delivered," Mohawk said. "You gave me your credit card, remember?"

Oh shit. He really needed to keep better track of things. Still, he was happy to have the pizzas. He had never thought about having his lunches delivered to school. That might open a whole new world of culinary options for him.

Mohawk made a big production of opening the doors and escorting Tony into the cafeteria, crammed as usual with freshman boys, trapped on campus until they got their driver's licenses. When the boys saw Tony holding the pizza boxes, they all cheered his name and started clapping. It ranked pretty high on Tony's list of his all-time favorite greetings, just behind the time he met The Rock at a celebrity golf tournament his parents took him to when he was younger.

Mohawk led Tony over to the usual brunch table. They opened the pizza boxes and let the smell of the baked dough and cheese and tomato fill the space. The delicious aroma drew every munchkin toward their table, looking for a hand-out. Tony grabbed a couple slices before these advancing little dudes devoured everything.

"Don't forget to sign the petition," Mohawk said, thrusting a clipboard and pen into the hands of the first boy in line. The boy signed the page and passed it to the kid behind him.

"What petition?" Tony asked, mouth full of pizza.

"To bring back Space Cow," Mohawk said. "I'm gathering signatures for you to present to the administration your first day of office."

"Awesome," Tony said, chewing.

After everyone had signed the petition and grabbed a slice of pizza, Mohawk made his way around the tables, meeting and greeting and squirting chocolate syrup into everyone's milk. Tony had to give him credit. He was a great talker. He seemed to know just what the crowd wanted to hear. *Freshman boys are the most disenfranchised group at high school*, Tony remembered him saying. *In the span of a summer vacation, they go from being big men on campus to the bottom-feeders of the school. All their girls are taken by upperclassman boys, and they can't go anywhere without being stuck in a toilet by some asshole. The cafeteria is their sanctuary. If you win over this corner of the school, you've locked in at least fifteen percent of the vote.* Was that this morning? Yeah, just before Mohawk told him about this campaign event. He didn't forget. He just remembered too late. Well, not too late. He was here, and things seemed to be going well.

"Dude, I think you need to say something," Mohawk said, returning from his rounds. "The people want to hear from you."

"You said no speeches," Tony said.

"It doesn't have to be a speech. Just some acknowledgment that you appreciate their support."

"I wish you had told me about this earlier. I'm kinda high right now."

"From brunch?"

"I snuck an edible in fourth-period biology."

"Come on, you can do it," Mohawk said, grabbing Tony by the shoulder and lifting him up. "Just a few words of thanks."

Tony steadied himself and gulped down the chocolate milk Mohawk had given him. Mohawk pounded his fist on the table to get the room's attention. Within seconds, all twenty tables in the cafeteria fell silent in anticipation of Tony's remarks.

"Greetings, munchkins," Tony said, which prompted some low, confused murmuring at the tables. "You might not believe this, but I was once a miserable turd like you. Back in middle school, I actually got bullied. A lot. But then, in the summer before ninth grade, I grew, like, four inches. Suddenly, I was taller than all the assholes who made my life so miserable. I couldn't wait to grab them by the waistbands and hang them from goalposts. But then I got to Lincoln, and guess what? There were giant dudes here too. These upperclassmen continued the bullying that started in middle school until I was forced to retreat here, to the safety of the cafeteria. Every day I sat alone, feeling sorry for myself. I thought I was always going to be small and weak and no one was ever going to protect me. The only thing that consoled me was Space Cow. The chocolate milk made me strong. I grew so tall, I could buy beer at the local liquor store. You know, the one on El Camino?"

"Wrap it up," Mohawk whispered. "The bell's about to ring."

"What I'm saying is, chocolate milk changed my life, and it can change yours too. But only if we bring it back to the cafeteria. If you support me, I promise to never stop fighting until you see Space Cow back on the refrigerated shelves of this, our beloved institution. This is a solemn promise. Even though I am no longer a pathetic munchkin such as yourselves, I will fight on your behalf. Together, we can make milk great again."

The boys at the tables all stood in unison and gave Tony

a standing ovation. It was the sweetest sound in the world, Tony thought, waving to his people as they walked out the cafeteria doors.

"Well done, boss," Mohawk said. "Well done."

OPPOSITION
RESEARCH

19

STACEY SAT IN her car outside Mr. Park's Academy of Tae Kwon Do and wished she could return to the studio. When her mom announced she was leaving Dad to move in with Stacey's instructor, Stacey had just received her brown belt. According to Mr. Park, she was one of his finest, most disciplined students, but she couldn't continue taking classes with him after he helped break up her family. She didn't blame him as much as she blamed her mom, and she didn't blame her mom as much as she blamed herself. Why hadn't she seen this coming? Her mom always gushed about Mr. Park's strength and self-control after every lesson. She obviously saw in him a heightened version of her own demeanor. Stacey too had a predisposition toward perfectionism and disapproval, but unlike her mom, she saw those qualities as defects to be corrected.

Right now, she would love a session with her former

master. The workout might help her take her mind off the election, which was quickly spinning out of control. Despite Priya's support for Stacey on social media, Julia's campaign continued to surge. Yesterday in Spanish, Stacey heard two girls talking about some kind of quinceañera protest, which could only be interpreted as a campaign rally for her rival. These were the same girls who just last week asked Stacey for help on the *pluscuamperfecto*! Now it was Stacey who people were talking about in the past tense. She needed to do something to shake things up, which was why she was now parked outside this Korean gingerbread house. Her mom had transformed this ailing business into a mini-empire. Stacey needed some of that magic now, even if it was dark magic.

Asking for Mom's help was hard though because, outside of a few text messages, Stacey hadn't really spoken to her since she announced her engagement. She had told Stacey she was getting remarried over the phone, probably sandwiched the call between appointments with city officials and contractors helping her expand Mr. Park's chain of studios. Stacey assumed Mom had already told her father about husband number two, but she hadn't. She wanted Stacey to break the news. *I just don't have time for his whining right now,* her mom had explained before hanging up. Stacey had told her dad over dinner, and rather than whine, he'd poured himself a large Scotch and pretended to be supportive. *Your mom deserves to be happy,* he'd said. Later that night, Stacey'd heard him crying in the bathroom.

Stacey took a deep breath and left the metallic cocoon of her car. Crossing the street to the studio entrance, she saw that the interior was dark. There were no Saturday classes until ten a.m. After breakfast, the place filled up with tiny children in white robes looking adorable while they practiced their fighting stances. Before then, the studio was closed except for private lessons. Stacey hoped her mom would be working in the small office in the back.

A tiny bell rang as Stacey pushed open the door. Within seconds, Mr. Park appeared in the open doorway at the opposite end of the studio, dressed in his black robe and pants. Stacey had never seen him in any other attire, now that she thought of it. She wondered if he'd get married in this outfit.

Mr. Park didn't move, probably trying to make out the shadowy figure standing at the entrance. When he recognized her, he beamed and crossed the polished floor in giant steps. Stacey watched his reflection in the wall-length mirrors, rather than try to maintain eye contact. When he was within six feet of her, he stopped and bowed curtly. Stacey made sure she bowed a little more deeply than her former teacher.

"*Ahn-nyong-ha-se-yo*" he said in his deep, gravelly voice.

Stacey repeated the greeting. Mom had wanted her to call him Young-jin, but Stacey couldn't call her former master by his first name. It was too informal, like an army private giving a congratulatory slap on the ass to his first sergeant. Of course, Stacey felt weird calling him Stepdad too.

"Is Mom here?" she asked.

Mr. Park nodded. "Yes, she's in the back." He extended his arm toward the open doorway he had just exited. He didn't escort Stacey to the office, probably because he knew this meeting was going to be awkward and tense and it would be better for him to use this time to get a bagel. He left the studio as Stacey moved toward her mom's back office.

Just outside the open door was a large display case holding all the trophies won by students at the studio. Stacey peered at the statues but didn't recognize any of the names. Her trophies would never be housed here. Stacey laughed bitterly. To psych herself up for this meeting, she had demolished most of the ones she'd found stored in the garage. The gold statuettes now lay scattered across the oily cement floor like the victims in some Rob Zombie–Pixar film.

"Hi, Mom," Stacey said, sticking her head through the open doorway.

Stacey's mom was sitting in her Aeron office chair at a tiny desk, responding to emails. At Stacey's greeting, she spun around and regarded her daughter with a confused smile. "This is a surprise," she said, standing up. She crossed the room and grabbed Stacey by the shoulders. She was still in her morning workout outfit—thin Lycra pants and a neon orange tank top that showed off her tanned, toned arms. Her tight ponytail sat on the back of her head like a child being given a time-out for misbehaving.

"I need your help," Stacey said. "Can I sit down?"

The office was tiny and cramped with barely enough room for the two of them. Stacey's mom stood and leaned her toned butt against her desk.

"You'd better not be in trouble," she said, crossing her arms. Without makeup, her mom looked a little aged. There was no fat on her face to soften it. It was all hard edges and lines like something drawn with a fine pencil.

"When have I ever been in trouble?" Stacey reminded her.

"Then what is it? Why are you here?"

"Nice to see you too, Mom," Stacey said, bristling at the brusque tone.

"I'm sorry," her mom said. "You just should have called first. I'm in the middle of a very important application that's due in two days."

"Sorry to bother you," Stacey said, turning to go.

Her mom pushed Stacey down into her chair and ran an invisible rolling pin across her face to smooth out its wrinkles. She looked at Stacey with the same light-blue eyes Stacey saw in the bathroom mirror every morning. "What's up?" she said.

"I think I'm losing the election for student-body president," Stacey said. "There's this new girl everyone likes more than me."

"What has she done to make herself so popular?"

"She's Latina. At least I think she is. Someone wrote something racist on her campaign poster."

"And now everyone's flocking to her defense."

"Pretty much."

"You think she vandalized her own poster?"

Stacey was shocked how quickly her mom had reached her conclusion. This just confirmed, once again, that her own brain came from this side of the family. She wasn't sure how she felt about that. But was it possible to use her mom's powers for good? Barack Obama probably had a paranoia streak in him too, but he managed to be a kind, generous, and intelligent person.

"I mean, you gotta give her credit—it's a smart move," Stacey's mom went on. "Especially from someone new to the school with no support."

Her mom walked over to the door and removed a black training jacket off the hook on the back. When she zipped it up, she took on the appearance of a ninja warrior. This is what Stacey needed right now: some assassin squad that would kill the lights at the pity party raging inside her.

"'All warfare is based on deception,'" her mom said.

"Excuse me?"

"It's from Sun Tzu's *The Art of War*. You should read it." Her mom walked back to her desk and pulled the book off the shelf that held her wedding-planning binders. She threw the tome in Stacey's lap. Stacey wondered briefly why a military treatise was sandwiched between her mom's collections of floral arrangements and bridal gowns but didn't say anything. Instead, she leafed through the book's many dog-eared pages.

"I don't think that really applies to my situation," Stacey said.

"Of course it does. Think about it. This girl. What's her name?"

"Julia."

"She wouldn't have anyone following her if she hadn't deceived them by vandalizing her poster."

"I guess that's true. But we don't know for sure—"

"What makes you think she might not be Latina?"

"She's a French-speaking immigrant from Canada."

"So, she may also be deceiving people about her ethnicity."

"She's evil," Stacey said.

"She's winning," her mom corrected.

"But why? You know how much of my life I've devoted to that school? I've been in student government since I was a freshman. I'm the president of, like, seven different clubs. I go to practically every sports event, even the JV games! It's not fair that someone can come in and win the hearts and minds of my people with one vandalized poster."

"You've misjudged the loyalty of your subjects."

"They're not my subjects. They're my peers. They may not

like me, but I thought they at least respected me."

Her mom took a breath. "People are selfish, Stacey. They will support you as long as they think you can do something for them. What's your campaign slogan?"

"'Stacey Wynn: Too Good to Waste,'" Stacey said. Every line on her mom's face seemed to stretch in disapproval. "It's meant to play off my promise of a zero-waste school."

"You're running on a recycling program?" Her mom cringed subtly.

"Yes," Stacey said. "The environment is very important to people at my school."

"Is it? Or is it important to *you*?"

Stacey paused. Of course the environment was important to everyone. Everything depended on the health of the planet, just like everything depended on the health of the body. Stacey had just assumed people accepted that, just as she had assumed people accepted her.

"What should I do?" Stacey's body slid into a slouch. Her mom kicked her feet to send her upright.

"'If you know the enemy and know yourself, you need not fear the result of a hundred battles,'" her mom said.

"What?"

"Page a hundred and seventy-nine," she said, pointing to Sun Tzu's book. "It's highlighted."

Stacey groaned. How did everyone suddenly get so adept at quoting famous people? First James with his Baldwin quotes and now Mom with Sun Tzu. Were these historical figures so inspirational or was it just safer to repeat someone else's ideas rather than come up with your own?

"You need to know your enemy," her mom went on. "This girl's power right now is that no one knows anything about her. She's a blank slate people can project anything on. You need to help people see her for what she really is."

"You mean spy on her?"

"I don't know if I'd go that far," her mom said. "But everyone's got a digital footprint these days. Follow her steps back to Canada. No one moves to a new country because they're happy at home. Something must have brought her here, and I bet it's not good."

"Seriously, Mom?" Stacey said. "Lots of immigrants come to America looking for a better life, not because they did something wrong. Look at Mr. Park."

Her mom bristled. "Please stop calling him that. He's not your teacher anymore. In a few months he'll be your stepfather."

Stacey sighed. She didn't know why she was arguing with her mother. Her mom was telling her what she wanted to hear. Why didn't she like hearing it?

"All I'm saying," her mom continued, "is that you should find out what brought this girl to California. Is this a temporary or permanent move?"

"I don't know."

"Did her father transfer here for work?"

"I don't know. I think Brian said something about her living with an aunt."

"Well, there you go," her mom said, snapping her fingers. "Start with that. Why transfer schools in the middle of your junior year to come live with your aunt? That's suspicious if you ask me."

Her mom was right. Students at Lincoln spend most of junior year preparing for AP tests, sucking up to teachers for letters of rec, and building résumés of community service. Who interrupts this process to start over? Shifty girls with French accents do, that's who.

"Thanks, Mom," Stacey said, going in for a hug.

Her mom's body stiffened like Stacey had interrupted some plank exercise. Stacey backed off.

"Sorry," she said, and bowed curtly at the waist, just as she had to her former instructor earlier.

"Don't be sorry," her mom said, grabbing Stacey by the shoulders and steadying her. "Be smart."

"I will," Stacey said.

"And don't forget, we're going bridesmaid dress shopping next Sunday," her mom said.

Stacey acknowledged the reminder with a wave and then left the building before getting drawn into a conversation about color combinations and accents. She was more comfortable discussing *The Art of War* with Mom than *Eat, Pray, Love*.

20

BEFORE BRIAN DID anything, he scanned the area. The public library was not a hotbed of activity on Sunday afternoons, but occasionally, the librarian would sponsor a gaming tournament that would draw crowds of boys looking to sneak in extra screen time outside their restrictive households. Kyle came to these occasionally if Mom was home revising her latest manuscript. If Brian saw his brother here, he would ignore him as usual, grab a study carrel, and do some homework.

So far, the coast was clear. The place was quiet and empty except for some retirees getting their magazine fix. A couple tech workers typed away on laptops on the desks near the east-facing windows. Brian walked past the librarians manning the reference section and made his way to the nonfiction stacks in the back. The bookshelves were practically floor to ceiling and offered little tunnels of privacy for clandestine meetings.

Brian walked to the designated meeting place—the 500 section, where all the science books were located. The area offered an ideal space to hook up, er, study. It was located in the middle of the stacks, away from the popular social science and biography sections. A wide support beam blocked the window, making it darker and more private. If someone did venture into the area, Brian and Julia would hear the person approach in enough time to separate and go back to browsing the biology texts for their project on genetic variation in giraffes.

No one was in the stacks when Brian arrived, so he threw his backpack on the ground and tried out a few poses while waiting for Julia to show up. Should he be reclined on the floor in a sexy, suggestive pose or thoughtfully browsing one of the many hefty tomes on the shelves? He tried out both positions and found he was more comfortable leaning back, holding a light paperback. The book he chose to pretend-read was called *Charles and Emma: The Darwins' Leap of Faith*. There were three silhouetted figures on the cover: a man, a woman, and an ape. It was a love story, Brian surmised scanning the back. Charles and Emma were opposites—he, devoted to science; she, to religion. Maybe he could learn something from this impossible relationship. If the Darwins could overcome this hurdle, maybe he and Julia could find a way to be together, despite their political opposition.

"Why are we meeting all the way back here?" Julia

asked, appearing suddenly at the end of the row of books. She looked amazing, as always. Her brown hair pulled back in a ponytail gave Brian full access to her face, which was a bit flushed from her bike ride. She was wearing a light flannel button-down over a low-cut T-shirt. Her shorts stopped just at mid-thigh. Brian felt his pants leg vibrate, and knew it wasn't his phone.

"Uh, this is where the bio books are?" Brian said lamely.

Julia arched an eyebrow and approached. "What are you reading?" she asked, throwing her bag down next to Brian's backpack.

"It's really interesting, actually," Brian said. "About Charles Darwin and his religious wife."

Julia plucked the book out of his hands and opened to a random page. "'One's tendency to kiss, and almost bite, that which one sexually loves is probably connected with flow of saliva, and hence with action of mouth and jaws.'" Julia paused. "That's hot."

Brian felt like he might drown in the flow of saliva his body was producing right now. He swallowed and tried not to look at Julia running the tip of her tongue along her upper lip.

"You want to get started . . . ?" Before Brian could finish his sentence, Julia pressed her lips and then her body against him. Instantly, he was transported out of the musty library and into a field of strawberries and honeysuckles. Their mouths opened, and Julia's tongue started slow dancing with his. Brian reached behind Julia and pulled her closer. He wanted their bodies to do the thing their tongues were doing—break through the barriers of skin and share the softest places of themselves.

The squeak of a book cart brought them back to reality. They quickly separated and sat down next to each other on the carpeted floor. Julia picked up the Darwin book and Brian rested his binder on his lap to hide his erection.

"Don't think I don't know what's going on back here," the clerk said as she passed by with her cartload of books. She was an older Asian woman with streaks of white in her hair, as if she had just walked through a cobweb. There was a hint of a smile when she stopped to address them. "Just so you know, I'm going to be shelving books in this section in about fifteen minutes."

The woman pushed her cart down the center aisle toward Ancient History.

"I thought we were being so discreet," Julia said, wiping the saliva off her lips.

They both laughed.

"Is this why you chose this spot for us to work?" Julia said, leaning her head against Brian's shoulder. "So you could have your way with me?"

"Yes," Brian said. "There's no better aphrodisiac than

scientific studies on sexual reproduction."

"Seriously," Julia said, lifting her head and looking at Brian with her beautiful brown eyes. "Why are we here?"

"I wanted to be alone with you," Brian said. "Away from all this election . . . bullshit."

"Is that any way for a campaign adviser to talk?"

"Can we make a deal not to talk about the campaign when we're together?" Brian asked.

"You worried you might reveal one of Stacey's secrets?"

"It's not for Stacey. It's for me. I want this time to be about us."

"You don't want Stacey to know you're with me," she said flatly.

"No. Well, yes. That would be problematic. But more important, I want you all to myself. I don't want to think about the election while we're together."

"That's going to be difficult."

"I don't think so," Brian said, and leaned over and kissed Julia on her neck. He hadn't kissed her there yet, and now he had. He planned to work his way through every part of her body, cataloging the distinct flavors of her arms, legs, and chest. Her neck tasted salty and sweet. A mixture of sweat and perfume, Brian guessed. He liked the combination. Julia moaned softly in response. "See?" Brian said. "Not thinking of the election."

"How long are we going to have to do this in the library?" she asked.

"We could go to your house," Brian said, caressing Julia's bare arm.

"My aunt would flip. She's only given me this much freedom because she thinks I'm campaigning right now. If she caught me at home with you, I'd be under house arrest again."

"It's crazy. We can't be together unless you're running for president, but while you're running for president, we can't be together."

"A real Catch-22," Julia said. "And what's wrong with your house?"

"I told you. My mom works from home. Plus, my brother might be there."

"I'd like to meet your brother."

"Trust me. You don't."

"What's wrong with him? I'm picturing a smaller version of you."

"Picture a scabby kid with a blue Mohawk."

"*That's* your brother?" Julia said, laughing. "I've seen him around school. I would have never guessed you two were related."

"My mom wrote a book about us. It takes place in a world where baby factories supply the military with soldiers. One woman rebels and refuses the drugs the government feeds her and gives birth to a pacifist."

"Let me guess," Julia said. "That's you?"

Brian nodded. "The government punishes her by giving her extra doses of testosterone powder during her next pregnancy, and she gives birth to a fighting machine."

"Your brother."

"Only in her story, the brothers end up working together to bring down the government and restore balance to the universe."

"I like happy endings."

"Yeah, me too. Unfortunately, I don't think there's one in store for my brother and me. Kyle's in therapy now, trying to work through his issues, but it's not helping. I overheard my mom talking to my dad about putting him on some anti-anxiety medication."

"I'm sorry," Julia said, grabbing Brian's hand.

"It could be the best thing for him," Brian said. "But Kyle has shown no interest in 'inviting Big Pharma into his body.'"

"That must be hard," Julia said.

Brian's phone buzzed, showing an incoming text from Stacey. "Shit," he said.

"That from Stacey?"

"Yeah. I promised her I'd help her frost her campaign cupcakes tonight. She's making, like, a thousand."

"Campaign cupcakes?" Julia asked.

"Yeah, you know, to pass out at brunch. People love them."

Julia was silent.

Brian realized he had just broken their rule of not talking about the election while they were together. Maybe this was an impossible situation after all. How could they keep the election out of their relationship if it controlled where they could meet and what they could say to each other?

The two stayed silent and stared at the rows of books neatly stacked in front of them. Julia pulled down the title *DNA Is Not Destiny* and started thumbing through its pages. Before long, she was immersed in the book and had forgotten all about the horny lab partner sitting next to her.

"Anything there on giraffes?" Brian asked, gently running his hand along Julia's leg. Her skin was soft and slightly goose bumpy from the library's air-conditioning.

"What?" Julia said, looking up.

"The book," Brian said. "Can we use it? Cohen loves when you include additional sources on projects."

Julia shook her head. "It's on human DNA."

"Humans are so boring compared to giraffes. Did you know scientists now think there are four distinct giraffe species?"

"I don't get it. All giraffes look alike to me. Humans seem way more diverse as a species."

"But we're not. Whenever people try to say we are, it gets into troubling eugenics territory."

"You sound like my mom."

"Is your mom supersmart with smoldering sex appeal?" Brian leaned in for a kiss and was blocked by the hardcover in Julia's hands.

"Don't ever use the words 'mom' and 'sex' in the same sentence again," she said emphatically. Julia continued with her reading, making little sighs and grunts as her eyes scanned the pages. Brian looked in his book for another passage that would get them making out again.

"If there's so little genetic variation, why are these DNA tests so popular?" Julia said after a few minutes of silence.

Brian shut his book and considered Julia's question. "I don't know. I guess people want to know about their geographic ancestry. That can be interesting." He paused, because suddenly Stacey's voice was whispering in his ear, *Ask her about her geographic ancestry, you idiot. Find out if she's really Latina!* Brian groaned. Clearly, the library was not the demilitarized zone he hoped it would be.

"What's wrong?" Julia asked.

"Nothing," Brian said.

"I wonder if our families would be from the same hemisphere," Julia said.

"They would, if we went back far enough. That's what I

like about genetics. How it connects us all together."

"Yes, but it's complicated," Julia said. "What if you were black and found out none of your DNA came from Africa? Would that make you any less black?"

"No, because race and DNA are different things."

"But your geography determines your race, right?"

"It's a contributing factor."

"So if you know your geography, you should know your race."

Ask her! Stacey screamed in Brian's ear. *Ask her what race she is right now!!*

Brian shook his head clear of Stacey's screaming. "Then how can someone who's black not have any African DNA?" he asked instead.

"I don't know. Maybe the tests are flawed. Maybe they can't go back far enough."

Okay, do this, Stacey's voice suggested. *Just ask, "What would you do if your DNA didn't identify you as Latina?" Just ask her that.*

"Just stop," Brian said.

"Excuse me?" Julia said, taken aback.

"What?"

"It sounded like you said, 'Just stop.'"

"What? No, I didn't say 'Just stop.' What I said was, uh, 'one drop.' You know, the one-drop rule?"

"What about it?"

"It was used to categorize people as black. Which is to say, that race, you know, is usually defined for you, most often by some other dominant group."

Julia nodded, accepting his point. Brian thought it was a quite excellent save on his part. He silently gave thanks to Ms. Watkins, his freshman history teacher.

"DNA may not be destiny," Julia said, putting the book down between them. "But race certainly is. Depending on where and when you grew up, your race determined your future."

"What about here and now?" Brian asked.

"Most definitely," Julia said.

"So why would anyone need a DNA test?"

Julia paused. She tapped her toes together. The gesture reminded Brian of trying to start a fire by striking two stones against each other.

"It's part of your story," she said finally. "Like the table of contents in a book. The DNA results give you the broad outline but none of the specific details.

Brian nodded. "I'd like to know that," he said.

"So would I."

A minute later, the library clerk appeared at the end of their row and beckoned Brian and Julia out.

"I just remembered I need to do something at home," Julia said. "Can we finish this thing online tonight?"

"Sure," Brian said. "Everything okay?"

"Yeah," Julia said, shoving her laptop and textbook in her bag and throwing it over her shoulder.

While Julia checked out the DNA book, Brian left through the sliding glass doors. He waited for Julia down by the bike racks. She arrived a few seconds later and unlocked her chain, coiled like a snake around her front tire.

"So, I guess we'll have to find another secret rendezvous," Brian said.

"Please don't speak French," Julia said, smiling. She took out a pair of sunglasses from her bag and put them on. "What about the bathroom stalls in the park?" she suggested, nodding in the direction of the playground off in the distance.

"Gross. One of us would have to stand on the toilet seat."

"What about the back row at the movies?"

"Too public. I know at least three people who work at the AMC. There's the darkroom at school. I don't think anyone uses it at lunch."

"Deal," Julia said. "I'll meet you there tomorrow."

"It's a little chemical-y," Brian said. "But it's dark, obviously. And quiet."

"Sounds perfect," Julia said.

Brian looked around once more, and seeing the coast was clear, he leaned in and kissed Julia on the lips. "Until then," he said.

"Until then," she repeated, and then pedaled away.

21

JULIA RACED HOME from the library, hoping to arrive before Gloria and her husband, Donald, got back from the twins' ballet recital. She wanted the house to herself when she ordered her DNA test. She could go online while pretending to do her homework, but the twins had an uncanny ability to detect when people were lying. The other day, after her ice cream date with Brian, she had to bribe them both with gummy bears to keep them from snitching. The girls could have figured out where she'd been based on the dribble of melted ice cream on Julia's top, but more likely they read her mind and knew just what price Julia would pay for their silence.

When she got home, the minivan was nowhere to be seen. Julia threw open the side gate and ran to the backyard, depositing her bike on the dried lawn. In a second, she was inside and rushing down the hallway to her room.

She left her door ajar and pulled open the curtains to keep an eye out for Gloria's arrival. Julia still wasn't allowed to have electronic devices in her bedroom, and if her aunt saw her, she might start threatening to deport her again. Running for president had given Julia some freedom outside the home, but inside, she was still treated with suspicion.

She typed "DNA test" into Google and scanned the hits for a reputable organization. The cost ranged from seventy to five hundred dollars and took between six to eight weeks. All of them required a credit card to ship a test kit. This was going to be problematic, Julia thought. She had a credit card, but her mom paid it, which meant she would see this charge on the next bill.

Julia leaned back and stared at the screen. Maybe it was time to discuss this with Mom again. She had always promised Julia could get a DNA test when she was eighteen. What difference could a year and a half make? She must understand how important this information was for her. She dialed her mom's number in Canada.

"Hi, Mom," she said when her mom picked up.

"Mon chéri!" she squealed. It was good to hear her mom's voice. They hadn't spoken in about a week, and Julia realized suddenly how much she missed speaking French with another native speaker.

"How are you?" Julia asked.

"Ugh, not good. I've taken in a family of Haitian asylum seekers, and the refugee agency is being very slow to find them permanent housing."

"Wait, you what?"

"Didn't I tell you? Now that you're gone, I have the space, so I put Tamara and her two boys in your room."

"My room?" Julia said. "But, Mom, that's *my* room."

"Don't get mad at me. If you want to blame anyone, look to the president in your newly adopted country. His anti-immigration policies have made these vulnerable people come to Montreal seeking refuge from the land of the free."

Ugh. As usual, her mother stood on the moral high ground, which made it impossible to argue with her without sounding like a selfish asshole.

"How are you doing?" her mom asked.

"Fine," Julia said, walking over to the window and peering outside. Aunt Gloria would be home any minute now so she didn't have much time. "I want to know something about my father."

Her mom sighed. "Don't call him that."

"Fine," Julia said. "My donor."

"You don't need to know anything about him. You're my child. I raised you."

"But he's a part of me. Like it or not, I inherited half his

DNA. I deserve to know something about him."

"When you're eighteen you can do a DNA test."

"Do you think he was Latino?" Julia asked.

"Julia, we've been over this."

"I know . . . I just . . . Well . . . with the election and all. People are asking."

"They're asking if you're Latino? Why would they do that?"

"They want to know what I am."

"*What* you are? Do you hear how offensive that question is, Julia? You're not an object to be classified. This is why I think running for office is a bad idea."

"But, Mom. I want to know what I am too."

"Why? So you can check a box on a form?"

"Race isn't just a box on a form, Mom. It's something I live every day. You don't get that because you're white."

Her mom sighed. Pointing out her white privilege was the best way to make her question the logic behind her social experiment.

"It's part of who I am," Julia said, repeating the argument she'd made the last two years. "What if I have some horrible genetic disorder? Like schizophrenia? Or lupus?"

"Your doctors would have picked that up in your regular checkup, don't you think? Honestly, Julia? Lupus?"

"We're studying genetics in biology right now. It's weird

having half your Punnett square blank."

"What's a Punnett square?"

"A diagram scientists use to calculate the probability of inherited traits."

"Listen to you. You didn't get those smarts from me."

Now it was Julia's turn to sigh. "Mom, I need to know."

There was a long pause, and then her mom said, "When you come home this summer, we'll get you a DNA test. Okay?"

"But—" Julia was about to object, but then the full weight of her mom's statement registered. "Wait. I'm coming home this summer?"

"Of course. I miss my baby. I'll take some time off, and we can go someplace fun. There's a meditation retreat in Montebello that looks fantastic."

Julia started pacing the room. Summer was only a few months away. She had already envisioned spending most of it with Brian, biking around town, making out in air-conditioned venues. "I was kind of hoping to stay here. If I win the election, I'm going to have a lot of work to do before school starts in the fall."

"But I miss you."

"Why don't you come out here and visit me?"

"You think my sister is emotional now," her mom said, laughing. "You should see her when she's with me. She's bought into the whole suburban mom thing. That's just not my scene."

"We can road-trip somewhere then?" Julia said. "Go see Uncle Seth." She was pretty sure her uncle lived in a church basement in Seattle, but Julia was desperate to stay in-country.

"Julia, when we talked about this arrangement, it was never a permanent move. You're only in California while things settle down here."

"But you can't just bounce me from place to place. I like it here. I'm not ready to go back to my old school. Everyone still hates me there."

"Maybe we can find another school for you, then."

"Mom, I want to stay."

Julia heard Aunt Gloria's minivan pull into the driveway. She ran over to the window and watched her and Uncle Donald emerge, talking about some obnoxious parent filming the performance with an iPad. A few seconds later, the twins got out, still dressed in their tights and tutus. They stopped in front of Julia's window and stared at her. From Julia's vantage point, they looked like immobile porcelain figures in a music box, something that when opened played the theme from *Jaws*.

"I gotta go," Julia said. "Can we talk about this later?"

"Fine," her mom said. "Let's Skype. I want you to meet Tamara and her family."

Julia hung up and raced to the front to greet everyone. She needed to start working harder to become indispensible to her host family. She wasn't much different from the Haitian refugees her mother had taken in. If she wanted to stay in this country, she would need someone to advocate for her. Aunt Gloria and her mom didn't get along, but she was the best hope she had.

"Bonjour!" Julia said to the twins.

"Bonjour," Madison and Olivia responded flatly.

"Comment était le récital de danse?"

"Très bien," the girls answered in unison.

"Do you need any help with dinner?" Julia asked Gloria, now pulling out some Tupperware containers from the refrigerator.

"Well, aren't you nice to offer," Gloria said.

"She wants something," Madison said.

"Or she's in trouble," Olivia said.

Julia turned on them with surprise. She wished she knew how rusty her aunt's French was because she'd love to tell these little shits to go fuck themselves.

"Mon Dieu!" Madison gasped, reading Julia's mind or her expression.

"I just want to help," Julia said.

"That's nice, dear," Gloria said. "I've got everything under control. Why don't you work on your homework?"

"Can I call my friend Jenny?" Julia asked. "I need to ask

her a question about the campaign."

"Who's Jenny?" Gloria asked.

"She's the ASB secretary," Julia said, hoping the title would impress her aunt. "She's kind of become my campaign adviser."

"Of course," Gloria said. "But keep the door open."

Julia walked back to her room, wondering how long Gloria was going monitor her behavior like this. Even if she won the presidency, her aunt would probably never fully trust her. The scandal that brought Julia here was just too horrifying. She wasn't a refugee escaping persecution; she was a parolee who might re-offend at any moment.

As soon as Julia reached her room, she dialed Jenny's number. She hoped her new friend wasn't weirded out about what Julia was about to do. Gloria needed to hear Julia talking about the campaign, but Julia needed to ask something much more private. Before she dialed Jenny's number, though, she texted her the message: Calling you in a sec. But need to text you something private too.

Jenny texted back a confused emoji face.

Julia dialed her number.

"What's up, girl?" Jenny said.

"I need to ask you a question about the campaign," Julia said as loud as she could while still sounding natural. After she finished talking, she texted Jenny, Can you order the

DNA testing kit for me? I can't have Mom know I'm doing it.

"Sure, what's up?" Jenny said. No prob, she texted back.

"Are campaign cupcakes a thing?" Julia asked. Thx so much! she wrote. Here's the link. She copy and pasted the URL of one of the sites she had looked at earlier.

"Totally," Jenny said. "Everyone bakes something to buy votes." Got it, she wrote. I'll order today.

"What should I make?" Julia asked. Pay you back tomorrow, she wrote. Can you have it delivered to your house?

"You should make conchas," Jenny said. Done, she texted.

"What are conchas?" Julia asked.

"Mexican sweet rolls," Jenny said. "They're delicious. I'm going to text you my mom's favorite recipe."

A link to a page on Hispanic Kitchen appeared on her screen. Julia scanned the ingredients and was pretty sure Gloria had them in the kitchen. Flour, milk, eggs, sugar—the ingredients were like genes. There was very little variation from one breakfast roll to another. Whether something came from Hispanic Kitchen or European Kitchen depended on how they were combined and packaged.

"Thanks," Julia said. "These look delicious."

"I'll meet you at brunch tomorrow to help pass them out. In case you're worried about culturally appropriating my favorite breakfast treat."

"Gracias," Julia said.

"Shut the fuck up," Jenny said, laughing.

Julia hung up and smiled. Jenny was another reason she wanted to stay in California. In the short time she'd known her, Julia already trusted her more than any of her girlfriends back in Canada. Her former crew had turned on her so quickly after Julia was hauled into the police station for questioning. Not one had reached out to her since she left for California. The thought of facing them again, after all that had happened, made Julia's stomach turn.

"Julia? You still on the phone?" Gloria called from the kitchen.

"No," Julia said, walking back down the hall to the common area. Gloria was stirring a brownish mixture on the stove, bathing her face in the steam rising from the pan. "Can you help me make these?" Julia asked, showing her aunt the recipe page on her phone.

Gloria put on the glasses dangling from a chain around her neck. "Hmm," she said. "I think so. Are these for tomorrow?"

"Yes," Julia said, remembering what Brian said about Stacey's cupcakes. She felt a pang of guilt about acting on that information, but according to Jenny, this kind of bribery was common practice in American elections. "Can we make, like, a hundred?"

"I don't have enough flour for a hundred," Gloria said,

walking over to the cabinet and scanning the shelves. "How about fifty?"

"That's fine," Julia said. She walked over to where Gloria was standing and wrapped her arms around her broad shoulders. "Thanks, Auntie, you're the best."

"Told you she wanted something," Madison said from the carpet on the other side of the kitchen counter.

"I still think she's in trouble," Olivia responded.

"POSTERGATE INVESTIGATION STALLED BY ADMINISTRATION"

by Lance Haber

It's been five days since an anonymous assailant viciously attacked Julia Romero. Many of my readers are asking for updates on the investigation. Here's what I can tell is currently happening.

Nothing.

After confiscating the poster as evidence, the administration hasn't questioned a single suspect or witness about the crime.

When asked about what appears to be a stalled case, Principal Buckley issued the same standard talking point.

"This is an ongoing investigation, and I'm not at liberty to share details with you at this time."

The one question that broke through Buckley's impenetrable armor concerned her much beloved protégé Stacey Wynn.

"Have you determined the exact whereabouts of Stacey Wynn on the evening in question?" I asked.

"Mr. Haber," Buckley said. "I know you see yourself as a journalist in a crusade for truth and justice, but what you're doing is treading very close to the school's definition of cyberbullying."

So there you have it: a clear warning from officials— shut down this investigation, or we will trump up charges against you. That's the kind of democracy we're living in today, people.

Clearly, my work has hit a nerve with the powers that be. Am I getting too close to the truth? Is there a larger cover-up happening here? What does the administration have to gain by placing someone like Stacey Wynn in one of the most powerful student positions in the school?

Stacey has never tried to challenge the status quo in the ways that Julia has. Julia wants to see greater inclusion of underrepresented minorities across our curriculum. What does Stacey Wynn want? More compost bins—a clear payback to the powerful custodial lobby that has been helping her cover up her crimes from the start. More composting means less trash. Less trash means less work for the custodians. You do the math.

What has Stacey promised the administration in return for their help in the cover-up? We can only guess. But don't be surprised if we start to see more "volunteer opportunities" for students to participate in litter patrols throughout campus.

BAD PUBLICITY

22

8 DAYS TILL ELECTION DAY

STACEY STARED AT the Tupperware trays of cupcakes in her back seat, a chocolate-frosted reminder of the time she would never get back. She and Brian had spent hours baking, frosting, and decorating these spongy flyers, thinking there would be lines of people clamoring to get their hands on them. Who doesn't like a cupcake after a long day at school? Apparently, a lot of people, judging from the amount of leftovers she and Brian were taking to the rec center downtown. The center's after-school programs were popular with kids, and hopefully, those kids would want their dessert before dinner.

"I don't understand it," she said, grabbing one of her cupcakes off the tray and sampling it. "These are delicious. Why didn't people gobble them up?"

Brian shrugged and shoved a whole cupcake into his

mouth. "Mmmm," he groaned, chewing the moist cake and throwing the used paper liner on the ground.

"Brian, we can compost those," Stacey said, bending down and picking it up. They were parked in the school's parking lot, having just broken down Stacey's cupcake stand that she had set up across the street. She had gotten as close to campus as the state's education code allowed and made a giant banner saying *Free Cupcakes!* to lure exiting students to her campaign headquarters. Priya had advertised the give-away on all her feeds, posting photos of Stacey's cupcakes with the hashtag #letthemeatcake, which Stacey thought was a clever, albeit not entirely complimentary, historical allusion.

"Maybe my new slogan needs work?" Stacey said, rolling up her banner. Under the block lettering announcing free cupcakes, she had written "Protecting Your Digital Rights!" and decorated it with tiny cell phones. "What do you think?"

Brian, still chewing, just shrugged his shoulders.

A group of sweaty girls, fresh from a field hockey game, approached in their shorts and tank tops. They walked with exhausted limps, holding their sticks across their shoulders.

"You guys destroy Jefferson?" Stacey asked enthusiastically. While not their rival, the Jefferson Grizzlies had narrowly beaten the girls earlier in the season. Stacey knew this, just as she knew all the stats for Lincoln's teams. It was one of the ways she stayed connected to the athletes, despite her lack of participation in group sports.

The girls shook their heads, which sent their ponytails in motion like sad flags waving.

"Oh, that sucks," Stacey said. "You want a consolation cupcake?" Stacey reached into the back seat of her car and plucked a few out of their plastic container.

The girls all begged off, holding their hands in front of their flat stomachs.

"I couldn't," Jenny said. "I shouldn't have eaten that concha at brunch."

"Oh my God, those were *so* good," the other girl said.

"What's a concha?" Stacey asked.

"A Mexican sweet bun," Jenny said. "Julia made them. You didn't see her passing them out in the quad?"

Stacey wanted to object and say that wasn't allowed. California education codes prohibited anything with that much sugar and fat to be sold or distributed on campus. But she said nothing. Instead, she focused on keeping the smile glued to her face.

"I was at the Environmental Club meeting," Stacey said. "Brian, did you get a concha?"

Brian stuck another one of Stacey's cupcakes into his mouth, shook his head, and chewed vigorously.

"They were a big hit," Jenny said. "A nice way to share a

bit of Julia's culture, too."

Stacey fought the urge to shove the cupcake she was holding into Jenny's face. How satisfying it would be to see the frosting splatter against her perspiring skin. *How'd you like a taste of my culture, bitch?* But she restrained herself. "That's great," she said.

The girls wandered off to their cars, leaving Stacey alone with her culturally inappropriate cupcakes. Once the girls were a safe distance away, Stacey's anger surged, and she crushed the cakes in her hands, smearing her fingers with the blood of their chocolate frosting. Brian grabbed a stack of napkins from Stacey's car and rushed over to hand them to her.

"Did you hear that?" Stacey said. "Julia passed out sweet rolls at lunch."

Brian nodded.

"That's why no one wanted my cupcakes," she said. "I should tell Principal Buckley. That's completely illegal. It could get her disqualified."

Brian grabbed the wad of chocolate-stained napkins from Stacey's smeared hands and handed her a clean batch. "That's just going to anger her constituency," he said.

"Who cares?" Stacey said. "I don't need their votes."

"They could vote for Tony just to get even," Brian pointed out. "Better to take the high road."

"No one's on the high road, Brian," Stacey said. "It's just me zigzagging on a street filled with potholes. Everyone else is on the highway, speeding to the finish line. I hear Tony's passing out chocolate milk to freshmen, despite the school banning it from the cafeteria."

"Seriously?"

"And did you see that latest post from Lance? He's crucifying me on that stupid blog of his."

Brian reached for another cupcake, but Stacey prevented him from taking a bite. "Ease up on those things. You don't have to keep eating them to make me feel better."

Brian placed the cupcake back on the tray. "Maybe Julia's concha giveaway was just a coincidence?" he suggested. "We're in the last week of the campaign. Everyone rolls out some promotion now. Ryan Fujika passed out origami cranes in the library at brunch as part of his campaign for junior class treasurer."

"Origami cranes?"

"I guess if you make a thousand, your wish comes true."

"He made a thousand origami cranes?"

"I don't think so, but his campaign slogan was 'I'll Make Your Dreams Come True.'"

"That's what sucks about being a white candidate. All I've got are crappy cupcakes."

"First off, they're not crappy, they're delicious," Brian

said. "And second, there's a lot in your Swedish heritage you could share."

"I'm pretty sure passing out pickled herring would cost me the election," Stacey grumbled.

"Your dad's family is from England, right?"

"Yes, the great colonizers. Unfortunately, I don't have great-grandma's meat-pie recipe."

"Now you're just being difficult."

"Come on," Stacey said, slamming her trunk closed. "Let's get these to the kids at the rec center. If they don't want them, I'm going to fill a lot of trash cans."

When Stacey got home that evening, she was in a foul mood. The rec center wouldn't let her pass out the cupcakes to the children in their after-school program. (Apparently, you need a parental consent form to feed kids anything that might contain sugar, milk, or nuts in the state of California), so she ended up tossing the leftovers into some nearby garbage bins. Brian tried to make her feel better about the waste by saying she would be making some raccoons very happy. Stacey didn't like the idea of contributing to wildlife obesity, but it was better than leaving the remains on a landfill somewhere. Next time, she would make her promotion cultural *and* biodegradable, like English tea bags with the slogan "Steeped in Experience!" written on the front.

Opening the front door, she listened for sounds of life inside. The house was quiet, but the lights were on in the living room. Stacey gently called out, "Dad?" but got no response. She found him asleep on the couch, his laptop resting on his chest. She shut the screen, trying not to look at what her dad had been viewing. She would have been fine if it was a dating site, but she knew it was probably something to do with real estate. In their divorce agreement, her mother had demanded Dad sell the house after Stacey graduated high school and split the profits with her. Her mom tried to play this off as her being generous, but it was just another cruel trick. All her mom had done was plant a ticking time bomb in their basement that both Stacey and her dad could listen to every fucking day.

Stacey walked quietly upstairs, dreading her bridesmaid dress shopping date this weekend. She would love to boycott the upcoming nuptials, but she knew that her mom would take revenge on her dad in some way. Maybe force Dad to sell the house immediately, or worse, demand custody. So Stacey was forced to be complicit in her mom's new marriage and stand beside her along with an aging sorority sister and Mr. Park's twenty-four-year old daughter.

As soon as she reached her room, she collapsed onto her bed in a faint. Why was she losing at everything! She'd never experienced failure on this scale before, and it was . . .

paralyzing. She should follow her dad's strategy and just give up. There must be some relief in quitting, right? People wouldn't do it if it didn't make them feel good on some level.

She thought of her dad, asleep on the couch at six o'clock. He was ten pounds heavier since the divorce, mostly because the only appliance he knew how to operate was the microwave. Stacey should do more to help him, but she barely had enough time in her day to do her homework and run this election. Part of her feared that if she took over the cooking and cleaning her mom had done, she would come to resent her dad, just as her mom had. Instead, her strategy was to give him projects and pep talks. But so far, those didn't seem to be working.

Well, she wasn't going to end up like him, she thought, pushing herself off her bed. She needed to be more like her mom. She had created a whole new life for herself with a new husband, a new job, and new condominium. If she weren't such a bitch, Stacey would really admire her. What Stacey needed was her mom's ambition and her dad's kindness. In a perfect world, those were the qualities she would have inherited. Instead, she feared she got Mom's indifference and Dad's inertia.

What advice had her mother given her? "Know your enemy." Clearly, Julia had read *The Art of War*. Somehow she knew Stacey was going to bring cupcakes to school today and had concha-blocked her with her Mexican sweet rolls. It was a smart move, something that would have made Stacey's mom proud.

Stacey grabbed her phone and dialed Priya's number. Priya never answered her phone, preferring to communicate through texts or posts, but Stacey wasn't comfortable putting her request in writing. "Hi, Priya," Stacey said after Priya's outgoing message finished. "I was hoping you could help me find information about our competitors." She stressed the word "our" in that sentence. "Can you dig around their social feeds and send me any photos or posts you think might be useful?" She was sure Julia and Tony had some skeletons they wanted to keep in their digital closets. If Stacey could find out what they were, it might just help her tip the balance in her favor.

23

AFTER HELPING STACEY dump the cupcakes in the rec-center garbage bin, Brian drove home feeling sick to his stomach. He shouldn't have eaten so many of those things, but he felt so guilty. It was his fault Stacey's promotion was such an epic fail. If he hadn't sold her out for a little library lip action, she might have generated more enthusiasm for her campaign and not wasted so much Pillsbury Funfetti Premium Cake & Cupcake Mix.

Brian pulled over near the library and threw up the eight or nine cupcakes he had eaten as penance for his crime. When the last of them was out of his stomach, he wiped his lips and thought, You know, as barfing experiences go, that wasn't so bad. Turned out, partially digested cupcakes slide up the throat as easy as they slide down it.

He closed his door and continued driving.

Julia had betrayed him, plain and simple. He had told her about Stacey's promotion in a moment of weakness, and Julia used that information to her advantage. Brian couldn't believe it when he saw a group of senior guys on the baseball team swarming her and Jenny at brunch, trying to get their hands on Julia's sugar-frosted buns. Pedro Ruiz lingered much longer than necessary, talking to Julia in a way that looked borderline creepy to Brian. Julia didn't seem to mind though. She smiled and flirted with him, slapping a *Julia for President!* sticker on his broad chest.

When she texted Brian at lunch saying she was waiting for him in the darkroom, it took superhuman effort to ignore her and go to the library instead. Then he ditched sixth-period biology to avoid seeing her and drove to the Tea House to drown his sorrows in Earl Grey. Julia kept texting, and Brian kept ignoring her texts. Her last message to him was *I'm so sorry. Please don't be mad at me.* He ignored that one too.

Now he was stopped at a light and getting a text from a number he didn't recognize.

Hey, Brian, it's James. Can we talk?

Now?

I'm at the Tea House if you have a sec.

On my way.

Brian pulled a U-turn and headed back downtown. If James was contacting him, it must be important. Maybe he had some information that could be helpful. But helpful for whom? Brian was beginning to realize that supporting both players in a competition made the game less fun to watch or participate in. It just made it exhausting.

Brian pulled into the parking lot ten minutes later. He walked in and saw James waiting for him at a round table near the register. A metal teapot sat on a doily next to a plate of bite-size sugar cookies. James waved Brian over and then blew on his steaming porcelain cup. Not exactly a scene out of a John le Carré spy novel, Brian thought. He wished the room was a bit seedy—with fog, cigarettes, and trench coats—but this wasn't East Berlin at the height of the Cold War; it was the suburbs just before the summer blockbuster movie season.

Brian ordered his usual and sat down with James.

"Thanks for meeting me," James said.

"No, problem," Brian said.

"You want a breath mint?" James said, pulling a tin out of his messenger bag.

Oh right. The barf. It couldn't smell good. "Thanks," Brian said, grabbing a handful and popping them into his mouth.

"I didn't get a chance to thank you, you know, for coming to the GSA meeting," James continued. "I know you were there for Stacey, but you really seemed to care about our plans."

"I do," Brian said. "I want to come to the next meeting, if that's okay."

"You really like to play both sides of the fence, don't you?" James said, smiling.

"What's that supposed to mean?"

"I know the girl you told us about is Julia," James said. "I saw her in the darkroom today at lunch. She was pretty upset."

"What were you doing in the darkroom?" Brian asked.

"Unlike Julia, I actually take photography. My portfolio's due in a few weeks, and I was developing some pictures."

"What did she tell you?"

"Enough for me to connect the dots. She told me how she betrayed her boyfriend's trust by scheduling a campaign event on the same day as Stacey's. I don't think she knows I'm going to be vice president next year."

"She said 'boyfriend'?" Brian said, feeling good for the first time today.

"She did. That's when I knew the person you were talking about at the GSA meeting was Julia."

"Please don't tell Stacey," Brian said. "It would kill her."

"Yes. It would," James said.

Brian wondered if this was why James wanted this clandestine meeting. Was he threatening to blackmail him? Was he going to force him into ironing his shirts in exchange for his silence?

"You and I used to be friends," James said, "back in the day."

"Until you stopped talking to me."

"Do you know why I stopped talking to you?" James said.

Brian shook his head.

"It's because I hated you," James said.

"Okay," Brian said, standing up to leave. "Glad we cleared that up."

James grabbed Brian by the wrist and pulled him back down. "That night we kissed. You remember that, don't you?"

"Yeah," Brian said, looking around the room. "It was no big deal."

"It was to me. It's what confirmed what I long suspected about myself. I hated you for making me confront something I didn't want to confront. And the fact that it was so easy for you to laugh the whole thing off made it even worse."

"You could have talked to me," Brian said. "You could have said something instead of just making me think I'd done something unforgivable." It suddenly struck Brian that this was exactly what he was doing to Julia. She deserved a hearing, especially if she thought of Brian as her boyfriend.

"I couldn't talk to you about it," James said. "At the time, it was too painful. Once I had accepted myself, it was too late. When you came to the GSA meeting, I wanted to tell you that *you're* my coming out story, Brian. I don't mention you by name, but you're the one who helped me figure out who I am, and for that I have to thank you."

"Oh," Brian said. "Sure."

James laughed. "It's okay. I'm not going to kiss you or anything."

"No, it's not that," Brian said, staring at his tea. "It's just. We have very different reactions to what happened, is all. For you, it clarified something. For me, it just made me confused."

"I can understand that," James said.

"The kiss for me wasn't as intense an experience as kissing Julia," Brian said. "But it wasn't gross or anything."

"Gee, thanks."

"You know what I mean," Brian said.

"It's fine," James said. "I didn't ask you here to work through your sexual confusion. I mostly wanted to ask you if you knew your brother was working for Tony."

"Wait. What?" The change in subject matter was so abrupt, Brian's left leg involuntarily jerked up in surprise and nearly upended their table.

James nodded. "You've got to be careful what you say at home."

"I don't talk to Kyle at home. Like ever."

"Well, keep it that way. I honestly don't care who wins. I can work with either Stacey or Julia. The person I *can't* work with is Tony. We have to stop him."

"You really think he has a chance?"

"If the girls split the votes, he does. The freshmen love this guy. He's turned the cafeteria into a speakeasy for chocolate milk addicts."

"Fucking Kyle. I'm telling the principal about his little Space Cow operation first thing tomorrow."

"Does he know about Julia?"

"God no."

"I would keep it that way," James said. "Can I ask you why, of all the girls at Lincoln, you decided to go after that one?"

"Like I said at the GSA meeting, it was kind of decided for me," Brian said, indicating his pants.

"I can sympathize with your situation," James said. "It must be tough."

"I'm doing everything I can not to hurt Stacey's campaign, but I keep screwing up."

"I don't know Julia, but she seemed sincerely sorry about what she did today."

"Yeah, I'll call her," Brian said. "Thanks, you know, for talking with me about this."

"No problem. Let's just make sure one of your two girlfriends wins, okay?"

Brian raced home to confront Kyle, the traitorous little shit. He knew Stacey wanted the presidency more than anything, and he knew she was Brian's best friend. So why help Tony defeat her? Did he merely want to hurt Brian, or was he looking to destroy the school in a blaze of riots and protest? Knowing Kyle, it was probably a little of both.

Upon entering his house, he found his brother quietly reading *Atlas Shrugged* on the living room sofa. On the opposite end of the sectional was Brian's mom, rereading *Harry Potter and the Chamber of Secrets*. Shouldn't those books be in different hands? he thought. Shouldn't it be the child immersed in a story about wizards and the adult reading a political diatribe against big government?

"Hi, honey," his mom said. "How was your day?"

"Great," Brian said. "Kyle, can I talk to you for a sec?"

"Sure, what's up?" Kyle did not look up and made no indication that he was ready to leave the sofa.

"In private," Brian said.

"I'm pretty comfortable right now," Kyle said. "Besides, I don't want to turn our home into a Chamber of Secrets."

"Nice one," Mom said, gently nudging him with her foot. "But actually, I've got to get back to work."

She closed her book and set it on the coffee table, next to her empty cup. "Ten more pages, and I can call it a day."

She walked down the hall, like she was on her way to the electric chair, and entered her office, which was just a walk-in closet with a standing desk. The life of a children's book author was really kind of depressing.

Brian waited a few seconds for his mom to put on her noise-canceling headphones before he lit into his brother. "What the fuck, dude? You're working with Tony Guo?" he said.

"I believe in Tony's platform," Kyle said, smiling and putting down the book.

"What platform is that?"

"Individual rights. Capitalism. The downfall of the nanny state."

"Those are *Tony's* interests?"

"Those and chocolate milk." Kyle picked up the book and went back to reading. After observing his little brother for fourteen years, Brian had come to learn that Kyle used people's perceptions of him to his advantage. Most didn't see how smart he was because they couldn't get past his blue Mohawk. Brian was sure the Ayn Rand novel was a similar kind of subterfuge; he wanted Brian to see him reading it. Brian doubted he was *actually* reading it.

"You know you're not allowed to serve chocolate milk in the cafeteria," Brian said. "I'm telling the administration."

"Are you that desperate?" Kyle said. "I saw how many cupcakes Stacey had left over today. How many did you eat? Let me guess? Five? Six?"

Brian felt sick at the mention of the word "cupcake." His

brother must have picked up on his queasiness because he laughed and warned, "You better watch out, bruh, or you're going to be as big as you were freshman year."

"You know Stacey has been working since ninth grade to be president," Brian said. "She's the best candidate for the job."

"That's for the voters to decide, isn't it?" Kyle stood up and walked over to the kitchen and poured himself a glass of water.

"What has Tony ever done besides get high and be a horrible DJ?"

"I'll have you know DJ Space Cow is an excellent musical stylist. You can't criticize him for being ahead of his time." Kyle took a tiny sip and swished the water around in his mouth, like he was sampling a fine wine.

"You're just helping him because he's the worst candidate. This is like some big joke for you."

"Not at all. I take my work with Tony very seriously. He speaks for me and all the other disenfranchised voters out there whose voices have long been ignored by people like Stacey. Let's see how she feels when she's the one on the outside."

"Is that what this is about? Revenge?"

"Kind of," Kyle said. "Isn't all politics about revenge, mostly?"

"No, it's about doing good."

"But your good is my bad. Your utopia is my dystopia."

"How would Stacey's presidency affect your life in any way?"

"She wants to turn us all into little eco-warriors," Kyle said, dumping the glassful of water down the drain.

"What's wrong with that?" Brian asked.

"I don't give a shit about recycling, and neither does most of the school. With her in charge, my life becomes a living hell. Throw something in the wrong bin, and you're carted away to a reeducation camp where you shovel manure on local farms for a semester."

"You're an idiot," Brian said. "I guess you don't believe in global warming, either."

"I'm ready for Earth to destroy itself. Bring on the droughts and floods! When the apocalypse happens, I'll be ready. You and Stacey will be the first casualties." Kyle pushed past Brian on his way back to the couch.

Brian stared at his brother in disbelief. "Jesus, Kyle. Is the world really that bleak a place for you?"

Kyle threw himself back onto the cushions and picked up the Ayn Rand brick of a book. "All you people trying to make things better are just putting a Band-Aid on a festering wound. I'm ready to amputate."

"You need help," Brian said.

"I need help? *Me?*" Kyle threw the book onto the carpeted

floor. "I'm the only one prepared to save this family from another attack."

"An attack? From whom?"

"From the government, you idiot. Don't you remember what happened to Dad?"

"That was years ago," Brian said. "And Dad was fully exonerated."

"He was *innocent*, but that didn't stop the police from arresting him. They did it at my soccer game, remember? Hauled him off like he was some low-life scum."

It was a horrible time for their family. Brian didn't understand everything that happened. What he remembered was his dad did the taxes for some shady investment fund manager, who had been siphoning money from his partners and hiding it in offshore accounts. Dad knew nothing about what the guy was doing until the police came to arrest him for "aiding or assisting in the preparation of false tax returns." It took years of courtroom battles and thousands of dollars in legal fees to clear his name, which they did eventually. His dad's arrest was the start of Brian's weight problem. He saw now that his brother had internalized the experience in a very different way.

"Is that what all this is about?" Brian asked. "You want to bring down the government because they accused Dad of a crime he didn't commit?"

"It's not just Dad, you moron," Kyle said. "You see the news? We're living in a police state. Just ask any black dude with a car."

"But government is supposed to fix these problems," Brian said.

"Government *is* the problem," Kyle said. "Unless we elect buffoons like Tony who don't give a shit about anything. With him in office, no one is going to tell me what to do."

"I wouldn't be so sure of that," Brian said. "Every president has his advisers."

"Yeah, well then, I'll be the man in charge," Kyle said. "Which works out even better for me."

Brian was about to respond when his phone buzzed.

"Does Stacey need her lapdog to make a run for more markers and glitter glue?" Kyle asked, picking up his book again.

Brian peeked at his screen and saw it was Julia. He quickly pocketed his cell before Kyle could see her name flashing in bright, glowing letters and went to his room. Sitting at his desk, he called Julia back, making sure to keep his voice low, just in case his brother was listening outside the door.

"I'm so sorry," Julia said.

"It's okay," Brian said. "I'm not mad anymore."

"Oh good," Julia said. "Because I've got a surprise for you. Guess where I am?"

"We still need to talk about what happened," Brian said.

"I know we do. First guess where I am."

"Julia, I've had a horrible day and don't have the—"

"I'm in the changing room at Nordstrom."

"And . . . ?"

"And it's really private. I mean, *no one* is here. I've got the space all to myself."

"Which department?"

"Women's Activewear."

"I'll be there in fifteen minutes."

Brian hung up and banged his head against his desk. How could he be mad at his brother when he was helping Stacey's opponent as well? His espionage was much worse because he was betraying his best friend. Kyle at least had some principles he was fighting for; all Brian wanted was to see Julia in leggings and a sports bra.

Brian went to the bathroom, brushed his teeth, and washed the cupcake residue off his hands and face. Then he tiptoed down to his parents' bathroom and sprayed a bit of his father's cologne on his chest and belly. He still felt queasy from throwing up those six cupcakes. A penance he'd have to endure during his make-out session with Julia. This was probably fair, he thought. If he was going to betray Stacey, he shouldn't feel good doing it.

On his way to the front door, he passed his brother,

hiding once again behind his book on the couch. The cover depicted a naked man bent under the weight of world. Brian couldn't see the image without thinking of the burdens his brother must be carrying.

"You smell nice," Kyle said.

"Tell Mom I'm going out," Brian said.

"Hot date?" Kyle said.

"See you later, Kyle," Brian said, and closed the door gently behind him.

24

JULIA KNEW WHAT she was doing was wrong. If her mom had taught her anything, it was to never use her body to get what she wanted. Objectifying yourself was never a means to an end, just a way of losing your self-respect. But this wasn't like that, Julia told herself as she paced the tight confines of the changing room in the Activewear department at Nordstrom. She wanted to apologize to Brian *and* she wanted to make out with him some more. She couldn't go to his house and the library was closed, so the department store offered the next-best meeting place. It was better actually. If she wanted a romantic evening with Brian—and she did want it, very much—why not spend it in a place that spritzed you with perfume and serenaded you with soft Muzak?

Julia tried on a few outfits, but everything from Activewear was made of some synthetic material and covered her body in uncomfortable ways. So she took the escalator up one floor to the trendier Juniors department and looked for something softer and prettier. The department was fairly empty, this being the hour most families sat down for dinner. Julia told Aunt Gloria she needed a new outfit for her speech next week and had gotten permission to stay out later than usual.

She flipped through the racks, keeping an eye on the two salesclerks talking at the register. So far, they seemed more interested in the new Bardot collection than they were in a potential customer. Julia hoped they would leave her alone so she could make out with her boyfriend. She texted Brian the change of plan—Waiting for you in the Juniors department on third floor—and tried not to look like a shoplifter.

While she waited for Brian to arrive, she received a text from Jenny confirming the quinceañera protest-and-dance rehearsal this weekend. We're meeting at my house at two o'clock on Sunday, she wrote. Everyone's fired up to march since the administration hasn't done shit about your poster. It was true. It had been nearly a week since Julia's poster was vandalized, and there had been no word about an investigation or response from the school.

I'll be there, Julia wrote back.

When Brian arrived, bounding up the escalator like a man on a sexy scavenger hunt (find: one naked girl in a department store), Julia waved him over to where she was standing. "Hold these," she whispered, throwing a pile of summer dresses into his arms. Then she walked him over to the fitting rooms and waited for one of the salesclerks to come over and let her in. The young woman who helped them was only a few years older than Julia. Her heavy lidded eyes and plucked eyebrows made her look both bored and surprised at the same time.

"I want to try on every one," Julia said in her most aggressively girlie voice. While the salesgirl counted the items, she turned to Brian and added, "I'll perform my signature dance move in each, and you tell me which you like best."

"This may take a while," Brian said, rolling his eyes at their clothes chaperone.

"Tell me if you need any help," the clerk said, and promptly left the area.

Brian moved to follow Julia into the changing room, but she stopped him with a gentle hand to the chest. "Let me change first."

She closed the door and slipped out of her T-shirt and jeans and into the cute floral slip dress she was actually planning to buy. She knew before the silky fabric fell over her chest and hips that it would be perfect. Once on, she smoothed her hands over her hair and wet her lips. When she opened the door to invite Brian in, she pretended to welcome him into her studio apartment.

"You're early," she said, pulling him inside. "My place is a mess."

Brian seemed struck blind by the sight of her. "You're so beautiful," he whispered, holding her hand but keeping a safe distance, almost as if he was afraid to touch her and ruin the effect.

"I wanted this night to be special," Julia said, stepping forward into his arms. "I thought we could go dancing." She reached down and pulled her iPhone out of her purse and played "Your Best American Girl" by Mitski. She held Brian close and rocked gently back and forth with her lips brushing against Brian's neck.

"I'm sorry," Julia whispered to the song's slow strum of a guitar. "I shouldn't have done my campaign promotion the same day as Stacey. That was unfair to her. And to you."

"Why'd you do it?" he asked, holding her close.

"I don't know," she said. "I panicked, I guess. I didn't know baked goods were a part of campaigning. I'm new to this, remember?"

"It made me feel like you're using me," Brian said. "Like the only reason you're spending time with me is to get information on Stacey."

"That's not true," Julia said.

"I want to be able to trust you."

"Would it help if I told you my biggest secret?" Julia said.

"You don't have to do that," Brian said.

"I want to," Julia said. "I trust you with it. Even though you may hate me after you hear the story."

"I doubt that," Brian said.

Julia took a deep breath. "There's a reason I'm in the States with my aunt and not back in Canada with my mom." She paused, then said, "I almost killed a girl." Julia felt Brian start to pull away, probably so he could look at her, but Julia tightened her embrace. She didn't think she'd have the courage to tell him the truth if they looked each other in the eyes.

"It was last year," she began. "I was dating this senior named Felix, a real asshole, although I didn't know that at the time. I found a picture of a girl posing in her underwear on his phone, and he told me she was a stalker who wouldn't leave him alone. I believed him and posted the girl's photo for everyone at school to see. The girl, Alice, was so embarrassed, she tried to kill herself."

Julia felt Brian's body grow rigid, as if she had dripped poison in his ear that instantly paralyzed him. She continued to hold him close and rock him gently.

"Did she succeed?" he asked.

"No, thank God. I found out later she was just a freshman, and Felix had been flirting with her for months. He's the one who convinced her to send him the photo. But since I'm the one who shared it, everyone turned on me. Rightly so. Felix broke up with me. My friends disowned me. The school suspended me. Alice's family wanted to prosecute. They had all my texts and posts as evidence. Mom thought it would be better if I left for a while, so she sent me to live with her sister here in California."

Julia pulled away. Now that she had bared her soul in this Nordstrom confessional, she wanted to see its impact on Brian. If he had anger or disgust on his face, it would kill her. But all she saw was pity.

"That's horrible," he said.

"It's okay if you hate me," Julia said, turning away. She caught a glimpse of herself in the floor-length mirror and quickly averted her eyes. "I needed you to know. I don't want there to be any secrets between us."

The next song on the Spotify playlist came on; "First Love/Late Spring." Julia hoped it was true. Mitski had never gotten anything wrong before. But how could someone forgive a person for something so horrible? Julia couldn't even forgive herself.

Brian stepped closer and wrapped his arms around Julia's waist. She listened to him breathe softly in her ear. "I kissed a boy once," he finally said.

The admission was so surprising, Julia couldn't help but laugh. "So?" she said.

"I just . . . if we're being totally honest . . . I thought you should know."

"Did you like it?"

"I didn't not like it. But I prefer kissing you. Like by a billion times." Brian pressed his lips against Julia's and showed her how much he liked kissing her.

"Well, that's good. I like kissing you better than the girls I've kissed too."

"Girls?"

"That's a story for another time," Julia said.

And so, the two went back to kissing.

Twenty minutes later, the salesclerk knocked on their door. "How's everything?" she asked.

"Just great," Julia said. "I think I found what I'm looking for."

Julia bought the summer dress, and she and Brian walked hand in hand through the maze of clothes toward the escalators. She couldn't remember a time she was happier. Somehow, out of all the various outfits she could have put on, she had found the perfect fit. She felt as soft and light as the fabric in her shopping bag.

"This girl who tried to kill herself," Brian said as they made their way toward the escalator. "Did you ever, you know, apologize?"

"There wasn't time," Julia said, but then added, "That's not true. I was too scared to see her."

"I get that," he said, squeezing her hand. "You have to, you know, at some point."

"I know," Julia said. "How do you make amends for something like that?"

"You'll find a way," Brian said. "I have faith in you. Oh my God!"

Brian immediately pushed her away. And not in the typical way boys do when they suddenly become emotionally unavailable. He literally shoved her into a circular rack of summer sweaters as they were rounding the corner to the down escalator.

"What the—?" she said, regaining her balance.

"Brian!" a blond woman in her late thirties said. She was tanned and fit, like a personal trainer who anchored the evening news.

"Hi, Ms. Wynn," Brian said, stepping away from the sweater rack as fast as he could.

Holy shit! This was Stacey's mom. Julia could see the resemblance now. She suddenly became a Black Friday shopper and started frantically flipping through the items on the rack in front of her, hoping to duck behind the sweater curtain when no one was looking.

"You're going to have to get used to calling me Mrs. Park," the woman said. "The wedding's in three weeks."

"That's going to be weird," Brian rambled. "Not the wedding. The name. I'm sure the wedding's going to be awesome."

"You're Stacey's date, right?"

"You know it," Brian said. "I'm here, actually, shopping for something nice to wear."

"In the Juniors department?"

"What? Is that what this is? No. I'm coming down from the Men's department upstairs."

"The Men's department is on the bottom floor."

"I know. I got confused. Anyway, nice seeing you. Gotta get home for dinner."

Brian stumbled off, leaving Ms. Wynn with a bemused look on her face. Julia ducked down and crawled between the sweaters hanging on the rack in front of her. She prayed Stacey's mom would move on to Bridal and not find her. She didn't know how long she could hide in all this cotton before she started to suffocate.

After a few minutes, she poked her head out and saw that the coast was clear. Just to be safe, she grabbed a few sweaters and took them into the changing room to buy herself some time. That was a close call, she texted Brian when she was safely locked inside. She waited there for a response, but there was none. After five minutes, Julia left the discarded sweaters in a heap on the floor and told the salesclerk that nothing fit quite right.

25

TONY LISTENED TO Mohawk discuss the upcoming election with the five other munchkins sitting at his table and wondered if this is what it was like to have siblings. He was an only child and had grown accustomed to solitude, both at home and at school. Now he had to share everything with these underclassmen—from his chocolate milk to his thoughts and feelings. Most days, it wasn't so bad, but there were times he wanted to be left alone. Today, for instance. He could really use this time to review his Chinese vocabulary, but instead, he was forced to listen to these little dudes brainstorm about how to win votes.

"I've started sharing my homework in math in exchange for Instagram posts," a sleepy-eyed kid with a lisp said.

"What math class are you in?"

"Geo 9."

"Any of you guys in upper-division classes?" Mohawk asked.

The boy with the glasses that hung crooked on his face raised his hand. Were his ears lopsided? Tony wondered. It was hard to tell with all that dirty-blond hair hanging over them.

"What class?" Mohawk asked.

"Trig Honors," the boy said.

Shit, Tony thought. He's in a higher math class than I am, and he's not even Asian.

"What can you offer the kids in exchange for their support?" Mohawk asked.

The boy thought for a moment. In the ensuing silence, Mohawk refilled each of the boys' glasses with squirts of chocolate syrup from his bottle. They were drinking it straight now, as if it were tequila shots.

"Olivia Seto cheats off me on practically every test," the boy said, smiling diabolically. "I could make my help conditional for her support. A kind of quid pro quo."

"What's that mean?" Mohawk asked.

"One vote for every answer I give her," the boy said.

"I like it," Mohawk said, squirting more syrup in the boy's now-empty glass. "What about you, Roger?"

Roger was the only black kid at the table. Tony had asked his older sister to the junior prom this year and had been rejected, somewhat unkindly, to his recollection. After going to the trouble of painting his car with the promposal *Wanna go to prom?* she had ignored him until he blocked her exit from the student lot with his vehicle, at which point she took out a Sharpie and wrote a big *NO* on the driver's-side window. The paint, it turned out, was indelible, and he had to get a whole new paint job to remove the invitation from the passenger side of his dad's Mercedes.

"I've been sneaking on to my sister's computer," Roger said. "I got all sorts of shit I can blackmail her with."

"I like it," Tony said, speaking up for the first time since this meeting began. "Give this dude a double shot," he instructed Mohawk.

Roger slid his paper cup over to Mohawk, who made a big commotion of filling it with syrup.

In the middle of his generous pour, a murmur arose in the crowd around them. Assistant Principal Evans had entered the building, escorted by a campus security guard, the one who was always escorting Tony back to class after he got lost on his way to the bathroom. The guy—a giant who would easily blend into the 49ers defensive line—was carrying a large, black garbage bag.

Evans wasn't doing his normal meet and greet with students. He made his way through the circular tables like a professional skier doing a slalom run. Sammy, his security detail, did his best to keep up, but his large frame made it challenging for him to step between bodies without knocking them over. On their way to Tony's table, they confiscated all the paper cups Mohawk had distributed to give the constituents their daily chocolate fix. The chorus of boos grew as the two men moved toward the back.

Sammy turned to the room of munchkins and did his best to intimidate them with his snarl and bug-eyed stare. When the booing was reduced to an audible grumble, Mr. Evans turned to Tony and smiled. The man had the bland look of the first guy killed off in alien movies.

"Mr. Guo," he said, placing his hands on his hips. Tony's dad struck this pose whenever he wanted to convey he meant business. "I hear you're providing these students with chocolate milk, is that correct?"

"Don't speak without a lawyer present," Mohawk advised.

"I assume you know," Evans continued, "that the district has dropped chocolate milk from the cafeteria menu."

"I do, sir." Tony always added "sir" and "ma'am" when addressing adults. Most adults at his school hated it. "I'd like to know why students weren't involved in that decision."

"It wasn't their decision to make," Evans said.

"Do district officials eat their meals in the cafeteria?" Mohawk asked.

Evans nodded in Sammy's direction. The security guard

moved over to where Mohawk was sitting and placed one of his huge hands on the boy's shoulder.

"Mr. Guo," Evans went on. "We can have this conversation here or in my office. Which do you prefer?"

Tony looked around the room and saw all eyes were on him. Normally, having this many people staring at him would freak him out. It always did in class when he had to give a speech, or solve an equation, or ask to go to the bathroom. But now he felt strengthened by the audience's gaze. He was fighting for these small, pathetic creatures. For the first time in his life, he understood why people had babies or pets—their weakness made you stronger.

"Mr. Evans, sir," Tony said. "I am running for ASB president to protect the rights of these munchkins."

"*You're* running for ASB president?" Evans seemed genuinely shocked at hearing this, so much that he got on his walkie-talkie. "Can you confirm for me that Tony Guo is a candidate for ASB president?" he said. "Really? Well, yes. That is a surprise."

Evans clipped his walkie-talkie back onto his belt. "Be that as it may," he continued, still a little bewildered. "I cannot allow you to serve chocolate syrup to students when it has been removed from the cafeteria menu."

"What about Stacey's cupcakes?" Mohawk whispered.

"What about Stacey's cupcakes?" Tony said, louder.

Evans rolled his eyes. "Those are allowed under the Pupil Nutrition, Health, and Achievement Act, as long as she gave them away off school premises, which she did."

"And Julia's sweet buns?" Mohawk whispered.

"And Julia's sweet buns?" Tony said.

"I wasn't aware Miss Romero was giving out baked goods as part of her campaign. I promise to speak to her about this. In the meantime, you will no longer provide chocolate milk to any student here on campus," he said. "Do I make myself clear?"

"Mr. Evans, sir. You are denying these children their human rights!" Tony pounded on the table for emphasis. "I, for one, will not stand by and let you do it."

Evans sighed and nodded in Sammy's direction. In a flash, the security guard had Tony by the forearm and was hoisting him up. A few seconds later, Tony was being led through the tables to the exit.

"I promise all of you," Tony said as he was dragged from the room, "I will not let the Man stop me from helping the little guy. You are the future of this school, and no one will keep me from fighting for your interests."

Just before they reached the door, Tony glanced back and saw Mohawk leap from his chair, climb onto a table, and say, "Captain, my captain," in a voice that echoed through the cavernous space.

"Sit down, Mr. Little," Evans said. "You hear me, sit down!"

One by one, the other boys followed Mohawk up onto tables, until every boy stood in silent solidarity with their leader. Then one of the tables buckled under the weight, and five boys fell to the floor in a tangle of spidery legs and elbows. The boys erupted in laughter after that, which sort of dampened the majesty of the moment. The last thing Tony heard as he was escorted out of his makeshift convention hall was "Smooth move, dumbass!"

"CAFETERIAGATE DERAILS WYNN CAMPAIGN"

by Lance Haber

On Thursday, April 5, the administration marched into the school cafeteria and forcibly removed Tony Guo from the premises. His crime? Speaking to his constituents.

"It was a political gathering," Kyle Little told me in a recent sit-down interview. "I thought the administration was supposed to protect our freedom of assembly, not make it more difficult."

As usual, the administration declined to comment.

"It is not the school's policy to share information about student punishment with reporters," Buckley said. "How would you like it if, for example, you were suspended for inflammatory speech, and I told our student newspaper all about it?"

Again, it appears you can't ask the administration a question without them threatening you with disciplinary action.

"This was a clear retaliatory measure by the Wynn campaign," Little said. "Tony's campaign is gathering momentum, and she now sees him as a threat. She did the same thing to Julia when her campaign first started."

When asked to comment, Wynn was typically evasive and only responded to my questions via email. "I had nothing to do with the administration shutting down Tony's illegal chocolate milk distillery," Wynn wrote. "He was violating Education Code 49431.5, which requires all beverages sold to students on school grounds be approved for compliance with state nutritional guidelines."

"We weren't selling chocolate milk," Little said. "We were giving it away like Stacey did with her cupcakes, which by the way contain way more fat and sugar content than our tiny squirts of chocolate syrup. Did they shut her operation down and drag her away to the front office? No, they did not."

Again, it appears the powers that be have already voted in this election campaign. Their candidate: Stacey Wynn.

First they refuse to fully investigate her role in the now-infamous Postergate scandal of last week. Now they shut down rising star Tony Guo just as his message of limited government is striking a chord with voters.

And what do we make of Wynn's recent pivot to loosening the restrictive cell phone policy? That should put the principal's beloved candidate at odds with her administration.

Before you get too excited about Wynn's new platform, think about it for a minute: she wants us to be able to use our cell phones in class more, claiming they are valuable educational tools.

The reason we like our cell phones so much is because they are a digital safe zone *from* school. *We* get to create the world we want to appear on the screen. What do you think will happen if the school starts using our iPhones and Samsungs as learning tools, as Wynn advocates? Not only will we be inundated with homework reminders throughout the day, but our devices will turn into tracking mechanisms, a GPS narc, able to locate us at any time. Is that the kind of digital world you want to live in? To me, it sounds like the start of every dystopian novel where the beleaguered citizens are under constant surveillance by their totalitarian overlords.

Unless you're looking forward to being grouped into personality-type factions and asked to fight to the death at annual gladiator tournaments, you must resist Stacey's attempts to control our primary means of communication. Use your cell phones to text your local school board officials today with your concerns and complaints. I provide their contact info below.

ATTACK ADS

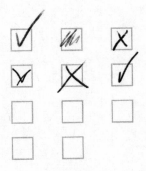

26

STACEY AWOKE TO the smell of something burning. She leaped out of bed and raced downstairs to stop the flames from spreading and found her dad making breakfast. He was dressed and grilling French toast, which was in some ways more alarming than the fire she had envisioned consuming her home. Breakfast was not her dad's thing given that he woke up most days after ten a.m.

"Dad? What're you doing?" she asked.

"Good morning, sweetheart," he said. "Sit down."

Stacey sat and watched her dad slide a couple crispy slices of French toast onto a plate and top it with powdered sugar and blueberries. Just how she liked it.

"You're making breakfast," she said.

"Yep! I'm taking the drone out for its maiden voyage," he said. "Thought I'd do it early, before class."

"Oh! You're done already?" Stacey said. She had hoped this project would keep him busy for at least another week.

"It wasn't that hard to assemble," he said. "Of course, now I have all these ideas for modifications."

It was great to see her dad excited like this. She hadn't seen him this engaged since he installed that electric awning in the backyard.

She stuck a forkful of toast in her mouth and chewed, listening to her dad go on about his ideas for increasing the machine's wind resistance. While she was eating, she received a text from Priya.

Found something interesting, she wrote.

On whom? Stacey typed back.

Both.

Meet in library @ lunch? Stacey wrote.

Priya sent her a thumbs-up emoji.

"Does the drone have a camera?" Stacey asked her dad, scanning the sky from the kitchen window.

Her dad nodded. "It's got a transmission range of up to four-point-three miles."

"What about sound? Can it pick up sound?"

"Not really," he said. "Why? You want to spy on your enemies?" He laughed.

"I don't have any enemies, Dad," Stacey said, deadpan, thinking of her mom's advice from their last meeting. "Just competitors."

...

Stacey had a hard time focusing on anything but her lunch with Priya. She texted Brian about the meeting, and he promised to be there. We can work on your speech too, he wrote back. I've got some ideas.

Ever since the cupcake fiasco, Brian had been working overtime to help Stacey regain some lost ground. Yesterday, he informed the administration about the flagrant health violations taking place in the cafeteria and effectively shut down Tony's campaign headquarters. He also went to another GSA club meeting to advocate on her behalf. Now he was helping her with her speech in anticipation of next week's school assembly, in which all candidates had three minutes to make their cases in front of the voting public. He really was a true friend.

As soon as the bell rang for lunch, Stacey sprinted to the library and grabbed one of the tables near the back, away from the prying eyes of the librarian. Brian arrived a few minutes later and sat down next to her.

"Based on my polling," he started, getting right down to business, "voters are most enthusiastic about your promise to change the cell phone policy."

"You're polling students?" Stacey asked, surprised.

"I conducted an informal focus group during English," Brian said, dropping his hand into his open backpack on the floor and removing an apple slice. The library had a strict no-eating policy, so they had to sneak their food while the librarian was monitoring the other side of the room.

"But I don't know if I *can* change the cell phone policy," Stacey whispered. She looked around and hoped no one was eavesdropping on their strategy session. The library was filling up with students, and the last thing she needed was another leak. "I spoke with Buckley about it in passing, and she's pretty inflexible on the topic."

"It doesn't matter," Brian said. "As long as people see you fighting for change, they will support you."

"What about my experience? Neither candidate has done as much for the school as I have. That should count for something. As vice president, I've nearly doubled the number of clubs on campus."

Brian looked at her. "So you're the one responsible for the Improv Everywhere Club?"

"I had no idea they would perform at every assembly!"

"Just sayin'. Be careful what you brag about. I think it's safer to run on the future, rather than the past."

Stacey sighed. "Fine. Oh look, there's Priya."

The two of them watched as the diminutive girl, eyes focused on her phone, stumbled into a book display on mindfulness. Without looking away from the screen in front of her, she redirected herself and moved toward Stacey and Brian's table.

"Is she following directions on Google Maps?" Brian asked.

"Maybe. She's probably got five or six screens open right now."

Priya bounced between tables like a slow-moving pinball until she reached where Stacey and Brian were sitting. Brian pulled a chair out for her, worried that she might miss the seat and land on the carpeted floor.

"Hi, Priya," Stacey said. "You know Brian, right?"

Brian felt his phone buzz and saw the Priya had just followed him on Twitter and Instagram. A second later, he got a friend request on Facebook.

"I do now," she said. "By the way, you don't have Snapchat?"

Brian rolled his eyes.

"Priya has been doing some opposition research for me," Stacey explained. "Digging into Tony's and Julia's digital pasts to see if there's anything useful."

"What? Why?" Brian said.

"Mom said I need to know my enemies," Stacey said.

"Oh, you talked to your mom lately?" Brian asked. Stacey noticed his voice went up a few octaves.

"Not since last weekend," Stacey said. "We're going bridesmaid dress shopping on Sunday." Stacey made a face like someone who's just swallowed a horsefly.

"I saw her the other day," Brian said. "Shopping at Nordstrom."

"Not in the Bridal section, I hope," Stacey said.

"Ha! Good one. Actually, I was shopping for a present. For my mom. For her birthday."

"Her birthday's not until July," Stacey said. She knew because it was two days after her own. They were both Cancers and gave each other crab-themed cards every year.

"Yeah, I know that. I like to start early. You know, for the sales?" Brian squirmed in his seat like he had to go to the bathroom.

"You want to hear what I found or what?" Priya said, staring at them with a bored expression. Given the speed with which Priya processed information, Stacey probably appeared to her like a slug does to a hummingbird.

"Yes, of course," Stacey said.

"Okay. Let's start with Tony. He was easy. There are, like, a billion selfies of him taking bong hits on his feed," Priya said. She slid her tiny fingers across her phone and sent Stacey a photo album filled with images of Tony smoking, drinking, and posing like a Chinese Snoop Dogg.

Brian scooted his chair next to Stacey to see the photos. "How many bongs does the guy have?" he asked as Stacey swiped through the montage of party shots.

"I like the one shaped like a bear-shaped honey jar,"

Stacey said, zooming in on a shot of Tony sucking smoke out of the yellow dispenser top. "These were just out there?"

"Yup," Priya said. "For a guy who parties as much as he does, he has surprisingly few followers, although that number has gone up recently. He seems to be trending high with freshmen boys."

"That's my brother's influence," Brian said.

"They seem to like his take on genitalia," Priya said. Her fingers glided over her screen again. Seconds later, Stacey's in-box was flooded with screenshots of Tony's tweets about his member.

"If there's a dick pic, please don't forward it to me," Stacey said.

"There's not," Priya said.

"What about Julia?" Stacey said, leaning forward.

Priya's large brown eyes crossed in response to Stacey's question. "She's weird," she said, swiping screens to the left to get to Julia's info. "Up until last week, there's nothing. I mean, zero. Is there, like, no social media in Canada?"

"There's definitely social media in Canada," Stacey said.

"Maybe she's just a lurker," Brian offered.

"She's got a good number of followers," Priya said. "Almost as many as you."

Stacey was about to say something, but Brian put a hand on her shoulder and stopped her.

"I did find one interesting thing," Priya said. "Julia's friends with her aunt, who's white by the way."

"Yeah, so?" Brian said, a bit defensively in Stacey's opinion. "Julia's biracial."

"She's not friends with her mom, but I was able to check out her mom's page through the aunt. Neither woman knows how to use privacy blocks. Adults are so lame with this stuff."

"What did you find?" Stacey said.

"No mention of Julia's dad. Like anywhere."

"Maybe they had a bitter divorce," Stacey said. Like her own parents. The day Mom moved out, Dad removed all the photos of her from the walls and replaced them with Dorothea Lange photographs of migrant farmworkers.

"Yeah, but wouldn't there be a shot of him somewhere? There are photos of nearly every one of Julia's birthdays, and there's not a brown guy anywhere."

"I don't think that means anything," Brian said.

"It's just weird, is all," Priya said, shrugging. "Especially with all the mom's posts on the rotting Y chromosome and the perfume of female power."

"What does that even mean?" Brian asked.

"She doesn't think men are necessary," Stacey said, quoting the title of a book she had long been curious about. The paperback was sandwiched between her mom's cookbooks and fitness guides until she moved out.

"So, her mom's a feminist," Brian said. "You want to use that against her?"

"Did you see any photos or posts reflecting Latino culture?" Stacey asked. "Any music, food, or clothing?"

"Nothing," Priya said. "Julia's upbringing, at least based on her mom's posts, was pretty white."

"Stacey," Brian said. "You can't use this information. It's worthless. You don't like tea and crumpets; that doesn't mean you're not English."

"I'm not running as an Anglophile," Stacey said.

"It's still wrong," Brian said, nearly shouting. He got an aggressive shush from the passing librarian. "And it will backfire, I promise," he continued, dropping his voice to a whisper. "You can win this race by not going negative."

"Not with two candidates splitting the vote," Stacey said. "If one of them drops out, I can win the majority."

"Then go after Tony," Brian said. "His crimes are clearly visible. He's been advertising his love of pot and dick for all to see."

"But don't you see?" Stacey said. "If Julia vandalized her own poster, her not being Latina makes her crime even *more* heinous. Not only did she appropriate the Latino culture, she also engineered her own victimhood in order to get a sympathy vote."

"Julia's voters will not come over to your side," Brian said.

"Especially if you accuse her of not being a 'real Latina.'"

Stacey didn't like how he put that last bit in air quotes, but she knew he was right. Tony was the safer one to attack. She just *so* wanted to expose Julia for the liar she was.

"Let's repost one of Tony's bong hit photos," Stacey said finally. "With the caption 'Is this who we want leading our school?'"

Priya tapped her phone. "Done," she said, and went back to swiping.

27

THREE DAYS TILL ELECTION DAY

"DUDE, CAN WE come in?" Doug said over the case of beer he was holding.

Tony stared at the four guys standing on his doorstep and hesitated. It was Saturday evening, and he hadn't received any communication from Doug saying he was bringing his buddies to the house, but then people often dropped by unannounced, especially when Tony's parents were out of town. He swung the giant front door open, and welcomed the foursome into his palatial home.

"Holy fuck," the pudgy guy holding the shopping bag full of mixers said. "This place is ginormous." Tony had seen the guy around school. He thought he remembered reading something about him winning a golf title.

Tony led them through the two-story entry and into the kitchen, where they began their opening, pouring, and mixing.

"Dude, what's with all this chocolate milk?" Doug asked, trying to find space in Tony's refrigerator for the beer. Tony had just figured out how to get groceries delivered through Amazon and had stocked his shelves with cartons of Space Cow. He walked over and created some room for the cans of Pabst Blue Ribbon that Doug had brought over.

"What'll you have, Tony?" Doug asked, holding up a beer and bottle of vodka. Tony had already gotten pretty high while watching *Walking Dead* reruns, so he grabbed the beer. Plus, he loved the sound of opening carbonated beverages.

After everyone had a drink, they moved out to the pool area and sat around a sparkling glass table. The setting sun tinted everything golden. The boys drank and watched Tony's terrier chase squirrels on the manicured golf course of a lawn. It was peaceful and quiet, and for a moment Tony was content just being present in the beauty of his backyard.

"Should we invite some girls over?" the short, stocky guy with the swimmer's hair said. Tony stared at the scrubby beard the dude was trying to grow and wondered why you never see swimmers with facial hair.

"Is that cool, Tony?" Doug asked.

Tony shrugged. "I guess." He hadn't invited these guys over; he supposed it didn't matter if they brought some dates.

"Cool," Doug said, and nodded in the direction of Swimmer Beard, who immediately started texting.

The boys finished their drinks, and Pudgy Golfer went to get refills. Before they started on their second round, Doug raised his glass and toasted Tony. "To our next school president," he said. When did Doug lose his braces? Tony wondered. His teeth seemed unnaturally white all of a sudden.

The guys cheered and slammed their glasses and cans against one another.

"I'm not going to be president," Tony said.

"People love you," the fourth guy said. Tony tried to think of a nickname for him, but there was nothing distinguishing about his appearance; he looked like every other white guy to Tony, so he called him Matthew McConaughey.

"Have you seen the comments on your photo?" Doug asked. He held his phone up to Tony's face. On the screen was a photo of Tony exhaling an insane amount of smoke from a bong hit. When was that photo taken? Tony couldn't recall. He was pretty sure it was back in September, when his parents left him for their cruise down the Yangtze.

Underneath the photo was the caption "Is this who we want leading our school?" Doug scrolled down the page so Tony could read the answers. Almost every one of the 143 comments was an enthusiastic yes.

"Tony's got my vote."

"Here's some change I can believe in."

"Make America baked again."

So this was why everyone had been high-fiving him in the halls yesterday, Tony suddenly realized. It seemed like he was especially popular Friday afternoon. Strangers called out his name and pointed in his direction. One girl asked him to sign her Spanish textbook. Tony thought all the extra attention was because the administration had banned him from the cafeteria for a week. But it was because of this dumb photo that had been posted and shared throughout the school.

"That's fucking . . ." Tony couldn't figure out how to finish the sentence—hilarious? Pathetic? Sad?—so he took a long drink of beer instead.

"You gonna have an election party?" Pudgy Golfer asked.

"A what?" Tony asked.

"Dude, you have to have a blowout when you become president," Doug said. "Make it epic and shit."

"Totally," Swimmer Beard said.

"I don't know," Tony said. "My parents are coming back soon."

"When?" Pudgy Golfer said.

Tony didn't know. His dad had told him, but it was so far in the future, Tony didn't bother to write it down. He was pretty sure it was in May sometime. "Not for a couple weeks."

"Bruh, the election is next week," Doug said. "You have to have a party to thank all your supporters." Doug raised his glass and toasted the other guys, supporters presumably, at the table.

"But not my brother," Matthew McConaughey said. "That little fucker threatened to tell my mom about the money I took from her purse if I didn't vote for you."

"No shit!" Pudgy Golfer said. "My brother said he'd do my chores for a week if I voted for Tony. How'd you get such a devoted army of slaves?"

"I'm fighting for their rights," Tony said, which caused everyone at the table to burst out laughing.

"You can't invite them to the party," Swimmer Beard said. "It's a serious liability."

Tony wanted to say he never invited anyone to his parties; people just showed up. He wasn't sure what point this response would make though. There was something in his head about nature abhorring a vacuum. Tony, like his empty house, was a thing that needed to be filled. It didn't matter who came over—Mohawk or Pudgy Golfer—it was all the same to him.

The distant sound of the doorbell made Doug and McConaughey bolt from their chairs to greet the new guests. A few seconds later, they returned with five girls and a new guy. Tony groaned thinking of all the nicknames he'd have to create to help him distinguish one guest from another. Easier to go get his bong and smoke upstairs.

Tony stumbled past his guests with barely a nod and trudged up the marble stairs to his bedroom. Someone had figured out how to link their phone to his Bluetooth speakers and was blasting some shitty pop music. Tony sealed himself off from the party downstairs and dug through his closet for his bear-shaped honey bottle bong—the one featured in the photo that Doug had just shown him. He'd forgotten how much he liked this bong. It was cute and compact, easy to reload. He found it on the upper shelf, tucked behind his chess set.

He walked over to the window and opened it wide. His room looked down on the pool deck, and Tony watched Doug and the others mix and mingle with their drinks. Dropping onto the beanbag on the floor, he filled the bong with some excellent Ghost Train Haze and lit up. He inhaled deeply and felt a goofy smile return to his face. Tony Guo, president of the ASB. It was hilarious and sad at the same time. His parents would flip out when he told them. They had pretty much written him off as a failure. A bad investment they had to live with. Or not live with as it turned out. He wasn't sure if he would welcome their renewed attention. In fact, it could be kind of a drag to listen to them nag him again about wasted potential.

Tony exhaled, being careful to blow the smoke out the open window. Maybe he should just quit. It's not like he wanted to do this. Mohawk had done all the work. Tony just sat back and enjoyed the attention. But did he really enjoy the attention? He wasn't sure. He kind of liked it in the cafeteria, where he could pretend to be someone important. Someone worth listening to. But at home, this interest bothered him. It felt more like an invasion of privacy than an honor bestowed on a great leader.

Tony took another hit, held it in, and blew the smoke outside. There *was* a difference between Mohawk and the guys downstairs. Mohawk saw a leader in Tony, someone with the potential to accomplish something great. All Doug and his friends saw when they looked at Tony was an empty house where they could get wasted.

The clouds drifting out Tony's window must have grabbed someone's attention from the pool deck, because people started chanting "Tony! Tony! Tony!" and holding their fists up to the beat of his name. Tony poked his head out the window and waved down to his guests, who broke into a loud applause. Maybe he could handle the crowds at home if he stayed up here and greeted them with a wave every so often. The help would always clean up any mess the guests left behind.

Tony dug into his pocket and pulled out his phone for a selfie. Before he snapped the photo, he lit the remaining flakes in the bowl and inhaled deeply. He took a picture with him exhaling the smoke, making sure he smiled broadly for the camera.

Satisfied with the self-portrait, he posted it to the comments section of the original post, asking if this was who people wanted leading their school.

"Yes we can!" Tony wrote under the photo, and shared it with everyone.

28

STACEY LOST AN entire Sunday afternoon that she was never going to get back, trying on bridesmaid dresses. She could have been memorizing her speech or ironing her clothes or working on her vocal fry, but instead, she was squeezing into hideous fashion and twirling in front of her mom like some homicidal debutante.

"Mom, I can't take this anymore," she said finally. "Just pick the one you like, and I'll wear it." Stacey pulled on the silk cross strap that felt like the sash pageants use to brand each girl with a state.

"I want you to love the dress too," her mom said, eyeing Stacey and wrinkling her nose. This had been her reaction every time Stacey stepped out of the dressing room. In response to her mom's lack of enthusiasm, Ashley, their weary consultant, dived back into the racks to dig out another selection.

"This one you could reuse for prom!" Ashley said, holding up a short, crinkled chiffon dress with a sweetheart neckline.

Ugh. Prom. Stacey hated the dress even more now because it reminded her of the worst part of the school year. After all the excitement of school elections came prom season. It was like following a great episode of *Washington Week* with a *Keeping Up with the Kardashians* rerun. Pretty soon, Stacey would have to suffer through an endless display of promposals, each one trying to outdo the other in a spectacle of bad puns. Then all the smart, capable girls stopped thinking about serious issues and became obsessed with finding the perfect dress, which they would only wear once. The waste was enormous. At least people carpooled in limousines.

"You going to prom this year?" Mom asked.

"Probably not," Stacey said. She hiked up her dress and struck a fighter's stance. Ashley and her mom exchanged a glance like people discovering stray hairs in their food.

"This one would probably look best on Soo Jung," Stacey's mom said, walking around and checking it out from behind. "She's a little pudgy around the middle," she whispered, as if Soo Jung's supersonic hearing made it possible to eavesdrop from South Korea.

Soo Jung was Mr. Park's daughter. The twenty-four-year-old would be flying in from Seoul to participate in the ceremony. There was some question regarding the length of her stay afterward. Mom hoped for a short-term student visa.

"Can I get out of this now?" Stacey asked.

Stacey's mom nodded and turned to consult with Ashley.

Stacey slid the dressing-room curtain shut and started the cumbersome task of removing her clothes. Why did she feel so uncomfortable in all these gowns? Did it have something to do with the dress, the occasion, or herself? Probably some combination of all three. She'd always hated wearing dresses. It didn't help that she had to wear one to celebrate her mom's marriage to her former Tae Kwon Do instructor. How could she ever repurpose this dress without it reminding her of the body blow that knocked her family onto the mat for good?

Changing back into her jeans and T-shirt made Stacey feel like herself again. This was the skin that felt natural to her. She placed the dress back on the hanger and held it in front of her like something a snake might have shed.

"I think we'll go with this last one," her mom told Ashley, snapping a photo of the dress with her phone. "I'll send this to Soo Jung and Tanya."

Tanya was Mom's former sorority sister flying in from Houston. It seemed a little unfair to pick a dress for an older woman based on how it looked on her teenage daughter, but Stacey wasn't about to question her mom's decision-making. This was her day; she could fuck it up however she chose.

"You're not going to make me plan a bachelorette party, are you?" Stacey asked as they headed back to the car.

"No," her mom said. "I didn't have one when I married your father. I certainly don't need one now. How is he by the way?"

"Great, actually," Stacey said, exaggerating Dad's recovery a bit. "He's helping me make a drone."

"Why do you need a drone?"

"For school," Stacey said, stretching the truth a little further. Her dad was the one who needed the drone, not her. "You know, to film games and activities."

"There's a camera mounted on it?" Mom asked. "Do you think I could borrow it for the wedding? I'd love to get some aerial shots of the ceremony. The winery is stunning."

Mom had rented out a winery in St. Helena at considerable expense. She justified the cost because getting married was supposedly a once-in-a-lifetime experience.

"I don't know if it will be ready in time," Stacey said, flat-out lying.

The two reached the car and got inside, which was cool and comfortable, thanks to the shade her mom had stretched across the windshield before leaving for the fitting. Her mom started the car, turned the stereo to her favorite eighties station, and drove to her apartment, where Stacey had left her car.

"You bringing Brian to the wedding?" her mom asked.

She pulled her water bottle out of her purse and placed it in the cup holder. Mom was a tropical plant that required constant hydration.

"Yeah."

"I saw him at Nordstrom the other day."

"I know. He told me."

"He was with a girl, I think."

"Brian? I don't think so. He said he was shopping for his mom."

"Hmm, I swear he was with someone. He looked embarrassed when he saw me."

"That's just Brian," Stacey said.

"You better lock that down before some other girl grabs him."

"Ew, gross. Brian's my friend."

"Yeah, but for how long?" Mom took a long sip from her bottle embossed with Mr. Park's studio's logo—a silhouette of a fighter in front of the American flag. "He's cute now that he's lost all that weight. Don't think other girls haven't noticed."

"So?"

"So, I'm just saying. As soon as he starts dating someone, you won't be seeing him much anymore."

"That's not true."

"Trust me. It is. Romance trumps friendship every time."

"I don't even know if Brian is straight."

"There are ways of finding out." Her mom smiled, forcing Stacey to focus on the song playing on the radio. "Don't you want me, baby? Don't you want me, Ahhhhhh!" the singer crooned.

"When I wanted to find out if Young-jin was interested in me," Mom said, tapping Stacey's knee, "I hugged him and rubbed his back in gentle circles."

"That's gross and sad."

"It got me this ring," her mom said, holding her hand in front of Stacey's face.

"It also got you divorced," Stacey said.

"This was after my marriage to your father was over," her mom said.

Stacey doubted it. Two weeks after Mom moved out, Stacey found a Starburst wrapper in the space between the passenger seat and door, and knew it could only come from one source. Her instructor was addicted to the fruity candy and chewed them like nicotine gum.

Mom pulled into her space in the basement garage of her condo complex.

"You want to come upstairs?" she asked. "We could have a little girl time? You could help me choose a nail color to match my wedding dress."

"That sounds like fun," Stacey said, as if her mom had just invited her to clean a toilet. "But I have to prep for my speech tomorrow," she said. She had had enough girl time with her middle-aged mother for one day.

On the drive back to her dad's, Stacey thought about what her mother had said. Was it time to "lock" Brian down? The phrase felt mildly offensive, as if Brian were a piece of hot real estate. She had never thought of him as anything but her friend. Could she imagine kissing him? Having him hold her? Feeling his— No, she could not go there. Time to think of other things. Gosh, that hedge was well manicured. Watch out, squirrel! That phone line looks wobbly.

She parked her car and walked in a daze to her front door. But what if Brian did start dating someone? Would she lose her best friend? It happened to girls all the time, didn't it? Stacey remembered watching a movie about a girl whose best friend starts dating her older brother, and it did not go well for them. Come to think of it, Brian was the one who recommended the film. That must mean he's gay, right? What hetero male chooses to watch coming-of-age stories that explore complicated female relationships?

Still, she couldn't imagine life without Brian. When they met as freshmen, he clearly needed her help. He was fat, friendless, and alone, and she took him under her wing and got him involved in school projects and activities. There was a whole scrapbook in her closet upstairs with photos of them making homecoming floats, playing in marching band, attending youth-in-government camps. Somewhere along the line though, she started needing him more than he needed her. She relied on him for practically everything now—making banners, decorating cupcakes, writing speeches. And he was always there for her. But what if he weren't? Then she would be the one friendless and alone.

She sat down at her desk and tried to distract herself by working on her speech. There was a lot riding on it now that her smear attempt had backfired. She logged on to the post featuring Tony mid–bong hit and saw even more likes and congratulatory comments. What was wrong with these people? Is this the kind of behavior we expect from our elected officials now? Next thing you know, Seth Rogen will be running for state congressman.

She really needed someone to help her with her performance. There were some complicated hand gestures that she didn't feel quite right about.

Hey, Brian, she texted. You free to help me practice my speech?

Sure. I'll come over after dinner, he wrote back.

Stacey looked at her grubby outfit and decided she should change. She wasn't going to wear jeans and a T-shirt tomorrow, was she? She should practice in her best suit. The one that showed off her tanned and toned legs and arms. Maybe a little makeup wouldn't hurt either.

29

WHEN JULIA SAW her reflection in Jenny's full-length mirror, she almost didn't recognize herself. The two girls had taken a break from the quinceañera protest practice to try on Jenny's sister's dress. The tight, bejeweled top and ruffled bottom of the gown didn't come close to anything in Julia's closet, but something about the outrageous style appealed to her. Rather than marking her transition into adulthood, the dress allowed her to experience a missing part of her childhood. Her mom forbade anything princess in their home, claiming the image reinforced unattainable standards of beauty and derailed any progress women had made toward self-actualization. So, no Disney movies or their accompanying paraphernalia were allowed. Instead, Julia got to dress up in Marie Curie lab coats or Simone de Beauvoir turbans for Halloweens.

"You're beautiful," Jenny said from behind her.

"It's weird how perfect it fits," Julia said.

"You and my sister are, like, the exact same size," Jenny said.

"Are you sure she won't mind me borrowing it?"

"Nah," Jenny said. "Vickie doesn't get back from college until late May. She'll never know. Oh, I got something else for you."

Julia expected Jenny to hand her a tiara or some other fancy accessory, but instead she dug under her pink duvet and pulled out a white cardboard box stamped with the brand name *AncestryDNA*. Her test had finally arrived.

"I don't think you need it," Jenny said, handing her the box. "Seeing you in this dress, there's no doubt in my mind you're Latina."

"You might think different if I were wearing a hijab," Julia said. Or a sari. Or even a colorful wrap. Julia's skin tone and features allowed her to become anyone she wanted, really, given the right outfit.

"Here, let's take a picture," Jenny said. Julia tossed the DNA test onto the bed and handed Jenny her phone. The two squeezed together for a selfie.

"See, we could be sisters," she said, looking at the photo.

"*Hermanas*," Julia said.

"I love how you're learning Spanish," Jenny said. "I've

never heard my language spoken with a French accent before. It's hella cool. Here, let me take one of just you."

Jenny held up the camera, and Julia struck her best Cinderella pose. After Jenny was done, Julia scrolled through the shots and sent the best one to Brian with the caption "Your Latina princess."

An urgent knocking drew her out of her narcissistic stare. "Can we see?" Rosa said from the other side of the door. Rather than wait for an answer, she burst into the room, followed by the rest of the girls who had come to Jenny's house to rehearse the dance they would perform at the protest. Jenny had been leading them through the steps in the backyard, trying to make it fun without losing the urgency of the message. The girls were tired and sweaty from marching and moving to Calle 13's "Pa'l Norte" all morning.

The group squealed in delight when they saw Julia standing in front of them.

"It's perfect," Rosa said.

"You're fucking gorgeous," Stephanie said. She was a senior with the stern expression of a flamenco dancer.

Julia did a little spin for the crowd. "*J'adore,*" she said. In her rotation, she spotted the DNA testing kit still on the top of the bed and panicked. She sat down quickly on top of the box before anyone could see and ask her about it.

"It's so weird hearing you speak French," Maria said. She

was wearing a black T-shirt with the image of a raised fist holding a microphone.

"I love it," Jenny said. "I wish I had a sexy accent."

"I just never heard of a Latina with a French accent," Maria said. "You sure you're one of us?"

Julia laughed and felt the box beneath her start to rattle. She was pretty sure the sound was in her head, but like the narrator and the ticking in Poe's "The Tell-Tale Heart," she felt the kit come alive from under the folds of her voluminous dress. She looked at Jenny for some assistance.

"Of course she's one of us," Jenny said. "Look at her. She's like a young Jennifer Lopez."

"Where's your family from anyway?" Maria asked.

Why had Julia done this to herself? She should have never let Jenny talk her into this masquerade. Under Maria's questioning, Julia went from 99 percent sure she was Latina to 99 percent sure that she was not. The box rattled some more beneath her, demanding to be heard. She should just tell everyone the truth about her ancestry and be done with it. They could remove her from their formation and do the dance without her. But Julia was kind of the centerpiece of this protest. "Build That Wall!" was written on *her* campaign poster. Did it matter that she wasn't Mexican herself? Julia wasn't sure it did. Everyone at Lincoln High School should be marching with these girls in the face of this kind of bigotry and hatred.

"My mom's family is from Quebec," she said. "Which is why I speak French instead of Spanish." Julia looked down and said, almost in a whisper, "I never knew my dad."

It was the truth. It wasn't the whole truth, but a bit of it. The box underneath her stopped shaking for the time being, satisfied with her admission, she hoped.

"Shit," Rosa said, flopping onto the bed next to Julia, wrapping her arms around her.

"I'm sorry," Stephanie said, joining the hug.

"My dad left when I was four," Maria said, in a quieter voice than normal. "It destroyed my mom. She married some loser 'cause she was so freaked out about being alone."

Jenny came over and put her arms around Maria and held her close. After a few minutes of silence, she clapped her hands and ordered everyone out so Julia could change back into her normal clothes. "Let's get back to dancing," she said, trying to inject some lightness into the room again.

Once everyone had left, she shut the door and turned to Julia, still seated on the bed. "*That* was hella awkward," she said.

"Can you help me out of this?" Julia said, standing and turning her back to Jenny. It was suddenly getting harder for her to breathe. Beads of sweat broke out on her forehead, and her skin began to itch. The dress must be rejecting her.

It must have sensed something deep inside Julia that was scheming and false like the Sorting Hat in *Harry Potter*. She was a Slytherin in a house full of Hufflepuffs.

Jenny's hands undid the straps in the back. As Julia felt the bodice loosen, she wriggled free and stepped out of the folds of ruffled skirt. After carefully laying the dress on Jenny's duvet, she put on her shorts and T-shirt and was able to breathe again.

"You still up for this?" Jenny asked.

"I think so," Julia said.

The girls practiced the rest of the day in Jenny's backyard. The plan was to walk in silence into the quad, holding their protest banners, and then transition to their choreographed dance. Maria had chosen the Calle 13 song, not because it was especially easy to dance to, but because its message was so on point. Jenny translated for Julia the lyrics that the girls wanted to shout out loud:

"A nomad without direction
I crush the negative energy
With my hooves like a lamb's
I set out to roam the entire continent."

Jenny did her best to match the rhythms of the song to some of Beyoncé's signature moves.

At five o'clock, Jenny's mom—a woman still gorgeous after an eight-hour shift at the hospital—sent the girls home for dinner. Julia hid the DNA testing kit in her backpack, hopped on her bike, and pedaled home.

She tried working on her campaign speech in the living room while her aunt prepared dinner, but couldn't concentrate. Uncle Donald hid behind a newspaper with a front-page story of a congressman facing ethics charges. Every so often, his hand would reach out from behind the fold to hoist a glass of sauvignon blanc to his lips. The twins lay on the carpet, coloring a picture of a house engulfed in yellow and orange flames.

Julia closed her laptop and joined her aunt in the kitchen. "Can I help?" she asked. When she first moved in with her aunt's family, she saw this room as a sweatbox, where Gloria slaved over a stove to prepare a hot meal every night. Now, she felt drawn to the warmth and smells of the place. She actually preferred eating something she had helped prepare, rather than having all her meals come from take-out boxes.

Her aunt handed her a brick of cheese and asked her to grate it into a bowl. Julia ran the wedge against the serrated metal while Gloria stirred seasoning into the ground beef cooking on the stove.

"How's the speech coming?" Gloria asked.

"I'm nervous," Julia said, taking some of her stress out on the block of cheese. She liked shredding its rubbery uniformity into thin slivers.

"You'll do fine," Gloria said. "I'm so proud of you, Julia. It takes a lot of guts to stand up in front of everyone and tell them what you believe in."

"Thanks," Julia said.

When Julia finished with the cheese, Gloria handed her a head of lettuce and asked her to cut it into shreds.

"Your mom would kill me if she saw you right now," Gloria said, laughing. "She always said the kitchen was a woman's prison."

"What was she like when she was my age?" Julia asked.

Gloria sighed. "She always did the opposite of what was expected of her. Even as a little girl, she rebelled against the kinds of things I liked to do. If I wanted a dress, your mom wanted army fatigues. If I wanted to take ballet, your mom wanted to box. If I wanted to attend the princess ball in a jeweled tiara, your mom wanted to 'reoccupy' Parliament Hill to draw attention to indigenous people's struggle for justice."

"That doesn't sound very twin-like," Julia said.

"It wasn't. I think in some ways, it was because we were twins that your mom worked so hard to distinguish herself from me. We're not like Madison and Olivia over there."

Julia looked over the counter at the two girls, now talking in their made-up language, a hybrid of English, French, and what sounded like Bantu.

"Do you know anything about my dad?" Julia asked. "Sorry, donor."

"Just what your mom told me," Gloria asked.

"It's frustrating not knowing where part of me comes from."

"I can imagine," Gloria said. "You know, that's another thing your mom and I don't agree on."

"What's that?" Julia said.

"Keeping your ancestry a secret. You deserve to have that information."

"Wait, what?" Julia dropped the knife on the cutting board, where it bounced and fell to the floor, missing Julia's foot by inches. "My mom knows who my donor is?"

Gloria bent down and retrieved the knife and placed it gently into the sink. Then she turned down the heat on the stove and pulled Julia away from the counter. Clearly, she didn't want to discuss this in front of the twins or Donald, although Julia didn't know why. It's not like her parentage was a secret in this household.

"She doesn't know who your donor is," Gloria whispered. "She just has your DNA analysis. The clinic paid for her to get the test done as part of the settlement."

"And she's been keeping it secret from me this whole time?" Julia had to stop herself from slamming her fist into the refrigerator door.

"Oh dear, I'm afraid I've said too much," Gloria said. "Your mother loves you more than anything. You know that, right? But I think she's always felt a little insecure about your, uhm, conception."

"My mother? Insecure?" Julia would never use that word to describe her mom. "Headstrong," "bitchy," "selfish," maybe. But not "insecure."

"Don't get me wrong. Your mom is the most opinionated person I know. She's driven everyone around her away with her inflexibility. You're the only person she wants to pull closer."

"And yet she sent me here."

"You know how hard that was for her? It just about killed her. But she knew it was the best thing for you, so she gave you up to keep you safe."

Julia felt her rage subside a bit. She no longer felt the urge to pick up the knife and stab that head of lettuce in any case.

"Your mom is terrified of losing you," Gloria said. "I think she thinks that if she shares your DNA results, you'll go running off to find your father."

"That's ridiculous."

"I know. It's not rational. And believe me, she will be the

first person to tell you that I'm crazy. She'll say she wants you to be able to create your future, untethered to your past. But deep down, I think she's just afraid you'll reject her in favor of some anonymous donor, and that would definitely kill her."

Julia leaned against the refrigerator, trying to absorb some of its coolness. "Do you mind if I go to my room?" Julia asked. "I need to be alone for a bit."

"Take all the time you need, honey," Gloria said, pulling her in for a hug. "I'll keep your dinner warm for you."

Julia trudged back to her room and fell onto her bed. In her heart, she knew her aunt was right about her mom, which made it difficult to be angry with her. Still, the fact that she would keep her DNA test results a secret for this long was hard to forgive. She knew how important this was to Julia, and yet, she strung her along with excuses for why they couldn't unlock the secret that lay in Julia's chromosomes. Well, no more, Julia decided.

Julia got off the bed and walked over to her desk to retrieve her backpack. Before leaving her room, she listened at the door to make sure the family had sat down for dinner. Once she heard them talking around the kitchen table, she tiptoed down the hallway and went into the bathroom. "I'm taking a bath," she yelled from the door.

"Okay," Gloria called out.

Julia locked the door and turned on the bath faucets. As the tub filled with water, she removed the DNA testing kit from her backpack and followed the instructions for where to spit into the plastic tube.

30

KYLE AND BRIAN'S mom and dad always made a big production of Sunday dinners. These were the only evenings of the week when everyone was home and not exhausted from school or work. Dinner prep was supposed to be a family activity, but the boys more often than not botched whatever sous-chef task they had been given and were sent to the table with some menial task like filling water glasses or salt shakers.

This Sunday, Brian seemed more engaged with his phone than in creating his signature pinwheel napkins. Kyle watched him out of the corner of his eye and noted every time he smiled in response to something he read.

His parents brought over the plates, loaded with slices of steak that Dad had grilled and an avocado salad Mom made with corn, tomatoes, and onions. After a quick grace, in which Mom thanked the Lord for all His blessings, the family tore into their meal.

Halfway through dinner, Kyle saw Brian smile in response to something in his lap.

"Mom, Brian's texting at the dinner table," he said.

"Hand it over, Brian," Mom said, holding out her open palm.

Brian passed her his phone and muttered "snitch" to Kyle.

Mom placed Brian's phone on the kitchen counter, where the family ate their meals Monday through Friday.

"Look who's talking," Kyle said.

"Boys," Dad warned. "Honey, this salad is delicious."

"Brian got my candidate banned from the cafeteria," Kyle said, ignoring Dad's cue to change the subject. He was still furious with his brother for stooping so low. If Priya hadn't posted that photo of Tony smoking a bowl, the campaign would be dead in the water.

"Your candidate broke the law," Brian said.

"What did he do?" Dad asked.

"He was giving kids chocolate milk," Kyle said.

"Which is against California's ed code," Brian said.

"Doesn't seem like that big a deal," Dad said.

"Thank you, Dad," Kyle said.

Kyle's Mom shot his dad a glare across the table that said,

Stay out of this. After a moment, Dad went back to complimenting Mom's cooking. "This avocado is really incredible."

"I bought it at the farmers' market," Mom said. "It goes well with the pickled onion, doesn't it?"

"You just squealed to Principal Buckley because Tony was pulling ahead of Stacey."

"That's not true," Brian said.

"Fun fact about avocados," Mom said. "Some people call them 'alligator pears.'"

"Interesting," Dad said.

"That's also why you had Priya post that photo of Tony smoking," Kyle said. "How'd that work out for you, huh? You just handed him the stoner vote, which is, like, half the school."

"Tony's a joke. Everyone will see it when he makes his speech tomorrow."

"Not if Stacey bores them to sleep first."

"Boys!" Dad said. "That's enough politics. Can we talk about something more pleasant?"

Kyle couldn't think of anything to say so he stuck a slab of meat into his mouth and chewed it as if it were glass. The fact was, he was worried about the speech. Public speaking was not Tony's strength; he could wax eloquent on the subject of chocolate milk, but not much else. And that was if he was sober, which wasn't a guarantee. Rather than turn Tony into a grand orator, he had to bring the girls down to Tony's level, especially Stacey, who had been training for this event for years. Now that she was finally at the Olympics, she wasn't going to blow it unless something threw her off her game.

"How's the book goin', honey?" Dad asked.

"It's taken a dark turn," Mom said. "I keep trying to keep things light, but this character wants to do despicable things."

"Speaking of despicable things," Brian said. "You should have Kyle tell you about turning the cafeteria into a *Lord of the Flies* base camp. He's encouraging freshmen to blackmail their older siblings into voting for Tony."

"That's a horrible misrepresentation of our 'Get Out the Vote' campaign," Kyle said earnestly. "Brian's just upset because I've mobilized an army of disaffected voters who feel shut out of the political process."

"Bullshit," Brian muttered.

"Brian! Language!" Mom said, throwing down her silverware and glaring in Brian's direction. Brian pushed back his chair and went to drop a dollar into the swear jar. The container was nearly full with crumpled bills at this point, mostly from Brian, who couldn't hide his anger the way Kyle could.

Brain sat back down and shoved a forkful of salad into his mouth. Kyle saw that his brother was at the tipping point.

Just a few more digs would get him banished from the table. The four of them sat in silence, listening to the clatter of silverware.

"Brian's like Cain trying to kill Abel," Kyle said, knowing his mom would appreciate the biblical allusion. "'Woe unto them! For they have gone the way of Cain!' Isn't that what the pastor said in this morning's sermon?"

"Actually, honey, I think the point of the sermon was about the corrupting influence of jealousy," Mom said.

"Exactly," Kyle said. "Brian's jealous because I'm winning."

"No, Kyle's jealous because I have friends."

"Friend," Kyle corrected. "You've got one. And she's a girl."

"How many friends do you have, Kyle?" Brian asked. "When was the last time you hung out with someone? Invited someone over? Isn't that why you're in therapy? Because you can't relate to people?"

"Brian!" Dad shouted. "Go to your room right now."

Brian shoved his chair away from the table and went for his phone on the counter.

"Leave that," Mom said. She was so angry she couldn't even look at him; she just stared at her plate like it was a bowl of slop she had to finish before she'd get to leave the table.

"Don't let him touch it," Brian said to his parents before storming off to his room.

The three of them sat quietly, waiting for stability to return. Mom and Dad both reached over and placed their hands on Kyle's shoulders.

"He didn't mean that, Kyle," Mom said.

"Sure he did," Kyle said, pushing the avocado chunks around his plate. "He's right, too. People don't like me."

"I'm sure they would if you gave them a chance," Dad said. He leaned over, and Kyle could smell the mixture of red wine and steak sauce on his breath. "You have to lighten up a bit, son. Let people get close to you."

"I don't know if I can do that," Kyle said, milking his parents' sympathy. The more he played the victim, the looser Mom and Dad were with their rules and punishments.

"You want to talk to the doctor about starting medication?" Mom said. "It might help ease some of this anxiety."

"I don't want to be sedated," Kyle said. Kyle had seen too many overmedicated kids at his school; he didn't want to be another pharmaceutical zombie.

"It's not sedation," Mom said. "It's medication to correct whatever chemical imbalance is affecting your mood."

"You just want me to be more like Brian," Kyle said. "Your perfect son with good grades and extracurriculars."

"That's not true," Mom said, grabbing Brian's plate and standing up from the table. "I just want you to be happy."

"Happiness is overrated," Kyle said.

"Happy people don't say that," Dad said, reaching over the table again and patting Kyle's hand.

"Can I be excused now?" Kyle asked.

"Finish your salad," Mom said, from the sink. Dad replenished both their wineglasses. Generously.

Kyle stabbed an avocado chunk with a fork and shoved it into his mouth. He tried to step outside his feelings, like his therapist recommended, and observe the situation objectively. He really was pretty lucky. His parents not only loved each other, but they loved him. They had never abused him, verbally or physically. They provided all the basic necessities—a roof over his head, regular meals, a cell phone. Even Brian wasn't so bad, most of the time. Why did he resent them so much? Was it because they made normal look so easy?

Kyle finished his salad and brought his plate over to the sink and handed it to his mom. Before leaving, he leaned in and gave her a kiss on the cheek. "Love you," he said. "You too, Dad."

"We love you, baby," Mom said, wrapping him in a tight hug. "So much."

On his way to his room, Kyle picked his mom's phone off the counter and snuck it into his pocket. He had maybe five minutes before she finished cleaning and started looking for it. Typing quickly, he logged in and opened My

Mobile Watchdog app, the one that allowed her to monitor the activities on both Kyle's and Brian's phones. It was the only stipulation she made when she got them their devices. She wasn't a helicopter mom, exactly. More like a satellite mom—someone who didn't want to see anything up close, but wanted access to information if she needed it. As far as Kyle could tell, she hardly ever checked it. Kyle, on the other hand, checked it often to see what Brian was up to. Brian was pretty good about deleting any data that might incriminate him, but tonight, he didn't have his phone to do that.

Kyle entered the password his mom used on all her devices (Brian's and Kyle's birthdays) and went to the screen showing Brian's text messages. There were a bunch of texts from Stacey asking him to come over tonight for more speech prep. Those weren't as interesting as the text that came from Julia an hour before they sat down for dinner. It was a picture of her dressed in what looked like a pink wedding gown and doing a duck face for the camera. "Your Latina princess," the caption read. Brian had responded with a row of heart emojis. Kyle took a screenshot of the exchange and sent it to his secret Gmail account. Then he logged off and went to the living room to place his mom's phone on the coffee table.

When Kyle was safely back in his room, he logged on to his computer and stared at the text exchange in disbelief. This was better than a smoking gun. It's was a nuclear mushroom cloud. It would incinerate Stacey and ruin Brian's relationship with her forever.

He quickly composed a text to accompany the photo. "This is who Brian's been seeing behind your back." He typed in Stacey's number and was just about to send when he paused. This wasn't the time to show her evidence of Brian's treachery. Kyle needed Stacey to see this when it would have maximum impact. He sent the image to himself instead so that it would be easily accessible when he needed it most.

CAMPAIGN
SPEECHES

31

"LET'S HEAR IT one more time," Brian said. It was Sunday night and he was sitting on Stacey's bed with a bowl of chips in his lap, being careful not to spill any crumbs onto her peach, down comforter. "This time, try to smile more."

Stacey flipped him off and then shook her hands to loosen up. She looked good in her sleeveless wrinkle-resistant top, Brian thought. It showed off her toned body. Brian envied her muscles and wished his flabby arms had her definition.

After doing her anxiety dance, Stacey closed her eyes and took a deep breath. "You are an incredible person, and people love you," she whispered.

"I can hear you," Brian said. "Keep that mantra inside your head."

Stacey took another deep breath and began. Was she wearing makeup? Stacey never painted her face with blush and eye shadow. Her features looked bolder somehow. Like someone went over them with a thicker Sharpie.

"Martin Luther King Jr. once said, 'Life's most persistent and urgent question is, What are you doing for others?' I've asked myself that question many times in the lead-up to this election. What am I doing for others? What makes me worth voting for? I'm happy to say, I've come up with a lot of great answers to that question.

"In my three years in the ASB, I've doubled the number of clubs on campus, giving people as diverse as the Gay-Straight Alliance to the Pottery Club a means to organize, fund-raise, and have their voices heard. I've increased attendance at JV and varsity home games through spirit competitions and other promotional activities. Most importantly, I've made us a cleaner, more eco-friendly campus through my school-wide initiatives to recycle and compost."

Brian made a big production of yawning.

"Fuck you. I want people to know what I've accomplished. None of the other candidates can say shit on this subject."

"Okay, okay," Brian said. At least Stacey had cut this part of her speech down from the ten-minute intro she started with.

Stacey took a deep breath and continued. "People say to me all the time, 'Stacey, you've done so much for our school. Don't you want to slack off? It's what seniors do, right?'"

Brian pantomimed a big smile like a pageant coach.

Stacey forced her mouth to stretch wide and curl up. Close enough, Brian figured.

"What I tell those people is, 'I'm just getting started!'"

Stacey leaned down and picked up the shovel lying at her feet. Brian didn't know how he felt about this prop. It kind made Stacey look like the stern prairie farmer in that *American Gothic* painting.

"There's a lot of waste I still want to get rid of," Stacey continued. "And not just the kind that fills our trash cans every lunch. The biggest waste I see is paper. Every day, we print out countless worksheets, papers, and tests. All this paper gets graded and then what? If you're like me, it's promptly recycled. We can do better. If elected, I promise to advocate for an all-digital campus, where tablets and cell phones are used as learning devices to take notes, do research, and complete assignments. The fact that I can't use this revolutionary device"—Stacey put down the shovel and raised her cell phone—"is a crime. Other schools let students use cell phones in class. It's time ours did too."

"Wait for applause here," Brian coached.

"In closing, I'd like to quote another line by the great Martin Luther King Jr. He said, 'We may have all come on different ships, but we're in the same boat now.' The candidates standing before you are different and unique, just like the students at Lincoln. But we are all Lions, and we need to come together to make this the best school it can possibly be.

I promise as your leader, I will not waste any time to make next year the best yet."

"Excellent!" Brian said, tapping the stopwatch on his phone. "Fifteen seconds under the time limit."

As Brian was staring at his screen, a text from Julia came in. *I'm freaking out,* she wrote. Brian clicked his phone off and stood up to face Stacey. "You feel good?"

"I feel good," Stacey said. "I wish we could debate like in a real election. Three minutes doesn't give me much time to distinguish myself from the others."

"You won't need to," Brian said. "Everyone already knows how awesome you are."

"What if I lose, Brian?" Stacey asked.

"You won't lose."

"But what if I do? I'll spend my senior year as a lobbyist, visiting the ASB as some club president asking for permission to hold a bake sale."

"Would that be so bad?" Brian asked. "It would allow you to really focus on what you're passionate about, rather than plan all those stupid rallies and class competitions."

"I just feel, if I don't win, it will be like a step down. Like I climbed Everest only to turn back before reaching the summit."

"That's your problem. You're judging your success on the distance to go rather than the distance traveled. That final step means nothing compared to journey it took to get there."

"Nobody remembers the explorers who almost got there," Stacey said. "They only remember the ones who reached their destination."

Brian saw fear creep into Stacey's eyes. For the first time in their relationship, he felt sorry for her. She looked worn out and defeated, like a boxer about to throw a title fight.

He stood up and pulled her into a hug. Stacey's embrace was stronger than usual, accompanied by some awkward hand-patting on his back. "How'd I get so lucky to have a friend like you?" she whispered. She must be really nervous about tomorrow. Was she nuzzling his neck with her nose?

"Ouch, you're hurting me," he gasped when her embrace had reached rib-cracking levels.

"Sorry," Stacey said. "It's just . . . I'm grateful is all."

"That's what friends are for," Brian said, and punched Stacey in the shoulder.

As soon as he left Stacey's house, Brian called Julia to see how she was doing.

"I'm freaking out," she said. "What do you think of starting with a quote from Martin Luther King Jr.?"

"I'd begin with a joke," Brian said, not wanting to get dragged into another coaching session. He didn't want to inadvertently reveal some campaign secret like he did last time.

"I'm not very funny," Julia said.

"Sure you are," Brian said. "Remember that joke you told me about Justin Trudeau. It was hilarious."

"Only because you knew who Canada's prime minister was."

"Listen, I can't really help you with this. I'm sorry."

"I understand," Julia said.

"And I can't, like, enthusiastically applaud tomorrow either."

"It's not like I'll see you," Julia said. "The gymnasium holds a thousand people."

"I'll do my best to grab a seat on the bottom bleacher," Brian said. "If you get nervous, look at me. Just don't, you know, blow a kiss my way or anything."

"I've got a line here thanking you for being my inspiration. Should I take that out?"

"See? You are funny."

32

ON MONDAY, BRIAN did his best to stay away from both Stacey and Julia at school, which meant he spent more time on his phone providing both with emotional support. *Everyone loves you*, he wrote Stacey, followed by *You've got this*, to Julia. His texts were both virtuous and sleazy at the same time. He honestly wanted to help both girls, but his supportive comments made him feel a little like a football coach betting against his own team at the Super Bowl.

The question Brian kept asking was: Who did he really want to win? Both girls were smart and hardworking. They would both make excellent ASB presidents. Stacey had earned the position through her years of service, but Julia probably needed the job more. When she told him this was her chance to reinvent herself (and stay in the country), Brian understood and sympathized with her completely. This job would be better for Julia, even though Stacey might be better for the job.

The bell rang, announcing the start of the assembly. Brian followed his second-period class to the cavernous space of the gym, hoping to find a seat in the front. When he saw all the candidates stationed in a neat row at the far end of the basketball court, he hesitated. The students were arranged by rank of office, with those running for ASB secretary on the left to the three candidates for president on the right. If he sat on the bottom bleacher as he had planned, both Stacey and Julia would see him and acknowledge him with a wave or smile. He couldn't risk Stacey thinking he was anything more than Julia's lab partner, so he hid with the rest of his class in the middle row and hoped to stay invisible.

The contrasts between the three candidates were visible even from afar. Stacey wore the navy blue jacket and skirt she used for Speech and Debate tournaments. She looked like an intern at some conservative think tank. Kids would either welcome her maturity or see her as a co-conspirator with the adults trying to curtail their freedom.

To her right, Julia sat looking beautiful, as always. Her long, curly, honeyed hair cascaded down her shoulders and stood in sharp contrast to Stacey's pulled-back blond ponytail. She was wearing the floral dress she bought at

Nordstrom, and Brian felt a pang of guilt as his boner stood up to salute the choice.

Tony Guo had bedhead and wore a T-shirt with what looked like a drunken cow in a space suit.

Continuing his visual scan of the gym, Brian saw his brother sitting on the bottom row of the bleachers opposite, a short distance away from where Tony was sitting. Brian had to hand it to Kyle. He was down there in the trenches with his candidate. If Brian didn't have such a huge conflict of interest, he would be down there with him.

Principal Buckley removed the mic from the podium and walked to center court to quiet the audience of nearly a thousand students. Brian winced when he saw she was wearing a jacket and skirt that nearly matched Stacey's. That optic would not be lost on his peers.

"Your fellow students are about to do something very few of us have the guts to do: speak to about a thousand teenagers in a crowded gymnasium," Buckley said. "Can you imagine how frightening that must be? I mean, seriously. One mistake, and everyone sees it. I for one wouldn't want to be in their shoes."

Brian assumed the principal's speech was meant to inspire sympathy in the crowds of teens, but all it really did was freak out the candidates. One girl running for treasurer started visibly shaking.

"We want to be the best audience for these boys and girls who have worked so hard to get where they are today," she continued. "Anyone shouting inappropriate things, or distracting the candidates in any way, will be promptly removed from the gymnasium and suspended. Am I clear? Silence means yes."

Buckley waited until everyone in the stands stopped talking.

"Terrific!" she said. "Let's get this party started, shall we? The first group of candidates you'll hear from are running for ASB secretary."

Even at three minutes each, the speeches felt long and boring, with each candidate reciting résumé items interspersed with inspirational quotes. By the time James grabbed the mic to make his vice president speech, four people had quoted Martin Luther King Jr.

"As the only black candidate up here, I should be the one turning to Dr. King for inspiration," James began. "But instead I chose a quote from Shakespeare to share with you. 'Woe to that land that's governed by a child.'" James paused here and made a big production of looking at Tony, who was slouched in his chair, staring at his sneakers. "That quote appears in *Richard III*, a play about a ruthless despot who sacrifices his humanity to be king. I thought this quote especially pertinent given the current leadership in the White House."

"Go Trump!" someone yelled from the audience.

"Without a proper adult role model, it's up to us to maintain the dignity of political office by treating one another with kindness and respect. We don't have to agree with one another. In fact, more often than not, it's better that we don't. Conflict can be healthy if it's used to argue and advance the best ideas for our country. As the great James Baldwin famously said, 'Not everything that is faced can be changed, but nothing can be changed until it is faced.' Rather than retreating into their own ideologies, political leaders should emulate how to have these hard conversations so that we can learn from their example. As your vice president, I promise to maintain the dignity of the office and foster a culture of collaboration and compromise. We can be the model for future generations of leaders and make this school a shining city upon a hill for all to see. Thank you."

James walked back amid some light applause and sat next to Stacey, who was rigidly upright in her chair. Did she think he was criticizing her in his speech? She hadn't behaved the most nobly of late, accusing Julia of vandalizing her own poster and leaking the party photo of Tony to the school. If she was concerned, she didn't show it. She leaned over and whispered something in James's ear, which caused him to smile.

Tony was the first presidential candidate called to the

podium to address the crowd. He hopped up from his chair, pulled up his sagging jeans with his right hand, and swaggered to the open mic.

"Yo, Lincoln, wassup?" he said.

Holy shit, Brian thought. He's going to freestyle this.

"Man, these speeches are boring, right?"

The crowd erupted into thunderous applause.

"I know, man. I feel you. So I'll keep this short. I don't got no experience to brag about. Most of y'all know me. I'm that tall Asian guy defying the stereotype. I'm only up here because the administration took away my chocolate milk."

An audible wave of boos erupted from the audience.

"I know, man? That shit ain't right. Sorry, Mrs. Buckley. My bad."

The gym howled with laughter. Tony was killing it. Brian glanced over at Stacey and Julia, who looked like wedding guests listening to the best man confess his love for the bride during his toast.

"I mean, first they come for the chocolate milk. Then they come for the Pop-Tarts. Who knows what's next? Those crispy tater tots that show up every other Friday? I love those things. You can bet if something's delicious, it's gone. If you want someone to stand up against these nutritionists, then I'm your man. I'll fight until all the best munchies are returned to our cafeteria. Peace! I'm out."

Tony dropped the mic onto the floor, where it hit with a boom. The space exploded with cheers and applause and the stomping of feet. It felt like a riot. Mrs. Buckley must have thought so too because she hustled over to the mic on the floor, picked it up, and stomped back to center court.

"Quiet!" she said. "Teachers, please control your students."

She waited until the room settled down. Then she spoke in calm, even tones into the mic. "We all appreciate Mr. Guo's passion, but the state sets strict nutritional guidelines for what schools can and cannot serve in their cafeterias. Those decisions are largely out of our control."

A lone student booed this response. Buckley somehow managed to identify the heckler in the sea of students packed in the bleachers. "Sammy, remove Mr. Turpin from the gymnasium and take him to my office," she said. A guy with a mop of black hair descended from the top tier of the bleachers and was escorted out of the building. The place got real quiet after that.

"Now, we have two more candidates we need to hear from," Buckley went on. "Please give them your utmost attention."

Brian's heart swelled. Whoever was called on next could never match the enthusiasm that came from Tony's speech. Here's where you learn who you really love, he heard some inner voice say. Who do you choose to go next? Julia or Stacey? Brian closed his eyes, trying to drown out the murmur of voices on all sides and came up with a name: Stacey. He wanted Stacey to go next.

"Julia Romero," Buckley said, and walked back to replace the mic on the podium.

Julia stood up slowly, holding her note cards in both hands. Why hadn't he sat in a more visible place? Brian should be there for her, not hiding in the crowds like a coward to protect his secret. The gymnasium was so quiet, everyone could hear the wobbly click of Julia's heels as she walked toward the podium. She was terrified, and Brian's heart went out to her.

"Viva Julia!" Brian shouted in the silence.

Buckley bolted from her seat and scanned the area where Brian was sitting. Before she could lock her laser eyes on him, another person on the other side of the gym repeated his cheer, then another, and another. Soon, the whole audience was chanting, "Viva Julia!" until Buckley walked back to center stage and threatened the crowd.

"One more interruption like this, and we'll stay in here during brunch. You want that?"

The students quieted immediately. Buckley stomped back to her seat, still scanning Brian's section of bleacher seats for the heckler. If she suspected Brian, she didn't show it. She knew he worked closely with Stacey and probably crossed him off her list of suspects.

Stacey, on the other hand, was staring right at him.

Brian leaned left and hid behind a volleyball player seated in front of him. Peeking around the girl's broad shoulders, he watched Julia smile from behind the podium.

"Thank you," Julia said. "It's not easy following a speech like Tony's." Julia nodded in Tony's direction. Tony took this opportunity to stand up and take another bow. Brian watched as Julia looked at the note cards in her hands, and he worried she had mixed up the order. She flipped through her prepared speech and then tossed the cards into the air. "He's right. Enough of these boring speeches. I want to speak to you from the heart."

"You go, girl!" someone shouted from the audience. Brian looked around and couldn't locate the fan. Everyone near him was leaning forward, anticipating what Julia would say next.

"You got this, Julia," Brian whispered.

"As much as I love chocolate milk, I don't think its absence is the biggest problem at our school," she said. "It's homework. There's too much, and we should get rid of it."

There was a moment of absolute silence as people contemplated the bomb that Julia had just dropped, and then the room erupted into deafening applause. The clapping went on for at least a minute, then it became feet stamping, and then it became a chorus of chanting, "Ju-li-a, Ju-li-a" over and over.

Buckley bolted upright from her seat, inspiring Julia to encourage the students to quiet down. "Please," she said. "I don't want to lose brunch any more than you do."

The room fell silent. Julia turned to Buckley, who nodded in approval at her like Mussolini in a wig.

"I take a few APs, but most of my classes are regular college prep," Julia continued. "I have on average four hours a night of homework. And I'm lucky. I don't play sports, or have a job, or have to look after siblings. My schedule is pretty free after school, and even then, I don't finish work until close to midnight every night. I don't think this is because I'm dumb. I think this is because our system is broken. The kids who want to succeed have to kill themselves to complete all their assignments. Either that, or they have to cheat, which they do. A lot. The kids who have other responsibilities besides school get farther behind because they can't keep up, which just reinforces the achievement gap between the Haves and the Have-Nots. I think we can change this. I've seen other schools do it. It starts with a commission made up of students, teachers, counselors, administrators, and parents working together to decide a reasonable amount of homework. The committee sets clear expectations, like no more than twenty minutes a night per class, and then holds everyone responsible for meeting those expectations. None of this will happen unless we demand it. As your student body president, I will demand it."

The LSU students rose to their feet and gave Julia a standing ovation, which inspired everyone else to do the same. Brian looked over at Stacey, who appeared bent and a little breathless. Her mouth dropped open like a slowly lowered drawbridge to a well-fortified castle.

Julia walked back to her chair and sat down with a giant smile on her face. Tony leaned across Stacey and fist-bumped Julia in a show of solidarity.

Poor Stacey, Brian thought. She was staring at the cell phone in her lap, probably wondering how her platform could compete against more junk food and less homework. Then she held her phone closer to her face. She was reading something on the screen. Something that upset her if her body language was any judge. She covered her mouth with her free hand and shook her head. Julia must have picked up on her distress as well because she put a tentative hand on Stacey's shoulder, which Stacey shook off violently. She stood up and stomped over to the podium, dragging her shovel behind her.

While she readied herself behind the mic, doing her deep breathing and repeating her mantra, Brian looked over at his brother, who was smiling and waving his cell phone in Brian's direction. He was trying to communicate something to him, but Brian wasn't sure what it was. Ignoring his taunts, he focused back on Stacey, who was about to open her speech.

"Martin Luther King Jr. once said . . ." Her voice was shaking, and she paused to get control of it.

"Sorry," she said, taking a deep breath. She stuck out her arms and shook them loose at her side. "Martin Luther King Jr. once said . . ."

The audience quieted out of respect, but the silence only made things worse. When someone coughed from the back row, it was a not-so-silent commentary on Stacey's performance.

"Martin Luther King Jr. once said . . . ," she began again. "Oh fuck it."

Stacey dropped her shovel, turned around, and walked out the back exit of the gymnasium.

"POLITICAL FORUM ENDS IN CHAOS"

by Lance Haber

"Fuck it."

It was probably Stacey Wynn's most effective campaign speech.

No statement more clearly revealed her character to the voters, at least. In two words she showed us everything we need to know about her: when faced with mounting criminal investigations and a losing campaign, she turns into a petulant, potty-mouthed princess.

It's hard to tell what finally broke the troubled Wynn campaign. Was it the ongoing Postergate and Cafeteriagate investigations conducted by yours truly? Probably. It could also be the fact that people are seeing through her treasonous attempt to take control of our electronic devices. Or maybe it's that no one wants to live in a world where you're forced to rake through fecal-infested compost bins as part of your PE class.

In contrast to Stacey's train wreck of a speech, came Julia Romero's eloquent and personal account of the effect homework has had on her life and the lives of others. Judging from the thunderous applause, this issue struck a chord with the audience. (It did with me—my grades have suffered horribly because of my commitment to you, dear readers. If it weren't for homework, I would be passing all my classes right now.)

Perhaps this is the real reason the administration has been favoring Wynn in this election. Romero and Guo, both nonwhite candidates, want to disrupt the existing system with their calls for greater freedom from tyranny.

Wynn, on the other hand, wants to give the administration more control over our lives, first by telling us where to put our trash, and second by telling us how to use our phones. It was an obvious attempt to curry favor with dictators that blew up spectacularly in her face.

DAMAGE CONTROL

33

STACEY PEELED OUT of the school parking lot and drove straight home. Her phone kept buzzing with incoming texts, from Brian presumably, but she didn't dare pick up that device again, not after what she had seen on it: three hearts from Brian in response to Julia's selfie. Three hearts! It was like the winning combination on some doomsday slot machine.

She came to a stoplight and screamed her head off. How could Brian have betrayed her so cruelly? He was her best friend. There wasn't a day she didn't see him, talk to him, rely on him to guide her with his wise counsel. And this whole time he had been a secret agent! It was like finding out your boring parents were KGB assassins assigned to kill Waffles, your pet hamster.

At least she finally understood why she was losing this election so badly. Brian had sabotaged her, probably from the beginning. Oh my God! Was he the one who defaced Julia's poster? It was all starting to make sense now! Why hadn't she seen it? She'd been so blind because she was such a kind and trusting person.

She wanted the house to herself to cry and yell and break things, but her father's car was still parked in the driveway. The digital clock on her dashboard said it was 10:30. Why wasn't Dad at the university?

She raced inside, letting her concern for her father replace the horror of what she'd seen on her phone, what she'd just done in front of the entire student body.

"Dad!" she hollered. "You home?"

"In here, dear," he said from the kitchen.

Stacey walked in and found her dad nursing a cup of coffee at the table. He smiled at her, not at all embarrassed by the fact that he was still in his pajamas.

"What are you doing home?" he asked.

Oh that's right. She's the one who shouldn't be here, not him. His class wasn't until after lunch. She had just been used to him leaving early to fly the drone.

"I forgot something," she said, hoping Dad wouldn't press her for specifics. "Why are you still in your pajamas?"

"I went to the lab last night after you'd gone to sleep and must have stayed later than I should have. I'm trying to find a way to increase the hovering time for your drone. This got me thinking about which thermodynamic cycle would be best for using the relevant source of energy."

"You've lost me, Dad," Stacey said.

"Never mind. It's complicated for me too, so I met with a colleague who specializes in robotics, and we got a little carried away."

Stacey's mind envisioned an army of drones and robots descending on her school. Their heat-seeking missiles all aimed at Brian and Julia.

"Stacey?" her dad said.

Stacey looked up at her dad's smiling and hopeful face. Had some *Freaky Friday* curse caused them to switch places, giving him all her strength and her all his weakness? She wanted to fall into his arms and let him comfort her like he used to when she fell and skinned her knee at the playground. But she couldn't be weak now. She had to be like a shark and keep moving.

"I'm just gonna grab that thing and get going," Stacey said.

She bolted upstairs, expended some of her anger furiously opening and closing her bureau drawers, and then ran back down again. "Bye, Dad!" she yelled, slamming the door behind her.

She needed to see her mom. She'd know how to help her channel this rage more effectively.

Stacey pulled out in a screech of tires and skidded

around the corner. At the first stop sign, she punched her horn, frightening a new mother crossing the street. "C'mon, woman!" Stacey shouted. "Some of us are in a hurry here."

She weaved through the suburban streets, tailgating retirees and coming dangerously close to oblivious cyclists. When she reached the more populated downtown area, she slowed her pace so as not to attract the attention of the police officers on the lookout for truant students. For all she knew the school had issued an APB for her arrest for besmirching the reputation of our greatest civil-rights leader.

She pulled up in front of the Tae Kwon Do studio and tried to get control of herself. After some deep breathing, she felt a little calmer. Then her phone buzzed. Another text from Brian. *Please write back and tell me you're okay.* Stacey tried to crush the phone in her hand, but these things were made of very resistant metal and plastic. Instead, she just threw the device on the floor, screamed "Fuck you, *Brian*," and bolted from the car.

The door to the studio was locked, so Stacey tapped on it gently, hoping her mother was in the back office. Her knocks began as gentle whimpers and then grew into fist-pounding fury. Her mom rushed to the front before Stacey's greeting shattered the glass.

"What is wrong with you?" she asked, ushering her inside the darkened space. Stacey stormed in and started pacing around on the hardwood floor. The mirrored wall reflected a crazed person Stacey didn't recognize. Who was this girl with the wild hair and red, blotchy face? Stacey kicked off her heels and peeled out of her jacket, as if she were an angry stripper.

Her mom led her back to her office and left her in the Aeron chair. She came back holding a cup of tea. "Drink this," she encouraged.

Stacey breathed in the herbal steam and imagined her lizard brain baking on a rock in the desert. When she had calmed down somewhat, she told her mom everything.

"So, the enemy was never Julia," her mom said. "It was Brian."

Stacey nodded.

"What are you going to do now?" she asked.

"There's nothing I can do," Stacey said. "I blew it on an epic scale today. I'm done."

"That's loser talk. Let's think about this." Her mom closed her eyes and started rubbing her temples with her manicured fingers. "Who do you think sent you that photo of Julia?"

Stacey paused. She had been so consumed by the betrayal, she hadn't stopped to consider who the leaker was. The number was in her area code, but it wasn't one she recognized.

"I don't know," Stacey said.

"Whoever it was, they executed the attack brilliantly. They found something to hurt you and then shared at the perfect moment."

"It sounds like you admire them."

"I do. That doesn't mean I'm not sorry this happened. But I think you can learn from this to plan your next move."

"My next move? Voting is tomorrow."

"That gives us twenty-four hours. The battle isn't over yet. Now, who stands to gain the most by having you out of the race?"

"Both Julia and Tony do."

"The text was designed to do two things: to throw you off your game before your big speech and to drive a wedge between you and your closest ally. Do you think Julia is ruthless enough to seduce your best friend, gather evidence of their affair, and rub your face in it in front of the whole school?"

Stacey thought about it. Put in such stark terms, the plan did seem diabolical.

"Yes," Stacey said. "Julia would totally do that."

For the first time, she felt her frozen heart melt a little for her friend. Brian was as much a victim here as Stacey. Could she really blame him for falling for Julia's treachery? He had never had a girlfriend before. Of course he's going to fall for the exotic foreigner with long legs and a French accent. It was just like one of those film noir movies her dad loved so much, where a weak man is brainwashed by a femme fatale to drown her husband in a bathtub.

"Well, then. You've got to find a way to ruin her," Stacey's mom said. "Do it today. I'll excuse you from all your classes."

Her mom was right. Julia was evil and had to be brought to justice. But how? Stacey sat in her car and tried to figure out a plan. Know your enemy, her mom had counseled. What did she really know about Julia? Nothing, except what Priya had uncovered. There was a feminist mom in Canada and no evidence of a dad. Something was off there, but Stacey didn't know what it was. She had less than twenty-four hours to figure it out.

She picked her phone off the floor and texted Priya. Do you have a name of Julia's aunt? she asked. Priya had mentioned that Julia was Facebook friends with her aunt and hoped it wouldn't take Priya long to—

Gloria O'Brien, Priya texted back.

O'Brien? Seriously? It doesn't get more Hispanic than that. Thanks, Stacey wrote.

What happened today? Priya said. Everyone's talking about how you lost it.

I lost it, but I'm getting it back, Stacey said.

Don't stress. Half my followers think your "oh fuck it" speech was the best one.

Stacey laughed bitterly. All that work, all that preparation, and all she had to do was swear into the microphone to win people's approval. It was almost enough to make her quit politics.

She punched in Gloria O'Brien's name and zip code and found her listed address. A few seconds later, Stacey was following the Google Maps directions to her home.

Julia lived in a single-story ranch-style home with a wide, empty driveway next to a tiny patch of lawn. The curtains were open in the front window, but Stacey couldn't see anyone inside. Stacey grabbed her phone and got out of her car, hoping a plan would come to her as she walked up the cement walkway to the front door.

She rang the doorbell and waited. No one was home.

She looked up and down the street, but the neighborhood was empty. There were no signs about a security system on the front lawn, so Stacey walked over to the side of the house and undid the latch on the wooden gate and slipped inside. She listened for the sound of a dog in the backyard. When she was convinced she was alone, she made her way back along the side pathway, testing the windows to see if any of them opened. They were all secure, as was the glass door on the back patio. Shit, Stacey thought. Now she'd have to look for a spare key.

She started with all the usual places. Under welcome mats, in flowerpots, but she didn't find anything. Then she saw the garden gnome, standing proudly amid a raised flower bed full of leafy greens. It was almost like the porcelain midget spoke to her, saying, *Hey, idiot! Over here!* Sure enough, the key was right under his red ceramic boots. Stacey ran back to the glass door and opened it with ease.

Stacey was about to step in when she heard her dad's voice counseling her against this course of action. Unlike Mom, her father always spoke of the opportunity cost of winning. *What are you sacrificing to succeed in this thing?* he'd ask. *If you spend all your time training for the Tae Kwon Do tournament, will you be able to do your best at the piano recital?* He wanted Stacey to think about her priorities. Standing at the threshold of Julia's home, Stacey heard him ask, *What are you sacrificing to win this election? Is it worth your friendship with Brian? Is it worth betraying your own ethical standards of decent behavior?*

"Shut up, Dad," Stacey muttered, and stepped inside. "You were decent, and look where that got you."

Before doing anything, Stacey scanned the area for any video surveillance equipment. Not seeing any glowing red dots, she carefully made her way into Julia's family room. The house still smelled of buttery pancakes from the morning meal, and Stacey's stomach growled in response.

Stacey ignored her hunger and moved down the hallway toward where she thought the bedrooms would be. As she passed the framed photos of twins that lined the walls, Stacey felt unnerved by the girls' blank stares. It almost felt like they were tracking her as she peered in doorways, trying to locate Julia's bedroom. She found it at the end of the hallway and went inside.

The room was fairly nondescript, with Ikea furniture, a floral-print bedspread, and framed prints of watercolor landscapes on the walls. It felt like the kind of room you might create if you knew nothing about the occupant. Like a hotel room. Julia hadn't done anything to personalize the space, either, except toss a few discarded dresses on the floor, which made Stacey wonder if she planned on living in it for long.

The desk's surface was empty, which meant Julia had a laptop she must take to school. Stacey pulled open all the drawers in the desk and didn't find anything helpful. Nothing in the wastebaskets either. She pulled open the drawers of the bureau and carefully picked through Julia's clothes, trying to remain focused on the mission at hand, which was hard given her desire to set the garments on fire.

Checking her watch, she saw it was almost noon and worried that someone might be coming home for lunch. There was nothing in Julia's room that could help Stacey anyway, so she decided to leave. Exiting the room, she noticed something weird about the doorknob. It didn't lock. The latch bolt that kept the door closed was there, but the deadbolt was missing, so the door couldn't be secured. Stacey checked the other doors on her way back to the living room, and all of them had functional push-button locks on the inside. Only Julia's door didn't. Not a lot of trust here, Stacey concluded. Julia's aunt must know something to take such precautionary measures.

She decided to investigate the aunt and uncle's room. Maybe there was something to explain why they didn't want to give Julia any privacy. The room was neatly made up, with not a piece of clothing on the carpeted floor. The surfaces of the bedside tables were nearly reflective in their high polish. Stacey jumped when she saw someone standing on the other side of the room, but then realized she was just looking at her reflection in the mirrored closet doors. She walked over and slid the doors open. If she knew anything about parents, it was that this was where they hid the things they didn't want their children to see.

She rummaged through the clothes on the racks, and shoeboxes on the floor. Then she looked up and found a set of photo albums lining the top shelf. These were all labeled by location and date and set in chronological order. Stacey was beginning to realize Julia's aunt was a bit of a neat freak.

Stacey pulled down the binder marked *Boucherville, 1980–2000*. Flipping through the cellophane-sealed pages, she saw images of two girls experiencing the decades in very different ways. The one on the pages marked with "Gloria" stickers fully embraced the aerobics look with headbands, loose sweatshirts with torn collars, and tights, while the other, identified as "Susan," adopted an edgier look with a Mohawk, piercings, and heavy eyeliner. As she flipped through the album, Stacey noticed the sisters were rarely in the same photos. Julia's aunt had dance recitals, cheerleading competitions, and prom pictures. Julia's mom had a band called Rabid Pussy that performed in a dodgy basement nightclub. By the end of the album, photos of her were replaced with news clippings of her run-ins with the law. There was a story about her getting arrested at an animal testing facility. Another about her throwing a pie in the face of a governor. Another detailing a protest at a petrochemical plant in which she chained herself to a fence. On the last page, there was a newspaper clipping about a woman who was suing a fertility clinic. "Sperm Bank Accused of Lying About Donors" the headline read. Below the byline was a picture of the former lead singer of Rabid Pussy, now grown up with long, stringy, blond hair and thin, brittle features. "Susan Romero has filed suit against a Quebec fertility clinic, claiming the facility lied in the marketing of its sperm."

"Holy shit," Stacey said, the reels in her mental slot machine spun and rested on Jackpot, Jackpot, Jackpot.

She read the story. After she was done, she took a picture of the article with her phone. It was going to look perfect next to the text Julia had sent Brian: *Your Latina princess.*

34

IT WAS OFFICIAL, Brian realized. Stacey was ignoring him. That could only mean one thing: she knew about him and Julia. But how? They had been so careful. They only met in secret, and Brian quickly deleted any texts he received from Julia as soon as he read them. Was it his outburst at the assembly? If she saw him cheer for Julia, it might be enough to throw her off her game, but it wouldn't wreck her so completely. It had to be something else. Something she saw on her phone made her misquote Dr. Martin Luther King Jr. Maybe Dr. King did say "Oh fuck it," at some point in his life, but it's not a line people typically associate with a Nobel Peace Prize winner.

After fifth period, Brian raced to the ASB classroom. He poked his head in the door and scanned the crowds for Stacey, but all he saw were student leaders congratulating themselves on their performance at today's assembly. In the center of the backslapping was James, gracefully accepting compliments on his speech. When he saw Brian standing in the doorway, he extricated himself from the crowd and walked over.

"Stacey's not here," he said. "No one's seen her all day."

Brian pulled James out into the hallway, where they could talk without the prying eyes of the school's Little and Big Brothers.

"It's all my fault," Brian whispered. "She must have found out about Julia."

James nodded. "I was sitting next to her at the assembly. Just before she was called up, she got a text that really upset her."

"What was it?"

"A photo of Julia in a pink dress. I couldn't read the text, but it looked like a screenshot of a conversation with a lot of heart emojis."

"Oh shit," Brian said, remembering the photo Julia sent him in her quinceañera dress.

"Yeah," James said. He put a hand on Brian's shoulder. "You okay?"

"This is all my fault."

"No, it's not. You didn't send that photo. I'm guessing your brother did."

Brian nodded.

The two stood there in silence, letting all the late students rush by on their way to class. James showed no urge to leave Brian's side, but instead closed the classroom door and led him to the bench across the hallway. The two sat on the metal frame and watched the seagulls circle overhead, still scavenging food left on the ground from lunch.

"I feel bad for Stacey," James said after a minute. "That's a dirty trick to play on anyone. But maybe it's for the best."

Brian shook his head. "Stacey wants to be president more than anything."

"I know. But that doesn't mean she *should* be."

"She'd be great and you know it."

"I agree. Stacey's a fighter. She's got conviction and tenacity. When she believes in something, nobody's gonna stop that girl from getting what she wants. It's probably why you two are such good friends."

"What do you mean?"

"She believed in you back when you were just a chubby, insecure boy. Now look at you. You're a confident, some might say reasonably attractive young man. Her friendship transformed you."

"Thanks," Brian said. He'd never thought of himself as one of Stacey's projects before, but what James said was true. Their friendship had been one long campaign to help Brian take control of his life instead of feeling completely powerless to change it.

"I'm just not so sure she'd make the best president," James said.

"Why not?"

"Don't get me wrong. She'd probably do a great job on the issues she cares about. She's just not interested in the issues other people care about."

"But you can't ask one candidate to care about every issue. That's impossible."

"I know, but look at our school. We're only forty percent white. You know what ASB is? Eighty percent white. There's an imbalance there that needs to be corrected."

"No one's stopping students of color from running for office," Brian said.

James rolled his eyes. "C'mon, Brian. You and I both know there are tons of things stopping people of color from running for office. Stacey's just one of those things. As long as she's in charge, people will always associate student government with whiteness. Julia could change that. I think you know that too."

"It just seems unfair that Stacey's color should be held against her. She has the most experience."

"She got that experience *because* of her color."

"She got that experience because she cares about the school."

"Then she should step aside and let the candidate who better represents the school be president."

"Julia might look like more of the students, but Stacey's grown up with most of them. She knows them better."

James sighed. "Listen, I get it. She's your friend and it's noble that you're defending her. And you're right. She'd be a great president. But her presidency wouldn't change anything for people of color at this school. Julia's would."

"You just see Julia as a symbol."

"Maybe. You obviously know her better. What do you think?"

Brian paused. "She'd be great," he said. "Really great."

A blond-haired, freckle-faced girl poked her head out the door and told James they needed him inside.

"You're late for class," James said, standing up and moving toward the door. "If you find Stacey, tell her I'm sorry about what happened. I hope you two work things out."

"Thanks," Brian said, and walked to his biology class.

Cohen was mid-lecture when he arrived. Brian wrote his name on the miniature whiteboard tacked to the door for tardies and squeezed through the narrow aisle to his empty desk.

Julia picked up on his distress as soon as he slumped in his chair.

"You okay?" she asked.

"I'm worried about Stacey," Brian whispered. "She hasn't responded to any of my texts."

"She's probably just upset," Julia said. "Have you seen this?"

Julia held up her phone for Brian to see. On the screen was a meme with Dr. Martin Luther King Jr. and the quote "Oh fuck it" written in the bold Impact font at the top.

"Priya's posting this everywhere as part of Stacey's rebranding," Julia said. "People love it. I think it's made her more relatable, you know?"

"Stacey knows about us," Brian said.

"Because of what you yelled at the assembly?" Julia said. "Thank you, by the way." Julia put a tentative hand on Brian's thigh. Brian knew the students seated behind them might see, but he didn't care. Julia's touch mattered more than his peers' curiosity right now.

"You saved me," Julia said.

"I had to do something," Brian said.

"Maybe it's good if she knows," Julia said. "I'm tired of keeping our relationship secret."

"She'll never forgive me."

"She will if she's a real friend. You just have to talk to her."

"Easier said than done."

After class, Brian texted Stacey and told her that he was coming over. When he showed up at her house, Mr. Wynn's car was the only one parked in the driveway. He pulled over and texted her again. I'm at your house and not leaving until we talk. Digging into his backpack, he removed his worn copy of *The Great Gatsby* and started reading.

At around four o'clock, Stacey's dad emerged from the front door, dressed in his usual short-sleeved button-down and khaki pants. Draped over his shoulder was the leather messenger bag Stacey got him for his birthday last year, its heavy contents tilting his body slightly to the right.

When he saw Brian parked in front of his home, he waved and walked over.

"You waiting for Stacey?" he asked. Mr. Wynn was looking better than the last time Brian saw him, although he wasn't sure how he felt about the mustache. Mr. Wynn probably had to do something to mark his transition back into single life, but the facial hair made him look like a contestant in *The Voice: Barbershop Quartet Edition*.

"Do you know if she'll be home soon?" Brian asked.

"She texted me thirty minutes ago to say she's staying at her mother's tonight."

"That's weird," Brian said.

"I thought so too." Mr. Wynn straightened his glasses and looked up at the sky. Brian wondered if the mention of his ex-wife made him anticipate some cataclysmic weather condition.

"I think she's mad at me," Brian said.

"How could she be mad at you?" Mr. Wynn said. "There's a plate of cookies with your name on it in the kitchen."

"When did she bake those?"

"Last night, I assume. I worked late at the lab and saw them when I got back. Just to be sure I didn't think they were for me, she wrote 'For Brian' on an index card and taped it to the cellophane wrapping."

"Shit," Brian said. "Sorry, it's just . . . I think I did something really bad."

"You don't strike me as the kind of person who can't be forgiven."

"I've been secretly dating her opponent in the presidential race."

"Oh," he said. This was clearly not the confession Mr. Wynn was expecting. His bushy eyebrows arched like electrocuted caterpillars. "That *is* pretty bad."

"I know," Brian said. "But I never helped Julia with anything. Well, not intentionally anyway. Until today, but that was only out of desperation. It's all so confusing."

"Listen, Brian," Mr. Wynn said, placing a hand on Brian's side-view mirror. "You and Stacey have been friends for a long time. You were here for her every day after her mom moved out, taking care of her when I was, well, let's just say I was a bit of a mess."

That's putting it mildly, Brian thought. This man cried through the first two seasons of *Modern Family* after the breakup.

"I'm sure your friendship is more important than this election," he said. "You just might have to give her time to realize that."

"Thanks, Mr. Wynn," Brian said.

Mr. Wynn reached inside the open car window and patted Brian awkwardly on the shoulder, and then got into his car and drove away.

Brian put his book down and picked up his phone. He wanted to send Stacey one last text before driving home. I know you're mad at me right now, he wrote. I want you to know one thing, and then I'll stop bothering you. Tomorrow, I'll be voting for you.

35

BIKING HOME FROM school, Julia soaked in the quiet. She pedaled through the empty suburban streets, listening to the spring breeze shake the trees awake from their afternoon nap. Off in the distance, there was some light hammering, some final touch on a home-improvement project.

Her speech had gone better than planned, mostly because Brian had risked everything to call out her name. Because he believed in her, she had the courage to ditch her prepared remarks and speak from the heart and it made all the difference.

She was a couple blocks from her home when she sensed a car trailing her from behind. Turning her head, she saw Lance holding his camera out the driver's side window, filming her.

"Here's Julia Romero, doing what she can to save the environment," he said loud enough for her to hear. "Does Stacey

Wynn, so-called champion of the environment, bike to school? Of course not. Wynn talks the talk, but drives the walk."

Julia turned her head so Lance wouldn't see her roll her eyes. She debated taking an alternate route home, but then realized she wasn't comfortable with Lance knowing where she lived, so she pulled over instead. "Hi, Lance," she said.

Lance parked his Range Rover behind her and got out. He was wearing a tank top, a ridiculous shirt for any guy to wear, especially a guy with that much back acne. "Great speech today, Julia," he said. "You really nailed it."

"Thanks," she said.

"I was thinking we could celebrate your victory tomorrow at Sushi Boat on Main. You been there?"

Julia shook her head. "I don't think I'm going to win," she said. "Tony killed it today."

"Sure you are. And if you don't, we can strategize our next steps. I've got a post ready to go about voter fraud. The school uses a Google form to tally the votes. Those things are so easily hacked it's ridiculous."

"You should publish that now," Julia said. "*Before* the voting."

"Nah," Lance said, smiling. "If you win, I don't want anyone questioning your victory. I've invested a lot of time in your campaign."

Lance stepped closer to Julia. His head tilted, his eyelids

drooped, and his lips puckered. Either he was coming in for a kiss or he was having a mini-stroke.

"I've got a boyfriend," she said, pulling away.

Lance stopped his approach. His eyes bulged as if Julia had slapped him. "No, you don't."

"What do you mean?" Julia said. She slowly rotated the right pedal on her bike upward, in case she needed to press down hard and accelerate away from this creep.

"I've been following you pretty closely these last few weeks," Lance said. "If you had a boyfriend, I'd know about it."

Julia didn't want to know what Lance meant by "following you pretty closely." She only knew this street was emptier than she'd like it to be. With a swiftness that surprised her, she pressed down on her right pedal and left Lance standing there with arms at his sides and a confused expression.

"I built you up!" he screamed from behind her. "I can bring you down too."

Julia raced home, constantly looking behind her to make sure Lance wasn't following. When she reached her side gate, she fumbled with the latch and practically dived behind the protective barrier. Once she was safely hidden, she leaned against the fence, too winded to go any farther. After catching her breath, she peered over the top and waited for Lance's Range Rover to do a slow drive by. But he never showed. Julia breathed a sigh of relief, walked her bike to the backyard, and went inside.

Just as she was unlocking the back door, her phone started buzzing. It was her mom. *Not now,* Julia groaned. She wasn't ready to end the silent treatment she had begun after learning her mom had Julia's DNA results. But she also knew Mom wouldn't stop calling until Julia told her about the speech.

"Hi, Mom," she said.

"How did the speech go?"

"Fine," Julia said. "It was fine."

"What's wrong?" her mom said, picking up on her brusqueness. Julia was probably channeling some of the rage she felt from Lance's harassment to her mother.

"Do you have my DNA test results?" Julia asked, turning around and walking into the backyard instead of the house. She wanted to be outside for this conversation. She didn't know why, but she thought it would be helpful to look at the clear blue sky.

"Yes," her mom said. Her mother didn't lie. She often didn't elaborate either.

"Why didn't you tell me?" Julia said, kicking a dirt clod against the back fence.

"I told you, I don't want you tethered to the past."

"That's not your decision to make," Julia said.

"Sure it is. I'm your mother."

"My *white* mother," Julia said.

"What's that supposed to mean?" her mom said.

"It means you don't understand what it's like to be me. You don't experience the world the same way I do because people see me differently than they see you."

"Trust me, Julia, I know what it's like to be different. I've spent my whole life being different."

"By choice!" Julia screamed. She put a hand on top of the wooden slats of the fence and shook the structure back and forth.

"Yes, by choice. I want you to have those same choices. I don't want you thinking you have to behave a certain way because you're Cuban, or Indian, or Iroquois."

"Let's talk about one of your choices, Mom. When you went to the fertility clinic, what race did you choose?"

"Excuse me?"

"What race did you choose? I want to know. You wanted a baby, what color baby did you want?"

"Julia, that's . . ."

"Tell me, Mom," Julia said. "I want to know. Did you want a white baby?"

"I wanted a *healthy* baby." Her mom stumbled. "There were other factors for me that were more important than race."

"But what color did you choose. Did you choose a white donor or not?"

Her mom paused. "Yes, I chose a white donor."

"That's what I thought," Julia said, and hung up. She threw the phone down on the ground and rushed inside so that the neighbors wouldn't hear her screaming.

36

"**YOU SEEM IN** an especially good mood today," Shirley said, taking a seat across from Kyle. She was probably responding to the hug he had given her in the waiting room. After the day he'd had at school, Kyle felt like hugging everyone. With one text, he had destroyed Stacey's chances of winning the election. Now all he had to worry about was Julia's little quinceañera protest tomorrow, but he had a plan to bring that down too.

"I *am* in a good mood," Kyle said, reclining on the couch, putting his hands behind his head. Today was probably the first day he had looked forward to going to therapy. Nowhere else could he talk freely about what had happened at the school assembly, and he needed to brag about it to someone. It helped that his therapist would keep his secrets. Even though Shirley wasn't a real doctor, Kyle was sure she took some oath protecting client-patient privilege.

"Tell me more," Shirley said, removing her glasses and folding her hands in her lap.

"Well, the candidates gave their speeches to the student body this morning," Kyle said. "It's their one time to address the voters directly."

"Your candidate must have done well," Shirley said.

"My candidate was awesome. I was a little worried he'd blow it, but he nailed it. He was himself, and people loved him."

"Did you coach him at all? I know how busy you've been working for his campaign."

"I helped in other ways," Kyle said, smiling.

"How so?"

"I made sure his closest rival went down in flames."

"And how did you do that?"

"I shared some information with her about her campaign that she needed to know."

"That doesn't sound too bad." Shirley looked down at her notes resting in her lap.

"I shared it with her, just before she gave her speech," Kyle said, choking back a laugh. "She got so freaked out, she misquoted Dr. Martin Luther King Jr. and told everyone to go fuck themselves. It was awesome."

"Sounds like she was pretty upset."

"Oh, she was, trust me."

"How do you feel about that?"

"About what?"

"About being the cause of her distress?"

"I don't feel anything," Kyle said. "It's politics. That's the game. If you can't stand the heat, get out of the kitchen, right?"

"Hmm." Shirley consulted her notes. "This is your brother's friend, right? The one you called an 'eco-lutionary.'"

"That's her."

"Do you think you dislike her so much because she's your brother's friend?"

"What do you mean?"

"Let's talk about why you're so invested in this campaign."

"You're the one who encouraged me to get more involved in school, remember?" Kyle sat up, preparing himself for a fight. Leave it to his therapist to ruin his good day by asking him too many personal questions.

"I did. But you're the one who chose to get involved in politics. Why do you think that is? Is it because you're interested in student government or because it's something that matters to your brother?"

Kyle shrugged. "Both, I guess."

"Talk more about that."

"What? You want me to say I hate government because my brother loves it?"

"I don't want you to say it if it isn't true." Shirley paused. "Is it true?"

"It used to be. Maybe. After what the government did to my dad, I wanted to see the whole corrupt system destroyed. But now that I've worked for Tony's campaign, I can see the appeal."

"What's the appeal?"

"I like manipulating people." Brian stared at Shirley. "Just like you."

"Oh?" Now it was his therapist's turn to squirm in her seat. "How do you see me manipulating people?"

"It's what therapists do, right? You make people relaxed and comfortable and then ask them questions to undermine their self-confidence."

"I ask questions to help people understand their motivation," Shirley said.

"Same thing," Kyle said. "I think you like being in control. These sessions probably benefit you more than any of your clients. At the end of the day, you must feel pretty superior after listening to all the fucked-up things people tell you."

"That's not how I feel at all." Shirley's ever-present smile vanished for a second, and Kyle knew he had struck a nerve.

"It's cool," he said. "I get it. I like being in control too. Most people are sheep. They need a good shepherd."

"You're the shepherd?"

"Yeah. The way I see it, you can either control people or be controlled by them. I'd rather be in charge of my own destiny than be at the mercy of someone else."

"So, you and your brother are more alike than you like to think."

"No, we're not," Kyle said, his hands clenching involuntarily into fists. "We may both like politics, but we disagree on the means and the ends. Criminals and police both like guns, but they use them for different purposes."

"Who's the criminal and who's the police in this scenario?"

"I guess we'll just have to wait and see, won't we?" Kyle said, leaning back down on the coach. "That's something for future generations to decide."

PROTESTS

37

ELECTION DAY

THE QUINCEAÑERA PROTEST was to take place in the quad at brunch before the students voted for their representatives in their third-period classes. The hope was that the performance would remind everyone about the important issues at stake in this year's election. Just two weeks ago, Julia's campaign poster was vandalized with a racist slur. The campus needed to deal with this hateful attack and not be distracted by Tony's desire to stock more munchies in the cafeteria.

Julia had begged Principal Buckley to give her back the defaced poster, but Buckley claimed it was evidence in an ongoing investigation and refused. "Why do you want it back anyway?" she'd asked, crossing her arms and staring at Julia with suspicious eyes. Julia had said something lame about wanting it for her scrapbook, and beat a hasty retreat. This protest required absolute secrecy, or the administration would shut it down. Instead of holding her original poster, Julia made a duplicate and smeared it with the same ugly message. This will do fine, she thought, folding it into her backpack and biking to school.

All the girls participating in the march met after first period to go change into their gowns. To avoid campus security, they drove to the public library five blocks away and used their larger and more private bathroom facilities. The girls cycled in and out of the room in groups of four so as not to drown in a sea of taffeta.

"We'll have Julia walk into the quad first," Maria said to the girls crowded around the bathroom mirrors, applying their makeup. "Followed by the rest of us in a show of solidarity."

Maria was the only one who looked uncomfortable in her billowing gown. She wasn't girlie like the others. She reminded Julia of that actress who kicks ass in all those *Fast and Furious* movies. It was easier to imagine her behind the wheel of a souped-up Lamborghini than waltzing in a tiara.

"After that, we march in a circle until a crowd has gathered," Maria went on.

"And then we do our dance!" Jenny said, snapping her fingers in the air.

"What do we do with our posters during the dance?" someone asked.

"As soon as you hear the music start, put them on the ground," Jenny said. "Just make sure not to step on them."

"What if security tries to shut us down?" Rosa asked.

"They won't," Maria said. "There was a flash mob last week for the dance show, and nobody did shit."

Julia pulled a stack of paper towels out of the rack and held them under her armpits. She was starting to get nervous. It didn't help that she was standing with five other girls in a cloud of hair spray and perfume. Once again, the enormity of her falsehood acted like a virus in her body, raising its temperature and constricting her breathing.

"Girl, let me add a little sparkle to those lips," Jenny said, dabbing Julia's lips with her fingers.

Up close, Jenny must have seen the beads of sweat on Julia's forehead and heard her gasps for air. "You okay?" she asked.

"I think I'm having a panic attack," Julia said, putting her hands on the sink and holding her head down.

"Let's clear the room, people," Jenny said. "Julia needs a moment."

Julia grabbed Jenny's wrist to prevent her from leaving. "Stay," she said. "Please."

The girls left the bathroom, and the atmosphere became more hospitable to human life. Julia breathed into the porcelain sink and felt Jenny's hand make tiny circles on her back.

Her heart slowed from a hyphy beat to a slow jam.

"What if I'm not Latina?" Julia said, keeping her head down, staring at the sink drain. "All this feels like such a big lie."

"You're not doing this to get elected," Jenny said. "You're doing it to make a statement."

"It feels like the same thing," Julia said.

"It's not," Jenny said. "You didn't ask for your poster to be vandalized. But it was. You're helping us take a stand against racism. That's a good thing."

Julia straightened up and looked at herself in the mirror. "I really hope I am Latina," she said.

"No matter what that test says, you'll still be my *hermana*."

"Gracias," Julia said, hugging Jenny and getting a mouthful of hair. "We'd know sooner if my mom would tell me."

"Yeah, I don't get that," Jenny said, looking into the mirror and adding a touch of lipstick.

"I don't either." Julia sighed. "My mom's always played by her own rules. Most of the time, it's what I like best about her."

Ten minutes later, the girls were crammed into Maria's car and heading back to school. Julia still felt a little lightheaded, but she attributed that to the excess of hair spray fumes trapped in the minivan.

The girls excitedly showed off their posters. Most of them had written some statement in support of immigration rights. Jenny, who couldn't pass up an opportunity to stand out in a crowd, wrote "We Were Here First!" in bold, sparkly letters.

The girls arrived at the student parking lot with fifteen minutes to spare. Maria opened the sliding side door, and the girls spilled out like brightly colored gumballs. Julia took her phone out of her purse to snap a few selfies with the pro- testing princesses when she saw a message from a number she didn't recognize. The text contained the photo Julia had sent Brian when she first tried on her quinceañera dress, along with a news article about the lawsuit her mom brought against the fertility clinic. Meet me behind the cafeteria, or this goes out to everyone, the text below read.

Julia stumbled backward in shock. "I've got to go to the bathroom," she said to the girls.

"We just came from the bathroom," Rosa whined.

"I know. Sorry. I'll be right back." Julia lifted her gown up and walked as quickly as she could in her heels through the parking lot toward the cafeteria.

The back of the cafeteria faced the school's marquee, near the pick-up-and-drop-off zone. Julia was terrified about who she'd find waiting for her there. The last person she expected to see was Brian.

"What are you doing here?" she asked.

"I got this text five minutes ago," he said, holding up his phone for her to see. It was the same message she had received. "What is this article all about? Is this your mother?"

"Yes," Julia said. "I'll explain later. How did this photo of me get out? Did you share it with anyone?"

"It was my brother," Brian said. "The other night at dinner, I left my phone at the table. It was the night you texted it to me. He's the one blackmailing you. Only he would do something so despicable."

"It's political, not despicable," a voice said off in the distance. Stacey emerged from behind the marquee and walked toward them slowly and deliberately. "Don't you look pretty, Julia!" she said, once she was standing next to them. "Like a real Latina princess."

Julia and Brian both gave yelps of surprise.

38

FOR A SECOND, Stacey almost felt sorry for Julia. She looked so helpless and weak in her quinceañera dress, as if she were a princess in need of saving. But if Julia were the princess, what did that make Stacey in this scenario? The evil stepmother? The wicked witch? Her mother? Stacey didn't like her options here, so she put a stop to this analogy.

"Stacey, what are you doing?" Brian asked.

"Do you want to tell him, or should I?" Stacey asked, turning to Julia.

"I don't have a father," Julia said finally.

"Well, scientifically speaking, that's impossible," Stacey said. "You have someone's DNA. We're just not sure the man's Latino."

"So?" Julia said.

"So, if your mom's white, it means you can't really lay

claim to the Latino cultural heritage. I think people at this protest would be interested in knowing what a liar and fraud you are."

"Stacey, come on," Brian said.

"I never lied," Julia said.

"You never told the truth, either. Look at you. All dressed up like you're one of them."

"Maybe I am Latina," Julia said. "You don't know that."

"But you don't either. Be honest. You only decided to become Latina when you realized it would help you win the election. It's the whole reason you vandalized your poster."

"That's not true," Julia said, turning to Brian. "You know I didn't do that, right, Brian?"

Brian nodded. He was completely brainwashed, Stacey realized. Even when confronted with evidence, he refused to believe his candidate was a liar.

"Stacey, who sent you this photo of Julia?" he asked.

"She did," Stacey said. "Just before I was about to make my speech."

"How could I do that?" Julia asked. "You were sitting right next to me."

"I don't mean you did it personally," Stacey said. "You had one of your supporters do it. Probably Jenny Ramirez. She worships you."

"I did not do this," Julia said. "Think about it. Why would

I want to hurt Brian by sending this to you?"

"Because you want to be president," Stacey said.

"I do want to be president, but I want to be with Brian too," Julia said. "He would never forgive me if I destroyed his relationship with you. You're his best friend."

"*Was* his best friend," Stacey said.

"Kyle sent you this photo, Stacey," Brian said. "I saw him at the assembly. He held up his phone to me and smiled. He wanted to ruin you because you were a threat to Tony. He's the one who vandalized Julia's poster, too. I would bet my life on it."

Stacey felt her moral high ground crumbling; the bedrock she thought she was standing on was starting to feel more like a swamp. "Even if that were true," she said, "which I'm not saying it is, Julia could have come clean at any point in the campaign, but she didn't."

Julia seemed to be having trouble breathing. She nodded in response to what Stacey said. "You're right," she said quietly. "I should have said something. But you can understand why that would be difficult, right?"

"You should have thought of that before you decided to run," Stacey said.

Stacey was hoping to feel vindicated in this moment. This was her triumphal scene. The part of the story where she confronted the liar and the cheat with the hard evidence she had gathered against them. So why didn't she feel heroic right now? She had done an excellent job channeling her mother's cold toughness. But that was the problem. Pretending to be Mom had come too easy. She didn't have to reinvent herself to impersonate her; it was a role she was born to play.

Stacey looked at Julia, in her pretty sequined gown and tiara. Brian was holding her up by her shoulders and whispering words of comfort into her ear. What was he saying now to make her feel better? Stacey felt her anger returning. Julia didn't deserve his support. She did. After all Julia had put them through, how could he be offering her consolation? Even after knowing the truth, he still supported her.

Oh God. Was it Brian the two of them were really competing over? It couldn't be. Stacey didn't have those feelings for Brian, did she? Things were so messy and confusing, and Stacey hated messy and confusing. She preferred organized and clear. Why couldn't she chart this all on a Venn diagram or spreadsheet? All she saw right now were two columns: gains and losses. Julia couldn't win both Brian and the election. She could have one, but not both.

Stacey pushed Brian out of the way and faced her rival, as if challenging her to a duel. "It's time to decide, Julia. Drop out of the race, or Priya sends the text to the whole school. Which is it going to be?"

39

BRIAN SQUEEZED BETWEEN the two girls, hoping he might absorb some of the tension that existed between them. The position probably struck Julia and Stacey as an appropriate one for a mediator. Or worse, a border wall. From his perspective, he felt like the toy two children were fighting over. Pretty soon his seams would tear and all his stuffing would burst from his body.

"Stacey, please," he said. "You can't do this."

Stacey turned and regarded Brian coldly. "I can and I will."

"You're just mad at me, and you're taking it out on Julia."

"Two birds. One stone."

"That's not who you are."

"How do you know who I am?"

"Because we've been friends since freshman year."

"That's right. I thought I knew who you were too, but

clearly I don't. The Brian I knew would never stab me in the back the way you have."

Brian could see Stacey struggle to hold back the tears welling in her eyes. In any other circumstance, he would reach out and pull her into a hug. Something told him that if he tried to do that now, she would punch him in the gut. "I never wanted to hurt you," he said.

"Why didn't you tell me you liked Julia?"

"I was going to tell you. I just didn't know how."

"You don't see this as a slight conflict of interest?"

"Not really. I mean, I guess it is, kind of."

"I feel like I've lost my best friend." Stacey turned, shielding her face from him. Brian reached out and put a tentative hand on her shoulders. He hoped this steadied her as much as it did him.

"You haven't lost me, Stacey."

"I thought you were gay," she said, her voice barely above a whisper.

"What? Why would you think that?"

"Because we're best friends."

"So?"

"So, that's not normal."

"Are you telling me you're gay?"

Stacey shook her head.

"But by your logic, it's the only way to explain our friendship."

"Why didn't you like *me*, Brian? What's wrong with *me*?"

"Nothing."

"Then why? Why her and not me?"

Brian turned Stacey around and stared at her. "Because you're my friend," he said gently. He dipped his head so that he came into Stacey's line of vision. Stacey's eyes darted from side to side but finally rested on his. "This is new for me, Stacey, so I'm a bit confused. I guess that's why I couldn't find the way to explain it to you because I didn't understand it myself. All I know is that I never felt anything like this before. The feelings I have for Julia are different from the feelings I have for you. You make me feel safe, and Julia makes me feel . . . scared."

"And that's why you like her?" Stacey whispered back.

"I think. Maybe fear's an important part of attraction. It's what makes people do crazy things. Julia's my tightrope, but you're my net. I need you both, but for different reasons."

"Oh Brian," Stacey said, leaning her head against his chest. "You have such a way with words."

Brian wasn't sure if Stacey was complimenting him or not. He proceeded as if she were.

"Life's complicated, Stacey. Elections demand that we simplify things, even simplify people, but sometimes that's impossible."

"So says the guy who can't narrow down his college wish list to twenty schools," Stacey said. "Sometimes you have to make a choice between two attractive options, Brian. I'm asking you to do that now. Her or me?"

"Stacey. I can't choose," Brian said, stepping back. "And I shouldn't have to."

"This is an election, Brian. If you don't choose, someone else will do it for you." Stacey nodded in Julia's direction.

Brian turned around and saw Julia moving across the parking lot like some disappearing balloon that had slipped through his fingers. By the time he realized what was happening, she was too far away for him to bring her back.

40

TONY WAS CONFUSED. He was about to take his reading quiz in second-period English when Mohawk arrived with a summons from the front office. His English teacher barely glanced at the slip. This was the third time this semester he'd been called out of class for some misdemeanor; it probably didn't surprise her that he was in trouble again. It surprised Tony though. As far as he could remember, he hadn't done anything wrong, except smoke a bowl before leaving home this morning. But since when was that a crime?

"Take your stuff with you," she told Tony after handing him the slip. "You can take the reading quiz during lunch."

Tony followed Mohawk dutifully out of class. Some kid in the back row shouted out "Vote for Tony," causing the students not stressing about the reading quiz to laugh. Before leaving the room, Tony turned and flashed a peace sign to all his supporters.

Mohawk led him down the hall toward the center quad. Rather than cross the empty space and head toward the main office, he ducked inside the boys' bathroom and motioned for Tony to follow. Once inside, Mohawk checked the stalls for any dangling feet and gave Tony a thumbs-up sign.

"What's going on?" Tony said.

"I got a present for you," Mohawk said, slipping the straps of his backpack off his shoulders.

The last time someone said this to him in a public bathroom, it didn't end well. Tony instinctively backed up against the door. "I thought I was in trouble," he said.

"Naw, I just forged the slip to get you out of class," Kyle said, unzipping his backpack.

"Dude, we were about to have a reading quiz."

"Did you *do* the reading?"

"No, but now I have to make up the quiz during lunch, which will be a total drag."

"Trust me. It'll be worth it. Wait till you see what I got you." Mohawk pulled out a thin white blanket with black spots and what looked like a pink helmet covered in dildos.

"What the . . . ?" Tony said, reaching for the door.

Mohawk lifted the garment above his head, and Tony saw it was a cow costume, complete with a rubbery set of udders. "Here, hold this," he said, passing the adult onesie to Tony.

He reached into his backpack and took out an astronaut space helmet.

"Whaddya think?"

"I'm not sure what's happening right now."

"It's Space Cow, you idiot. I got these for you to wear today."

"Why today?"

"It's election day, dumbass. We've got one last chance to remind voters that you're their man."

"Dressing up as Space Cow is supposed to remind them of that?"

"Uh, yeah. It's kind of your platform, remember?"

"What am I supposed to do in this thing?"

"What do you mean? Haven't you ever seen our mascot perform at rallies or football games?"

Tony shook his head.

"You go out into the crowds, do silly dances, and remind them to vote for Tony."

"Why can't *you* do this?"

"I didn't buy the suit in my size," Mohawk said. "Besides, it's traditionally the candidate's job."

"I don't know, dude. I kinda like what that chick said about getting rid of homework."

"Are you kidding me? That's never going to happen. Not in a million years. You have a better chance opening up a dispensary in the cafeteria before homework goes away."

"That would be cool."

"Let's just stay on message. A vote for Tony is a vote for Space Cow. You want to see it back in the cafeteria, right?"

"Yeah. I guess I was kind of hoping the principal would accept my demands to keep me out of the race. You know, like you said."

"They're playing chicken with you," Mohawk said. "You need to call their bluff."

Tony looked at the costume. It was pretty cool, like a giant version of the footed pajamas he used to wear as a kid, only instead of feet it had hooves. It also had a cow face on the hood, which he could pull down so no one would recognize him.

He took off his high tops and stepped into the legs. Mohawk zipped him up from behind, and he felt the costume envelope him like a soft blanket. The hoodie only covered half his face, but with the space helmet on, his features were impossible to see. Of course, it was impossible for him to see as well, but he figured he didn't need 20/20 vision to dance around the quad.

"Dude, I have five penises," he said, running his right hand over the plastic udders jutting from his waist.

"Yeah, be careful with those," Mohawk said. "Or not. Who gives a shit at this point, right?"

"Do we have time to get high?" Tony asked. "I've got a blunt in my right pocket, and I'd love to see what happens when I trap the smoke in my space helmet."

"Fire up, dude. The bell won't ring for another five minutes. I'll keep watch outside and make sure you aren't disturbed."

41

JULIA DIDN'T HAVE much time. The bell was about to ring, and she needed to walk her quinceañera sisters into the quad, poster held high. It might be the most humiliating thing she ever did—parading around with the other Latinas while everyone at school learned of her real heritage—but she wasn't going to back out now. These girls had gone out of their way to defend her; it was time for her to return the favor.

She met the girls in the area that separated the parking lot from the center quad. On the left of this corridor was the band room, and to the right, the theater. Both classes were full of performers, and she hoped the musicians and actors would cheer the fourteen girls as they passed by in their brightly colored dresses, holding banners for justice.

"Who's got the speaker?" Jenny said, looking around frantically.

Maria, at the end of the line, held up the Bose cylinder that would blast Calle 13's "Pa'l Norte," to which the girls would perform their choreographed dance.

"We circle the quad three times and then line up in formation," Jenny ordered. She should really be the one running for president, Julia thought. She's pretty good at bossing people around.

Julia clutched her sign to her chest and took a deep breath.

"You going to be okay, girl?" Jenny asked, touching Julia's shoulder.

Julia nodded and tried to smile.

"'Cause we've got your back," Jenny said. "Don't we, girls?"

The line of girls, a rainbow of silky pastels and sparkly tiaras, all whooped and hollered.

It was at this moment, at the end of her campaign, that Julia understood why she was running for president. For so long, she thought of this race as a means to an end. If she were president, she could stay in California. But that wasn't it at all. Standing in formation with these girls, she finally realized that real power comes when you stop thinking of yourself and start working for others. She loved these girls and wanted to fight with them and that purpose made her feel indestructible.

The bell rang, and students began streaming into the quad from all sides. Julia raised her banner and walked solemnly into the fray.

42

IT WAS ONE of the most beautiful sights Stacey had ever seen: kids flooding into the quad to enjoy the few minutes of freedom they had between classes and stopping dead in their tracks to watch a silent parade of beautiful girls walk by in silent protest.

"Wow," Stacey said.

"I know," Brian responded.

They stood on the quad's perimeter, near the front of the school, and watched the spectacle. It was a stunning bit of contrast. The girls were all dressed in their bubble-gum pink, purple, and red gowns, tiaras perched delicately on their sculpted hair, but they wore serious expressions like the royal families in *Game of Thrones*. Julia led the group, holding up her vandalized poster, a reminder of why this march was necessary. Behind her, each girl broadcast messages of love, acceptance, and unity. The campus was absolutely still as the girls marched in a wide circle, once, twice, three times. On the last loop, Julia looked up and smiled at Stacey as she passed. Stacey had never been prouder to call herself a Lincoln student. What she had been about to do to Julia seemed so ugly in contrast to this dignified display of nonviolent protest. Who cares if Julia is Latina or not if she's willing to support her fellow students like this? Julia respected these girls enough to participate in this protest, which Stacey had never even thought to do. Stacey had been so wrapped up in winning the election that she completely ignored the fact that someone had broadcast a message of hate to every Latino at her school. The fact that Stacey saw the slandered poster as a political maneuver, rather than a vicious attack, made her sick to her stomach.

"I'm sorry," she said to Brian.

"Me too," he said.

"My bridezilla mom must have gotten to me. What Julia's doing . . . It's really great."

Brian nodded, clearly proud.

That's when Space Cow came bouncing into the quad.

Stacey grabbed Brian's arm. "No," she said. Brian gasped in response.

Space Cow stumbled around the crowd, crashing into people and jostling them with pleas to "Bring back my chocolate milk!" The girls did their best to ignore him, which only got harder when they started their flash-mob dance. As soon as Space Cow heard the Calle 13 tune, he started gyrating his pelvis, Elvis Presley style, and stroking his udders suggestively. He got in the way of the girls' routine and caused them to break formation. Anger flashed across the girls' faces, but they refused to sink to Space Cow's level.

"Yeah, Space Cow!" a freshman yelled from Stacey's left. She turned on the boy who ignored her threatening glare. Instead, he encouraged the guys standing around him to start chanting "Space Cow! Space Cow!"

"No," Stacey said again. "No, Space Cow."

She stormed into the center quad and performed a roundhouse kick worthy of a black belt. It landed squarely in Space Cow's udders, causing the dancing bovine to collapse to the ground. There was an audible crack as his helmet hit the pavement.

Stacey stood over him and heard the crowd chant "Fuck it, fuck it, fuck it." Apparently, this was Stacey's new campaign slogan.

Before she shut her supporters up, Space Cow recovered and kicked Stacey's legs out from under her. She fell to the concrete with a thud, pain shooting up her ankle. Before she knew what was happening, she was drowning in cotton candy, or at least, it seemed like cotton candy to her slightly addled brain. More likely, it was a quinceañera princess rushing to her aid and pulling her away from Space Cow, who was now facing off with Julia.

Julia's transition to womanhood involved hitting Space Cow over the head with her sign and bringing him down with an aggressive punch to the stomach.

The two of them rolled on the ground in some bizarre rodeo reenactment. Julia somehow flipped Space Cow onto his stomach and then yanked off his helmet and threw it into the crowd. Space Cow tried his best to buck her off his back, but she straddled him like a cowboy and wouldn't be shaken loose. Four of her sisters came over and grabbed Space Cow's feet and started dragging him off center stage.

"Munchkins! Help!" Tony screamed in terror.

In an instant, a wall of freshman boys appeared and blocked the girls' path to the parking lot. A mangy-looking kid with a blue Mohawk, Brian's brother, locked his scarred arms with the boys on either side of him and bellowed, "You shall not pass," a rallying cry that seemed to fortify his army of dwarves.

Out of nowhere, Brian rushed this defensive line and tackled his brother onto the ground. After securing him in a headlock, he screamed out to the crowd, "Anyone else here been bullied by a younger sibling lately?"

Slowly, older brothers and sisters began breaking free from the crowd to approach the line of freshmen. As soon as they saw their siblings storming toward them, the boys scattered, opening up a wide path over which the girls could drag their prisoner.

"No! Please! Help!" Tony yelled.

Before the quince crew could take another high-heeled step, Sammy pulled up in his golf cart and put a stop to the mayhem. No one was going to mess with a man who looked like a CGI special effect from a Hobbit film. He grabbed Tony and Julia by the arms, put them in the back of his golf cart, and drove toward the principal's office.

The bell rang, and the crowds dispersed to their third-period classes. Stacey limped among her peers, who were too busy comparing video clips of the fight to notice her. Just as she was about to enter her classroom, Stacey stopped. She couldn't pretend to be a student right now. She needed a quiet place to figure out what her next move was going to be. Before her teacher could see her standing at the doorway, she turned around and pushed through the crowded hallways to the quiet space she had helped create when student government still mattered to her.

"SPACE COW MASSACRE"

by Lance Haber

Not since the infamous Boston Tea Party has such a dramatic display of civil disobedience been seen in our country.

Lincoln students from different classes and cliques rose up from their knees and spoke truth to power. Unfortunately, power had their noise-canceling headphones on.

First it began with the Latinas, led by Julia Romero, a girl whose beauty and integrity has been an inspiration to us all during this campaign. A group of Latina girls dressed in quinceañera dresses walked in solemn procession through the quad to protest the racist attacks either perpetrated or inspired by Wynn's xenophobic campaign. The crowds watched respectfully as the girls peacefully marched, much like the NAACP's Silent Protest Parade of 1917.

Amid this quiet ceremony, Tony Guo did a satiric dance in a Space Cow costume. The space helmet he wore served as a painful allusion to the administration's efforts to silence the growing voices of dissent on our campus.

Of course, Stacey Wynn could not allow such peaceful protests to continue. Not if they might cost her votes in the election.

If you need any more evidence of Wynn's naked ambition, just check out this YouTube clip of Wynn assaulting the Space Cow with a lethal kick to his abdomen. Prior to witnessing this, I always assumed Wynn got other people to do her dirty work for her, but it turns out I was wrong. Not only is Stacey a shifty political manipulator; she's also a Jason Bourne–level assassin.

The administration has refused to comment on what, if any, punishment Wynn will receive for her aggressive strongman tactics. Judging from the principal's response to past violations, my guess is that nothing will happen. At least everyone has seen Wynn for who she really is and will use their moral and ethical judgments to cast their votes next period. A vote for Julia or Tony is a vote for freedom.

Unfortunately, dear reader, this will be my last blog entry for a while. After committing myself so fully to exposing the crimes perpetrated throughout the campaign, I must now focus on my schoolwork so I can be eligible to graduate in June. (My parents have already confiscated my laptop and cell phone, and I write this on the library computer).

Even though I will not be posting on a regular basis, you can be assured that I will fight injustice wherever I see it, whether it's in the classroom, on the quad, or at home in the family living room with my dad reading over my shoulder.

Fight the power!

<u>VOTING</u>

43

JULIA RECEIVED HER DNA test results from her mother while sitting in the principal's office, waiting for Stacey to arrive.

"I'm not sending you this information to help you win an election," her mother wrote in her email. "I've always believed race is a social construction, but that doesn't make it any less real. You've helped me see that. I'm not sure what these percentages will mean for you, but I hope they help answer some of the questions you have about yourself and lead you on a journey of self-discovery."

Julia paused before clicking open the file. Was her mom right? Did she need these numbers to tell her who she was? Wasn't there some freedom in choosing the group you identified with, rather than letting a bunch of percentages do it for you? She made a silent promise that no matter what her

DNA results were, she would never leave the girls in LSU. They were her sisters, and no genetic code could take that away from her.

She clicked open the file and read the breakdown: 52 percent European, 26 percent Sub-Saharan African, 10 percent Middle Eastern and North African, 9 percent East Asian and Native American, and 3 percent unidentified. What did this mean? She was hoping to see a specific country identified, ideally one that fell under the racial category of Hispanic or Latino. But there was no such category on the page. Below the numbers, there was a world map, color-coded to match the breakdown of Julia's chromosomes. The map of South America was the same color as the Native American percentage, which Julia took to mean that 9 percent of her DNA could be traced back to that continent. It wasn't specific or conclusive, but Julia grabbed it as the answer she needed.

I'm nine percent Latina!!! she texted Jenny. Mom just sent me my test results.

Congratulations! Welcome to the club! Jenny texted back a few minutes later. Now get off your phone before Buckley sees you and you get into even more trouble.

A few minutes later, Stacey arrived, followed shortly by Buckley. Stacey insisted on taking the blame for the fight, despite Buckley's obvious desire to suspend Tony.

"It sounds to me that Tony was the one who created the

disturbance," Buckley said after Stacey provided a recap of the incident.

"No, it was me," Stacey said. "I struck the first blow."

"But you were protecting the girls from Tony's aggressive behavior."

"No, I just wanted to hurt him."

"Because you saw him as a threat," Buckley said.

"No, because he's obnoxious."

"Hey," Tony said. "We don't know each other well enough for you to say that."

"You're right," Stacey said. "I was wrong to judge you. That's why I deserve the blame for what happened."

Buckley's eyes bulged out of their sockets in exasperation. Clearly, she wanted to save Stacey but Stacey wasn't grabbing hold of the rescue buoy Buckley kept tossing her way. Eventually, she had to watch Stacey sink underwater and acknowledge the survivors. Buckley dismissed Julia and Tony with the directive to change out of their costumes before returning to class.

"That was weird," Tony said once they left the admin building.

"Yeah," Julia said.

"Why do you think she took the hit like that?"

Julia shrugged, although she had her theory. In the brief moment she and Stacey exchanged eye contact during the march, something passed between them—a shared under-standing of something bigger than the election. She imagined it was the same acknowledgment of respect athletes share after they've fought ferociously to win a game, a recognition that they were more alike than different.

The rest of the day passed in a kind of blur. The students voted for their class representatives at the end of third period. Stacey's name didn't appear anywhere on the Google form. The race was just between Julia and Tony now. Julia felt bad for Brian's friend, and a little guilty that she hadn't fought harder to take the blame. Truth was, Julia wanted to be president now more than ever. The brunch protest had only convinced her that she could do some real good if she were elected. So, she didn't fight Stacey as hard *not to be* president as she fought her *to be* president. Besides, if she got suspended, who knew how Aunt Gloria would react. Not only would she lose the election, she could lose Brian as well.

The results were announced at the end of sixth period. Brian and Julia were sitting in biology when the principal got on the intercom and started reading the names of the winners beginning from secretary and moving to president. Brian grabbed Julia's hand and squeezed it tightly. Her palm still felt rough from where she had scraped it against the pavement in the brunch melee.

"The ASB secretary is Ally Wu," Buckley said.

Julia couldn't stand the suspense. She turned to Brian and told him the other important news of the day. "I got my DNA analyzed," she said. "I'm nine percent Latina."

"Good for you," Brian said. "Now, shush, I want to hear the results."

Julia wanted to hear the result too, and she didn't want to hear them. She had a sudden premonition that her name would not be called. She didn't know how she knew this, but the knowledge settled on her bones like winter frost on tree limbs.

"The ASB treasurer is Mackenzie Zheutlin," Buckley said, botching the name a bit.

"I'm going back to Canada," Julia blurted out. Her admission surprised her as much as it surprised Brian.

"What?" Brian said. "No! You can't."

"Just for the summer," Julia said. "I need to see Alice. The girl I hurt." It was time for her to atone for her mistakes, like Stacey had done today in Buckley's office. Julia admired the way Stacey faced her faults instead of pretending they didn't exist. She needed to do that too.

"You're coming back though, right?" Brian said.

"If Mom will let me," Julia said.

"The ASB vice president is James Carter," Buckley said.

Brian squeezed Julia's hand a little tighter. "Can I come with you?" he asked.

"And for ASB president," Buckley said, pausing for dramatic effect.

"We'll see," Julia said.

"Tony Guo." Buckley was unsuccessful in silencing her heavy sigh after the announcement.

"No!" Brian said loudly. He pulled Julia's hand up and held it to his lips.

"It's okay," Julia whispered, feeling her whole body collapse like an inflatable tube man at the end of a sales event. "It's fine."

Gina Yuan got up out of her seat and came over to give Julia a hug. "Stupid freshmen," she said. "I'm going to kill my little brother."

The bell rang, and students packed up their things and left the classroom. Julia tried to distract herself by organizing her backpack. When Mr. Cohen came by and said *"Lo siento,"* Julia smiled, but then lost it as her teacher disappeared through the back door.

Brian bent down next to her and wrapped his arms around her shoulders. "We're going to fight this," he said. "Maybe there were some voting irregularities. Maybe the Russians are involved."

"I had a chance to do something good," Julia said, crying into Brian's T-shirt. "I thought I could really stand with Jenny and the LSU and fight for their cause."

"You can still fight for their cause," Brian said. "You'll be a great advocate."

"With Tony as president?" Julia said, shaking her head. "You think he cares about anything except himself?"

"He's not the only one in charge," Brian said. "James is vice president. He's going to be the one really running the show next year."

"You know him?" Julia said.

"Yeah, he's great," Brian said. "Trust me, he's on our side."

It made Julia feel a little better to hear him talk about the future as something shared, rather than something she'd have to face alone. She wiped away the tears with the back of her hand and stood up to go. When Brian reached for her bag, she stopped him with a gentle hand on his arm. "I got it," she said, hoisting her bag up and draping the strap over her shoulder. "Let's go."

The two left the classroom and walked into the blazing light of the afternoon.

"At least we won't have to sneak around anymore," Brian said, grabbing Julia's hand.

Julia smiled and squeezed his hand in response.

"Promise me you'll come back," Brian said. "After your apology tour."

"I promise," Julia said. "You understand why I have to do

this, right? You're the one who convinced me it was the right thing to do."

"I didn't mean *now*," Brian said. "I meant sometime in the future. Like ten years from now."

"I need to see her," Julia said. "I need to know she's okay."

The two strolled through campus like a real couple. A few people stared at them as they passed, but most were too busy heading to their seventh-period classes or gazing at their phones to notice. The guys who always congregated in the quad, waiting for their after-school lives to start, all applauded and shouted "Viva Julia!" when Julia and Brian approached. Julia waved like a queen, and the boys bowed in a deferential manner.

"Looks like you've earned their respect," Brian said.

"Yeah," Julia said. "Maybe I have."

Off in the distance, someone called out Julia's name. Brian and Julia turned and saw Stacey and Jenny racing down the hallway, trying to catch up with them.

Brian instinctively loosened his grip on Julia's hand but didn't let go.

Jenny ran up and nearly knocked Julia over with a bear hug around her neck. "Girl, I'm so sorry," she said. Her mascara had run, making her eyes look like flowers with black stems.

"It's fine," Julia said, trying to maintain her brave face. "How are you doing, Stacey?"

"I'm suspended for two days," Stacey said.

"I'm sorry," Julia said.

Stacey shrugged. "It will kill my mom, so it's not all bad."

"You didn't have to take the blame for us," Julia said.

"For *you*," Stacey said. "I didn't do anything for Tony."

"I bet you won the popular vote," Julia said. "If Buckley didn't suspend you, you'd be president now. The meme of you drop-kicking Tony is everywhere."

"Girl, you slaughtered that cow," Jenny said, wrapping an arm around Stacey. "Who knew a model student could be such a badass."

"I've got an idea for a new class next year that I wanted to talk to you all about," Stacey said. "What are you doing now?"

"Nothing," Brian said.

"Sorry, Brian," Stacey said, reaching out and putting a hand on his shoulder. "This one's just for the ladies."

"Oh, sure," Brian said. "I've got a little brother to kill anyway."

44

WHEN BRIAN GOT home, Kyle was waiting for him in the living room. He must have known Brian was angry because he was huddled next to their mom, feeding her nachos on the couch.

"Hi, honey," Mom said. "You hungry?"

"No," Brian said. "Did Kyle tell you what happened today?"

"He told me Stacey lost," Mom said frowning. "How's she doing?"

"She's fine," Brian said. He waited for his mom to elaborate, to say something about the fight and the suspension and the fact that a brain-fried boy was now the president, but she didn't say anything. Kyle must have kept those details to himself.

"How do you feel about the election, Kyle?" Brian asked.

"I feel empowered, thanks for asking, Brian," Kyle said.

"How so?" Mom asked.

"No one listens to the freshmen," Kyle said. "We've got no representation on the ASB because we come to school after everyone's been elected. This year, my class said 'enough' and made our voices heard."

"That's great, dear," Mom said. "Maybe you'll run for office next year."

"No way," Kyle said. "I'm more effective behind the scenes. Wouldn't you agree, Brian?"

"Definitely," Brian said. "Kyle really understands how to work the system."

Brian left his brother and mom on the couch and closed himself off in his room. He was never going to get back at his brother through the traditional means of fistfights and noogies. He had to think strategically, just as Kyle had done, and destroy him without leaving a mark. But to do this he needed an ally. He looked at the photo of him and Stacey pinned to his corkboard. Since Stacey was busy with Julia, he'd have to find another crime fighter, preferably someone with skin in the game. He pulled down the photo of him at the Scouts jamboree and dialed James's number.

"You want to help me take down Tony Guo?" he asked.

45

TONY COULDN'T BELIEVE it. He was president of the school. How did this happen? He thought for sure his Space Cow performance would have gotten him disqualified. But then that other candidate, the blond girl who brought him down like a Black Widow, demanded to be punished. There was something happening here that Tony didn't understand. Why would someone argue so forcefully to be suspended unless there was some benefit? It couldn't be that she just wanted to miss a few days of school. Girls like that don't like missing school and they certainly don't like having a stain like this on their permanent record. Maybe she knew something Tony didn't about the hassles of being ASB President and skillfully engineered her own disqualification. Maybe this white girl with the powerful roundhouse kick had played them all.

Tony spent the rest of the day avoiding the Latinos, who

were out for blood after what he did to their protest. He took some comfort in the fact that they would rise up against him and ensure his defeat at the polls. When Buckley announced his name as president, Tony, along with practically everyone else in his US history class, scratched their heads and said "Wha?!" His teacher immediately began an impromptu lecture on the failings of the democratic process.

As soon as the sixth-period bell rang, Tony sprinted to his car to avoid anyone looking for vengeance. Half the people he passed shouted congratulations; the other half, obscenities. When he finally reached his Mercedes, he saw someone had written "Pendejo" in the dust that covered his back window. Did the office of president come with round-the-clock security detail? Tony hoped so.

Now he was huddled in his room trying to think of what to do next. Why had he ever listened to Mohawk? It had all been a goof, hadn't it? A joke he and the little munchkins were playing on the school. A way to get back at the administration for their shitty cafeteria menu. Now half the school hated him, and he was stuck with all this responsibility he didn't want.

He pulled out his honey bear bong, loaded it with some Bruce Banner #4, and took a long hit. That should help. It might not solve his problems, but at least it kept him from stressing out about them too much.

The phone rang in the middle of his second hit. The only people who ever called on the landline were his parents, so he picked up the phone, trying to mentally calculate the time in Macao. If there was a fifteen-hour difference and it was six p.m. in California, then it must be either super early or super late.

"Hello?" Tony said, breathing out the smoke and trying not to cough.

"Why didn't you tell us you were running for president?" his dad asked in his typical abrupt style. Tony heard his mom arguing with the Chinese newscast in the background.

Was his dad calling to congratulate him? Maybe the election hadn't been a total loss if it got his parents off his back for a while. Maybe this would finally give them something to brag about to their friends at the country club and the strangers they met on vacation cruises.

"It was kind of a last-minute decision," Tony said. "Did you hear I won?"

"The Wus called to congratulate us. They said you want to sell marijuana in the school cafeteria."

"What? No!" Tony said. "I want to bring chocolate milk back to the cafeteria."

"They say there are photos of you smoking marijuana all over the internet."

"That's weird," Tony said. "It's probably someone who just looks like me."

"I'm looking at one now. It says 'Tony Guo for President' underneath a photo of you blowing smoke like a Chinese steel factory."

"Uh, that's a joke, Dad," Tony fumbled. "You know, to appeal to immature voters."

"This is very concerning to your mother, Tony."

"What? Why?"

"She's worried you'll bring more shame to our family."

Tony didn't think that was possible, but he had to concede the point. Before he was a public figure, all his misdeeds were mostly private family matters. Now he would be embarrassing them in front of their friends, whose children were actually on their way to becoming doctors.

"You need to drop out," his father said.

"Dad, I won. It's too late to drop out."

"Then we'll transfer schools," he said. "Send you to Saint Francis."

Catholic school? No freaking way. Those guys were stricter than Lincoln. Tony knew a guy who went there who told him the administration had replaced the pizza truck with a salad bar.

"Don't worry, Dad. I'll find a way out of this."

"We're coming home on the next flight," his dad said, and hung up.

Almost simultaneously, the front doorbell rang. Tony was confused. Were his parents home already? Why would they be ringing the doorbell? And since when do airport cabs broadcast Chinese news?

Tony opened the door and saw Doug and his white friends standing on his porch with alcohol. Lots and lots of alcohol.

"Ready to celebrate?" Doug asked, stepping over the threshold. Before Tony knew it, the guys had stormed into his kitchen and were shoving bags of ice into his freezer.

They were followed by a steady stream of kids Tony only half recognized. Most of them jokingly congratulated him on his victory. "Not my problem!" a number of seniors said after high-fiving him. A few admitted that they hadn't voted for him, but were happy to move past the acrimony of the election and focus on more important things like prom and grad night.

In the span of a few hours, Tony's house filled up with drunk teenagers who danced on his parents' Ming ivory rug and threw up in the guest bathroom. This party was just like the election—something that had taken on a life of its own until Tony felt powerless to stop it.

In the midst of all the mayhem, two guys who Tony had never seen before walked up and introduced themselves.

"I'm James, your vice president," the tall, skinny black guy said. Tony decided to call him Bow Tie.

"I'm Brian," the other guy said. He looked familiar, kind of like Mohawk, only with neatly parted hair. He wore a light blue polo and khakis, almost like he had dressed up for the party, not knowing that most people wore clothes they were fine barfing on.

"Nice to meet you," Tony said, looking at the crowds crammed into his kitchen. "You should get a drink."

"That's okay," the guy said. Tony had already forgotten his name. Was it Brain? He looked smart. Tony decided to call him Brain.

A girl bounced into Tony, nearly knocking him over. "Watch it, bozo," she slurred, and stumbled off.

Tony turned back to Brain and Bow Tie and rolled his eyes. He wondered if they were a couple. They'd be cute together, he decided, like those dudes on that TV show *The Big Bang Theory*.

"I'm excited to work with you next year," Bow Tie said, patting his hands together in rapid, tiny claps. "We've got quite the agenda."

"What are you talking about?" Tony asked. Off in the distance, he saw a dude pressing his butt against the kitchen's sliding glass door to moon a group of girls standing outside.

"The ASB is really going to pump up the volume at the spirit rallies," Brain said.

"Those things are lame," Tony said.

"I know, right?" Bow Tie said. "That's why were so excited to have you as our new emcee."

"Emcee?"

"Yeah. You *do* know the ASB president is like the master of ceremonies at every rally, spirit competition, and cultural celebration."

"I did not know that." If one more person hangs from that chandelier, it's going to come down, Tony thought, turning his attention to the living room.

"Next year we're doing something I think you're going to be really excited about."

"What's that?"

"You know the show *So You Think You Can Dance?* Well, that's going to be the theme of every assembly. You and a partner will compete against other school leaders to see who will reign supreme on the dance floor."

"I am *not* going to do that," Tony said.

"It's too late," Bow Tie said. "We've already voted to make it happen. We've got this great dance instructor, Alonso, who's going to be working with us all year long. You're going to love him."

"James does a mean rhumba," Brain said. "You better start practicing."

"I just wanted to bring chocolate milk back to the cafeteria."

"Oh, that's taken care of," Bow Tie said, swatting Tony's signature issue away like a pesky fly. "My dad's on the school board, and I got him to reverse his decision. Turns out milk sales plummeted when kids were just offered unflavored. So, problem solved."

"Now you can focus all your energies on the cha-cha-cha," Brain said.

"No, I'm out," Tony said.

"You can't quit," Bow Tie said.

"The principal will never accept your resignation," Brain said.

"Tough shit."

"You could force her to get rid of you," Brain said. "Like Stacey did."

"Who?"

"The girl who drop-kicked you today at brunch."

"Yeah, how do I get her to fire me?"

Bow Tie looked over at the girl drinking out of the fish tank. "If she finds out you were serving liquor to minors, that would do the trick," he said.

"What do you mean?"

"This party?" Brain said. "How many of your guests can drink legally?"

"Ha! You serious?" Then it hit Tony. He should call the cops on his own party! That would get him in enough trouble to have the principal fire him. He was ready for these people to leave him alone anyway. He had had enough of them invading his space and making disgusting mixed drinks with his chocolate milk.

"I've got an idea," he told the two guys standing in front of him with oddly impatient expressions. He pulled out his phone from his back pocket and dialed 911. "I'd like to report a party," he said.

"I'm sorry, that's not an emergency matter."

"The kids are drinking lots of alcohol," Tony said.

"And lighting fireworks," Bow Tie whispered.

"And lighting fireworks," Tony repeated.

"Near the fertilizer bins," Brain whispered.

"Near the fertilizer bins," Tony repeated.

"And paint-thinner storage facility," Bow Tie whispered.

"And paint-thinner storage facility," Tony repeated.

A few seconds later, Tony hung up the phone.

"Done," he said. "If I were you, I'd leave now."

NEW ADMINISTRATION

EPILOGUE

"IF WE OFFER a Spanish literature class, don't we need to offer other culturally specific classes as well?" someone in the back of the room asked.

"Not necessarily," Stacey said. "We're responding to demand. We don't have enough Russians to support a Russian literature class."

"So the largest clubs get to decide which electives the school offers? That doesn't seem fair."

"The admin asked us to gather student input," Julia said. "The LSU overwhelmingly voted for this class."

"The GSA wants a LGBT history class," Brian said. "Why isn't that on our list of proposals?"

"Because there are only five people in the Gay-Straight Alliance," Stacey said. "And they teach *The Color Purple* in American lit."

"One book!" Brian said, punctuating the point by raising his index finger to the sky.

"There's not one Latino author in the entire curriculum," Jenny said. "We deserve this."

A general murmur rose among the students in the class. They had been debating this for two weeks, and they had only eliminated seven of the proposed electives. The administration asked the leadership class to give them a list of five, and there were still eleven written on the whiteboard. Brian looked over at Ms. Callahan, their adviser, but she wasn't getting involved. She preferred to let the students "manage the debate" and only stepped in to remind them of class protocols if necessary.

"What if we change Spanish literature to Ethnic Studies?" Stacey suggested. "That would appeal to a broader group of students."

"I worry the curriculum might be too shallow," Julia said. "If we try to cover all ethnicities, students won't learn much about any of them."

"Not necessarily," Stacey said. "I think it depends on the teacher."

"Who's teaching these classes anyway?" Priya asked. "Do we get a say in that?"

"I can talk to admin," Stacey said. "But they usually like to control staffing."

"Tell them we want Ms. Dunlap," Priya said. "She never assigns homework."

"This raises a good point," Ms. Callahan said. "You may not have any say in who gets hired. But you could encourage the administration to consider important factors when making their decision."

"Like what?" Priya asked.

"Like do we want the teacher of the Ethnic Studies class to be white," Julia said.

"Are you saying a white teacher can't teach an Ethnic Studies class?" Stacey asked.

"I'm just saying, a teacher of color will bring a different perspective."

Brian leaned over to Cindy Po and whispered, "Here we go again." Stacey and Julia didn't agree on much and often used up class time defending their positions. Already this year, they fought over the new homework policy (Stacey thought AP classes should be exempt from the new time restrictions; Julia did not) and compost bins (Stacey wanted more bins around the campus; Julia wanted the cafeteria to switch to biodegradable plates and cups).

Their differences kept the new leadership class interesting, and always led to richer debates about what was better for the school. This is what Stacey and Julia promised when they promoted the new elective in May of the last school year. "You don't have to get elected," they told students in the classes they visited. "You just have to want to get involved." After all the drama of the spring election, people did want to get involved, and the counselors actually had to turn kids away when the class became overenrolled. Now there was talk of adding another section, although Brian wondered if the class would be as interesting without Stacey and Julia in it. Somehow, they found the perfect balance of discussion and decision-making to make every student feel they were making a positive difference.

Brian also liked that he didn't have to get people "psyched" for homecoming. School spirit still fell under the ASB's responsibility, and they did a good job with their event planning, especially with James as president. After Tony was suspended, James took over and implemented his own reforms, including making homecoming court more diverse by having nominations come through clubs rather than class council. The king and queen this year were James and a girl from the LSU. They both wore tiaras.

Brian took Julia to the dance, and Stacey went with a bunch of girlfriends, even though she'd been asked by a few guys, including Tony. He waited for Stacey to wander into the parking lot, then did a slow drive by with the message, *Don't fight me on this, girl. Let's go to prom.* painted on his Mercedes. When Stacey politely declined, he circled the lot a few times before finally getting a date. When the captain of the girls' volleyball team saw the message, she squealed in delight and did a mock striptease on the hood. They've been together ever since.

The bell rang, dismissing students from seventh period. Ms. Callahan reminded everyone to vote on the remaining elective choices by tonight since the deadline for submitting them to the administration was this Friday.

"Where are you guys headed?" Stacey asked, zipping up her jacket. The warmth of their Indian summer had disappeared last week, replaced by crisper fall temperatures.

"To the Tea House," Julia said. "Wanna come?"

"We could use your help narrowing down some of these college choices," Brian said. Applications were due in a few weeks, and Brian still had more than twenty schools on his short list.

"Think I'll pass," Stacey said. "Julia, where are you applying to?"

"McGill University," she said. "It's in Montreal."

"Well, then, Brian, you should go to Middlebury."

"It's on my list!" Brian said. "But it's just so cold in Vermont. I'm freezing now and it's only sixty-one degrees outside."

"I'll keep you warm," Julia said, snuggling up next him.

"Ugh," Stacey said, sticking a finger down her throat.

"You guys are worse than my mom and Mr. Park."

"Shouldn't you be calling him Dad by now?" Brian teased.

"Never," Stacey said. "I nearly bit my tongue in half when the minister asked if anyone objected to their union."

"I thought I saw you tear up on the wedding video," Julia said. "You looked overcome with emotion."

"A little passive-aggressive of your dad to fly that drone in low during the exchange of vows," Brian said.

"Mom was the one who wanted the ceremony recorded," Stacey said, smiling. "How was Dad supposed to know the drone would show up in practically every shot the wedding photographer took?"

"The surveillance looks like she's getting married in North Korea," Brian said, laughing at the memory of the photo Stacey shared just after the ceremony. Stacey's mom and Mr. Park are standing under a canopy of flowers. Just behind the minister's head is the drone, hovering like some gigantic mosquito ready to suck the blood out of all three of them.

"Actually, I think it's great that Dad has finally moved on to the anger stage of grieving," Stacey said. "That means he's healing."

The sky was overcast and gray as they left the classroom. The news had predicted rain all week, but so far not a single drop fell from the sky. On their way to the bike racks, Brian saw his brother skateboarding through the parking lot, slaloming through the stalled cars lined up to exit. Brian waved, but Kyle either didn't see or ignored him. That was okay. He was trying to be nicer to his little brother, both at school and at home. So far, it hadn't made a dent in the wall of silence Kyle had erected between them. Kyle had taken Tony's suspension and subsequent loss of the presidency pretty hard and retreated farther into his room than before. Brian figured his brother was channeling his rage about the "rigged system" into various chat rooms and social media platforms. Whenever someone reposted a hateful message or comment, Brian had to wonder if his brother was responsible for the anonymous post. It would catch up to him one day, Brian thought. Even the best trolls can't stay hidden forever.

Brian, Julia, and Stacey squeezed into the fenced-off area of the bike racks, along with the freshmen and sophomores at the school. Some boy holding a longboard the length of his body nearly decapitated Julia when he turned around.

"Watch it, dude," Brian said. The skater reminded Brian of Kyle, only this guy had a mop of red hair and freckles. Still, he and Kyle shared the same nervous energy that the board seemed perfect for channeling.

"It's too crowded in here," Stacey said, shifting the blame away from the boy and onto the environment.

"Hello? That's what I've been telling you," Julia said. "We need to expand the space."

"But where? The student lot already has a wait list for parking permits."

"Let the motorists find street parking, then," Julia said. "We should be rewarding those getting out of their cars, not into them."

"I just don't think that's practical," Stacey said.

"There you go, favoring the practical over the optimal."

"What if we gave the skateboarders their own storage space? We could build those racks anywhere. That might alleviate some of the crowding."

Brian looked at Stacey and smiled.

"It never ends, does it?" he whispered.

"No," Stacey said. "It never does."

ACKNOWLEDGMENTS

Writing a book is a little like running for office. The author gets all the attention, but he or she would be nothing without the hard work and dedication of people working behind the scenes. If it weren't for these amazing collaborators, I would be that obscure name on the ballot running on a platform of mandatory napping and dinner waffles.

This book wouldn't exist without the insight and encouragement of my editor, Karen Chaplin, the best campaign adviser I could ask for. She's the one who suggested I write an election story and then helped me channel my feelings about the 2016 presidential election into something that didn't sound like a giant scream for help. Anything you like here is the result of her input; anything you hate is me ignoring her advice.

Adriann Ranta Zurhellen is the best agent a writer could ask for. She's so good, I continually ask myself when she is going to fire me. Surely her talents are better used on writers who don't put murderous chickens and cows from outer space into their young adult novels.

Sheila Grau always gets the earliest drafts of my books

and *still* encourages me to keep writing. As my sister, she's not obligated to be nice, but she always is, which is weird because when we were younger she used to pin me on the floor and threaten to spit into my mouth.

Robie Spector and Poppy Livingstone worked with me throughout the process, providing ideas and feedback on the story and characters. Robie went so far as to invite me to her quinceañera party so I could better understand and appreciate the details of this cultural celebration.

Megan Gee is a talented writer I discovered back when she was in high school. When she becomes famous, I plan to take all the credit for being her inspiration. She made time in her busy college life to provide feedback that helped me shape the characters and story in important ways.

Lyn Fairchild Hawks is the best pen pal a writer could hope for. Thank you for continuing to swap drafts with me and for giving me such detailed and thoughtful feedback. Thanks too for always siding with me whenever someone criticizes my work.

Anne Battle, Donna Tracey, and Susana Herrera read later drafts of the book and provided much-needed feedback and also talked me down from the ledge when I wanted to hurl myself and this book into the ocean. Kym Sites also helped me work through some psychological issues, both personally and for the characters in the book.

This book looks as good as it does because of the talent

and hard work of Laura Eckes. Thank you for creating the pretty icing on my election cupcake.

I am so lucky to live in the Bay Area and have access to an amazing group of writers who looked at drafts and helped me see and correct flaws and errors. Rahul Kanakia, Mary Taugher, Eileen Bordy, Ann Gelder, Shelly King, Katy Motley, Beth Sears, Anita Felicelli, and Harriet Garfinkle make me a better writer by giving me access to their work and seeing how this should be done. Matthew Liu and Mariana Giron supplied me with some of my favorite lines here and didn't even need to be bribed with candy to help out.

I couldn't ask for a better school to work at than Los Altos High School. The students and staff there inspire me daily with their commitment to learning and social justice. While some of the details that appear in this book come from my school, the book does not reflect my lived experience of working there. The students and staff are examples of excellence in public education. I'm proud to be included in their ranks and hope to match their intelligence, empathy, and work ethic someday.

I love my family and wouldn't be able to do any of this without their encouragement and support. Thanks to Mom, Dad, Lisa, Jeff, Charlie, Cooper, Juan, Rachel, Ricky, Alex, and Daniel. Henry, you're the best son a dad could ask for. Kathleen, you're pretty great too. Maybe you'll read this book since it's dedicated to you.